ASIMOV'S FOUNDATIONS!

The three-volume Panther edition of THE EARLY ASIMOV contains twenty-seven stories by the greatest name in twentieth-century science fiction which have never before been collected in book form. They span the formative years of Isaac Asimov's writing career, from 1939 when Frederik Pohl accepted the second story he ever wrote (*The Callistan Menace*) for the magazine *Astonishing Stories*, to 1949 when, with the bulk of his famous robot stories and most of his epic *Foundation* saga already published, Isaac Asimov was firmly established among science fiction readers the world over as the foremost living SF author.

This first volume contains eight outstanding Asimov stories, from *The Callistan Menace* (first published in 1940) to *The Secret Sense* (first published in 1941). Each volume of THE EARLY ASIMOV will be an essential addition to the library of every true science fiction connoisseur and – as always with Isaac Asimov – first-rate reading entertainment in its own right.

D0892201

Also by Isaac Asimov in Panther Science Fiction

Earth is Room Enough
The Stars Like Dust
The Martian Way
The Currents of Space
The End of Eternity
The Caves of Steel
The Naked Sun
I, Robot
The Rest of the Robots
Asimov's Mysteries
Nightfall One
Nightfall Two

THE FOUNDATION TRILOGY
Foundation
Foundation and Empire
Second Foundation

Isaac Asimov

The Early Asimov

or, Eleven Years of Trying
Volume I

Panther

Granada Publishing Limited
Published in 1973 by Panther Books Ltd
Frogmore, St Albans, Herts AL2 2NF

The Early Asimov first published in Great
Britain (in one volume) by Victor Gollancz Ltd 1973
Copyright © 1972 by Isaac Asimov
Made and printed in Great Britain by
Richard Clay (The Chaucer Press) Ltd
Bungay, Suffolk
Set in Linotype Times

This book is sold subject to the condition that it
shall not, by way of trade or otherwise, be lent,
re-sold, hired out or otherwise circulated without
the publisher's prior consent in any form of binding
or cover other than that in which it is published
and without a similar condition including this
condition being imposed on the subsequent
purchaser.
This book is published at a net price and is
supplied subject to the Publishers Association
Standard Conditions of Sale registered under the
Restrictive Trade Practices Act, 1956.

To the memory of John Wood Campbell, Jr.
(1910–71) for reasons that this book will
make amply obvious

CONTENTS

Although I have written over a hundred and twenty books, on almost every subject from astronomy to Shakespeare and from mathematics to satire, it is probably as a science fiction writer that I am best known.

I began as a science fiction writer, and for the first eleven years of my literary career I wrote nothing but science fiction stories, for magazine publication only – and for minute payment. The thought of actually publishing honest-to-goodness *books* never entered my essentially humble mind.

But the time came when I did begin to produce books, and then I began to gather together the material I had earlier written for magazines. Between 1950 and 1969, ten collections appeared (all of which were published by Doubleday). These contained eighty-five stories (plus four pieces of comic verse) originally intended for, and published in, the science fiction magazines. Nearly a quarter of them came from those first eleven years.

For the record, these books are:

I, ROBOT (1950)
FOUNDATION (1951)
FOUNDATION AND EMPIRE (1952)
SECOND FOUNDATION (1953)
THE MARTIAN WAY AND OTHER STORIES (1955)
EARTH IS ROOM ENOUGH (1957)
NINE TOMORROWS (1959)
THE REST OF THE ROBOTS (1964)
ASIMOV'S MYSTERIES (1968)
NIGHTFALL AND OTHER STORIES (1969)

It might be argued that this was quite enough, but in arguing so, one is omitting the ravenous appetites of my readers (bless them!). I am constantly getting letters requesting lists of ancient stories out of me so that the letter writers can haunt secondhand shops for old magazines. There are people who prepare bibliographies of my science fiction (don't ask *me* why) and who want to know all sorts of half-forgotten details concerning them. They even grow distinctly angry when they find that some early stories were never sold and no longer exist. They want those, too, apparently, and seem to think I have negligently destroyed a natural resource.

So when Panther Books, in England, and Doubleday suggested that I make a collection of those of my early stories not already collected in the ten books listed above, with the literary history of each, I could resist no further. Everyone who has ever met me knows just how amenable to flattery I am, and if you think I can withstand this kind of flattery for more than half a second (as a rough estimate), you are quite wrong.

Fortunately I have a diary, which I have been keeping since January 1, 1938 (the day before my eighteenth birthday); it can give me dates and details.*

I began to write when I was very young – eleven, I think. The reasons are obscure. I might say it was the result of an unreasoning urge, but that would just indicate I could think of no reason.

Perhaps it was because I was an avid reader in a family that was too poor to afford books, even the cheapest, and besides, a family that considered cheap books unfit reading. I had to go to the library (my first library card was obtained for me by my father when I was six years old) and make do with two books per week.

This was simply not enough, and my craving drove me to extremes. At the beginning of each school term, I eagerly read through every schoolbook I was assigned, going from cover to cover like a personified conflagration. Since I was blessed with a tenacious memory and with instant recall, that was all the studying I had to do for *that* school term, but I was through before the week was over, and then what?

So, when I was eleven, it occurred to me that if I wrote my own books, I could then reread them at my leisure. I never really wrote a complete book, of course. I would start one and keep rambling on with it till I outgrew it and then I would start another. All these early writings are forever gone, though I remember some of the details quite clearly.

In the spring of 1934 I took a special English course given at my high school (Boys' High School in Brooklyn) that placed the accent on writing. The teacher was also faculty adviser for the semiannual literary magazine put out by the students, and it was his intention to gather material. I took that course.

It was a humiliating experience. I was fourteen at the time, and a rather green and innocent fourteen. I wrote trifles, while

---

* The diary began as the sort of thing a teen-ager would write, but it quickly degenerated to a simple kind of literary record. It is, to anyone but myself, utterly boring – so boring, in fact, that I leave it around for anyone who wishes, to read. No one ever reads more than two pages. Occasionally someone asks me if I have never felt that my diary ought to record my innermost feelings and emotions, and my answer is always, 'No. Never!' After all, what's the point of being a writer if I have to waste my innermost feelings and emotions on a mere diary?

everyone else in the class (who were sixteen apiece) wrote sophisticated, tragic mood pieces. All of them made no particular secret of their scorn for me, and though I resented it bitterly there was nothing I could do about it.

For a moment I thought I had them when one of my products was accepted for the semiannual literary magazine while many of theirs were rejected. Unfortunately the teacher told me, with callous insensitivity, that mine was the only item submitted that was humorous and that since he had to have *one* non-tragic piece he was forced to take it.

It was called 'Little Brothers,' dealt with the arrival of my own little brother five years earlier, and was my first piece of published material of any kind. I suppose it can be located in the records at Boys' High, but I don't have it.

Sometimes I wonder what happened to all those great tragic writers in the class. I don't remember a single name and I have no intention of ever trying to find out – but I sometimes wonder.

It was not until May 29, 1937 (according to a date I once jotted down – though that was before I began my diary, so I won't swear to it), that the vague thought occurred to me that I ought to write something for professional publication; something that would be *paid for*! Naturally it would have to be a science fiction story, for I had been an avid science fiction fan since 1929 and I recognized no other form of literature as in any way worthy of my efforts.

The story I began to compose for the purpose, the first story I ever wrote with a view to becoming a 'writer,' was entitled 'Cosmic Corkscrew.'

In it I viewed time as a helix (that is, something like a bedspring). Someone could cut across from one turn directly to the next, thus moving into the future by some exact interval but being incapable of traveling one day less into the future. My protagonist made the cut across time and found the Earth deserted. All animal life was gone; yet there was every sign that life had existed until very shortly before – and no indication at all of what had brought about the disappearance. It was told in the first person from a lunatic asylum, because the narrator had, of course, been placed in a madhouse after he returned and tried to tell his tale.

I wrote only a few pages in 1937, then lost interest. The mere fact that I had publication in mind must have paralyzed me. As long as something I wrote was intended for my own eyes only, I could be carefree enough. The thought of possible other readers weighed down heavily upon my every word. – So

I abandoned it.

Then, in May 1938, the most important magazine in the field, *Astounding Science Fiction*, changed its publication schedule from the third Wednesday of the month to the fourth Friday. When the June issue did not arrive on its accustomed day, I went into a decline.

By May 17, I could stand it no more and took the subway to 79 Seventh Avenue, where the publishing house, Street & Smith Publications, Inc., was then located.* There, an official of the firm informed me of the changed schedule, and on May 19, the June issue arrived.

The near brush with doom, and the ecstatic relief that followed, reactivated my desire to write and publish. I returned to 'Cosmic Corkscrew' and by June 19 it was finished.

The next question was what to do with it. I had absolutely no idea what one did with a manuscript intended for publication, and no one I knew had any idea either. I discussed it with my father, whose knowledge of the real world was scarcely greater than my own, and he had no idea either.

But then it occurred to me that, the month before, I had gone to 79 Seventh Avenue merely to inquire about the non-appearance of *Astounding*. I had not been struck by lightning for doing so. Why not repeat the trip, then, and hand in the manuscript in person?

The thought was a frightening one. It became even more frightening when my father further suggested that necessary preliminaries included a shave and my best suit. That meant I would have to take additional time, and the day was already wearing on and I would have to be back in time to make the afternoon newspaper delivery. (My father had a candy store and newsstand, and life was very complicated in those days for a creative writer of artistic and sensitive bent such as myself. For instance, we lived in an apartment in which all the rooms were in a line and the only way of getting from the living room to the bedroom of my parents, or of my sister, or of my brother, was by going through *my* bedroom. My bedroom was therefore frequently gone through, and the fact that I might be in the throes of creation meant nothing to anyone.)

* I told this story in some detail in an article entitled 'Portrait of the Writer as a Boy,' which was included as Chapter 17 of my book of essays *Science, Numbers and I* (Doubleday, 1968). In it, relying on memory alone, I said that I had called Street & Smith on the phone. When I went back to my diary to check actual dates for this book, I was astonished to discover that I had actually made the subway trip – an utterly daring venture for me in those days, and a measure of my desperation.

I compromised. I shaved, but did not bother changing suits, and off I went. The date was June 21, 1938.

I was convinced that, for daring to ask to see the editor of *Astounding Science Fiction*, I would be thrown out of the building bodily, and that my manuscript would be torn up and thrown out after me in a shower of confetti. My father, however (who had lofty notions) was convinced that a writer – by which he meant anyone with a manuscript – would be treated with the respect due an intellectual. He had no fears at all – but I was the one who had to go into the building.

Trying to mask panic, I asked to see the editor. The girl behind the desk (I can see the scene in my mind's eye right now exactly as it was) spoke briefly on the phone and said, 'Mr Campbell will see you.'

She directed me through a large, loftlike room filled with huge rolls of paper and enormous piles of magazines and permeated with the heavenly smell of pulp (a smell that, to this day, will recall my youth in aching detail and reduce me to tears of nostalgia). And there, in a small room on the other side, was Mr. Campbell.

John Wood Campbell, Jr., had been working for Street & Smith for a year and had taken over sole command of *Astounding Stories* (which he had promptly renamed *Astounding Science Fiction*) a couple of months earlier. He was only twenty-eight years old then. Under his own name and under his pen name, Don A. Stuart, he was one of the most famous and highly regarded authors of science fiction, but he was about to bury his writing reputation forever under the far greater renown he was to gain as editor.

He was to remain editor of *Astounding Science Fiction* and of its successor, *Analog Science Fact–Science Fiction*, for a third of a century. During all that time, he and I were to remain friends, but however old I grew and however venerable and respected a star of our mutual field I was to become, I never approached him with anything but that awe he inspired in me on the occasion of our first meeting.

He was a man, an opinionated man, who smoked and talked constantly, and who enjoyed, above anything else, the production of outrageous ideas, which he bounced off his listener and dared him to refute. It was difficult to refute Campbell even when his ideas were absolutely and madly illogical.

We talked for over an hour that first time. He showed me forthcoming issues of the magazine (actual *future* issues in the cellulose-flesh). I found he had printed a fan letter of mine in the issue about to be published, and another in the next – so he knew the genuineness of my interest.

He told me about himself, about his pen name and about his opinions. He told me that his father had sent in one of his manuscripts to *Amazing Stories* when he was seventeen and that it would have been published but the magazine lost it and he had no carbon. (I was ahead of him there. I had brought in the story myself and I had a carbon.) He also promised to read my story that night and to send a letter, whether acceptance or rejection, the next day. He promised also that in case of rejection he would tell me what was wrong with it so I could improve.

He lived up to every promise. Two days later, on June 23, I heard from him. It was a rejection. (Since this book deals with real events and is not a fantasy – you can't be surprised that my first story was instantly rejected.)

Here is what I said in my diary about the rejection:

'At 9:30 I received back "Cosmic Corkscrew" with a polite letter of rejection. He didn't like the slow beginning, the suicide at the end.'

Campbell also didn't like the first-person narration and the stiff dialog, and further pointed out that the length (nine thousand words) was inconvenient – too long for a short story, too short for a novelette. Magazines had to be put together like jigsaw puzzles, you see, and certain lengths for individual stories were more convenient than others.

By that time, though, I was off and running. The joy of having spent an hour and more with John Campbell, the thrill of talking face to face and on even terms with an idol, had already filled me with the ambition to write another science fiction story, better than the first, so that I could try him again. The pleasant letter of rejection – two full pages – in which he discussed my story seriously and with no trace of patronization or contempt, reinforced my joy. Before June 23 was over, I was halfway through the first draft of another story.

Many years later I asked Campbell (with whom I had by then grown to be on the closest terms) why he had bothered with me at all, since that first story was surely utterly impossible.

'It was,' he said frankly, for he never flattered. 'On the other hand, I saw something in *you*. You were eager and you listened and I knew you wouldn't quit no matter how many rejections I handed you. As long as you were willing to work hard at improving, I was willing to work with you.'

That was John. I wasn't the only writer, whether newcomer or old-time, that he was to work with in this fashion. Patiently, and out of his own enormous vitality and talent, he built up a stable of the best s.f. writers the world had, till then, ever seen.

What happened to 'Cosmic Corkscrew' after that I don't really know. I abandoned it and never submitted it anywhere else. I didn't actually tear it up and throw it away; it simply languished in some desk drawer until eventually I lost track of it. In any case, it no longer exists.

This seems to be one of the main sources of discomfort among the archivists – they seem to think the *first* story I ever wrote for publication, however bad it might have been, was an important document. All I can say, fellows, is that I'm sorry but there was no way of my telling in 1938 that my first try might have historic interest someday. I may be a monster of vanity and arrogance, but I'm not *that* much of a monster of vanity and arrogance.

Besides, before the month was out I had finished my second story, 'Stowaway,' and I was concentrating on that. I brought it to Campbell's office on July 18, 1938, and he was just a trifle slower in returning it, but the rejection came on July 22. I said in my diary concerning the letter that accompanied it:

'... it was the nicest possible rejection you could imagine. Indeed, the next best thing to an acceptance. He told me the idea was good and the plot passable. The dialog and handling, he continued, were neither stiff nor wooden (this was rather a delightful surprise to me) and that there was no one particular fault but merely a general air of amateurishness, constraint, forcing. The story did not go smoothly. This, he said, I would grow out of as soon as I had had sufficient experience. He assured me that I would probably be able to sell my stories but it meant perhaps a year's work and a dozen stories before I could click....'

It is no wonder that such a 'rejection letter' kept me hotly charged with enormous enthusiasm to write, and I got promptly to work on a third story.

What's more, I was sufficiently encouraged to try to submit 'Stowaway' elsewhere. In those days there were three science fiction magazines on the stands. *Astounding* was the aristocrat of the lot, a monthly with smooth edges and an appearance of class. The other two, *Amazing Stories* and *Thrilling Wonder Stories*, were somewhat more primitive in appearance and printed stories with more action and less-sophisticated plots. I sent 'Stowaway' to *Thrilling Wonder Stories*, which however, also rejected it promptly on August 9, 1938 (with a form letter).

By then, though, I was deeply engaged with my third story, which, as it happened, was fated to do better – and do it faster. In this book, however, I am including my stories not in the order of publication but in order of writing – which I presume is more significant from the standpoint of literary development. Let me stay with 'Stowaway,' therefore.

In the summer of 1939, by which time I had gained my first few successes, I returned to 'Stowaway,' refurbished it somewhat, and tried *Thrilling Wonder Stories* again. Undoubtedly I had a small suspicion that the new luster of my name would cause them to read it with a different attitude than had been the case when I was a complete unknown. I was quite wrong. It was rejected again.

Then I tried *Amazing*, and again it was rejected.

That meant the story was dead, or would have meant so were it not for the fact that science fiction was entering a small 'boom' as the 1930s approached their end. New magazines were being founded, and towards the end of 1939, plans were made to publish a magazine to be called *Astonishing Stories*, which would retail for the price of ten cents. (*Astounding* cost twenty cents an issue.)

The new magazine, together with a sister magazine, *Super Science Stories*, were to be edited on a shoestring by a young science fiction fan, Frederik Pohl, who was then just turning twenty (he was about a month older than myself), and who, in this way, made his entry into what was to be a distinguished professional career in science fiction.

Pohl was a thin, soft-spoken man, with hair that was already thinning, a solemn face, and a pronounced overbite that gave him a rabbity look when he smiled. The economic facts of his life kept him out of college, but he was far brighter (and knew more) than almost any college graduate I've ever met.

Pohl was a friend of mine (and still is) and perhaps did more to help me start my literary career than anyone except, of course, Campbell himself. We had attended fan-club meetings together. He had read my manuscripts and praised them – and now he needed stories in a hurry, and at low rates, for his new magazines.

He asked to look through my manuscripts again. He began by choosing one of my stories for his first issue. On November 17, 1939, nearly a year and a half after 'Stowaway' was first written, Pohl selected it for inclusion in his second issue of *Astonishing*. He was an inveterate title changer, however, and he plastered 'The Callistan Menace' on the story and that was how it was published.

So here it is, the second story I ever wrote and the earliest story to see professional publication. The reader can judge for himself whether Campbell's critique, given above, was overly kind and whether he was justified in foreseeing a professional writing career for me on the basis of this story.

'The Callistan Menace' appears here (as will all the stories in this volume) exactly as it appeared in the magazine, with only the editing and adjustment required to correct typographical errors.

1 : The Callistan Menace

'Damn Jupiter!' growled Ambrose Whitefield viciously, and I nodded agreement.

'I've been on the Jovian satellite run,' I said, 'for fifteen years and I've heard those two words spoken maybe a million times. It's probably the most sincere curse in the Solar System.'

Our watch at the controls of the scoutship *Ceres* had just been relieved and we descended the two levels to our room with dragging steps.

'Damn Jupiter – and damn it again,' insisted Whitefield morosely. 'It's too big for the System. It stays out there behind us and pulls and pulls and *pulls*! We've got to keep the Atomos firing all the way. We've got to check our course – completely – every hour. No relaxation, no coasting, no taking it easy! nothing but the rottenest kind of work.'

There were tiny beads of perspiration on his forehead and he swabbed at them with the back of his hand. He was a young fellow, scarcely thirty, and you could see in his eyes that he was nervous, and even a little frightened.

And it wasn't Jupiter that was bothering him, in spite of his profanity. Jupiter was the least of our worries. It was Callisto! It was that little moon which gleamed a pale blue upon our visiplates that made Whitefield sweat and that had spoiled four nights' sleep for me already. Callisto! Our destination!

Even old Mac Steeden, gray mustachioed veteran who, in his youth, had sailed with the great Peewee Wilson himself, went about his duties with an absent stare. Four days out – and ten days more ahead of us – and panic was reaching out with clammy fingers.

We were all brave enough in the ordinary course of events. The eight of us on the *Ceres* had faced the purple Lectronics and stabbing Disintos of pirates and rebels and the alien environments of half a dozen worlds. But it takes more than run-of-the-mill bravery to face the unknown; to face Callisto, the 'mystery world' of the Solar System.

One fact was known about Callisto – one grim, bare fact. Over a period of twenty-five years, seven ships, progressively better equipped, had landed – and never been heard from again. The Sunday supplements peopled the satellite with any-

Astonishing Stories, April 1940
Copyright © 1940 by Fictioneers, Inc.
Copyright renewed © 1967 by Isaac Asimov

thing from super-dinosaurs to invisible ghosts of the fourth dimension, but that did not solve the mystery.

We were the eighth. We had a better ship than any of those preceding. We were the first to sport the newly-developed beryl-tungsten hull, twice as strong as the old steel shells. We possessed super-heavy armaments and the very latest Atomic Drive engines.

Still – we were only the eighth, and every man jack of us knew it.

Whitfield entered our quarters silently and flopped down upon his bunk. His fists were clenched under his chin and showed white at the knuckles. It seemed to me that he wasn't far from the breaking point. It was a case for careful diplomacy.

'What we need,' said I, 'is a good, stiff drink.'

'What we need,' he answered harshly, 'is a hell of a lot of good, stiff drinks.'

'Well, what's stopping us?'

He looked at me suspiciously, 'You know there isn't a drop of liquor aboard ship. It's against Navy regulations!'

'Sparkling green *Jabra* water,' I said slowly, letting the words drip from my mouth. 'Aged beneath the Martian deserts. Melted emerald juice. Bottles of it! Cases of it!'

'Where?'

'I know where. What do you say? A few drinks – just a few – will cheer us both up.'

For a moment, his eyes sparkled, and then they dulled again, 'What if the Captain finds out? He's a stickler for discipline, and on a trip like this, it's liable to cost us our rating.'

I winked and grinned, 'It's the Captain's own cache. He can't discipline us without cutting his own throat – the old hypocrite. He's the best damn Captain there ever was, but he likes his emerald water.'

Whitefield stared at me long and hard, 'All right. Lead me to it.'

We slipped down to the supply room, which was deserted, of course. The Captain and Steeden were at the controls; Brock and Charney were at the engines; and Harrigan and Tuley were snoring their fool heads off in their own room.

Moving as quietly as I could, through sheer habit, I pushed aside several crates of food tabs and slid open a hidden panel near the floor. I reached in and drew out a dusty bottle, which, in the dim light, sparkled a dull sea-green.

'Sit down,' I said, 'and make yourself comfortable.' I produced two tiny cups and filled them.

Whitefield sipped slowly and with every evidence of satisfaction. He downed his second at one gulp.

'How come you volunteered for this trip, anyway, Whitey?' I asked. 'You're a little green for a thing like this.'

He waved his hand, 'You know how it is. Things get dull after a while. I went in for zoology after getting out of college – big field since interplanetary travel – and had a nice comfortable position back on Ganymede. It was dull, though; I was bored blue. So I joined the Navy on an impulse, and on another I volunteered for this trip.' He sighed ruefully, 'I'm a little sorry I did.'

'That's not the way to take it, kid. I'm experienced and I know. When you're panicky, you're as good as licked. Why, two months from now, we'll be back on Ganymede.'

'I'm not scared, if that's what you're thinking,' he exclaimed angrily. 'It's – it's,' there was a long pause in which he frowned at his third cupful. 'Well, I'm just worn out trying to imagine what the hell to expect. My imagination is working overtime and my nerves are rubbing raw.'

'Sure, sure,' I soothed, 'I'm not blaming you. It's that way with all of us, I guess. But you have to be careful. Why, I remember once on a Mars–Titan trip, we had –'

Whitefield interrupted what was one of my favorite yarns – and I could spin them as well as anyone in the service – with a jab in the ribs that knocked the breath out of me.

He put down his *Jabra* gingerly.

'Say, Jenkins,' he stuttered, 'I haven't downed enough liquor to be imagining things, have I?'

'That depends on what you imagined.'

'I could swear I saw something move somewhere in the pile of empty crates in the far corner.'

'That's a bad sign,' and I took another swig as I said it. 'Your nerves are going to your eyes and now they're going back on you. Ghosts, I suppose, or the Callistan menace looking us over in advance.'

'I saw it, I tell you. There's something alive there.' He edged towards me – his nerves were plenty shot – and for a moment, in the dim, shadowy light even I felt a bit choked up.

'You're crazy,' I said in a loud voice, and the echoes calmed me down a bit. I put down my empty cup and got up just a wee bit unsteadily. 'Let's go over and poke through the crates.'

Whitefield followed me and together we started shoving the light aluminum cubicles this way and that. Neither of us was quite one hundred per cent sober and we made a fair amount of noise. Out of the corner of my eye. I could see Whitefield trying to move the case nearest the wall.

'This one isn't empty,' he grunted, as it lifted very slightly off the floor.

Muttering under his breath, he knocked off the cover and looked in. For a half second he just stared and then he backed away slowly. He tripped over something and fell into a sitting position, still gaping at the case.

I watched his actions with raised eyebrows, then glanced hastily at the case in question. The glance froze into a steady glare, and I emitted a hoarse yell that rattled off each of the four walls.

A boy was sticking his head out of the case – a red-haired dirty-faced kid of thirteen or thereabouts.

'Hello,' said the boy as he clambered out into the open. Neither of us found the strength to answer him, so he continued, 'I'm glad you found me. I was getting a cramp in my shoulder trying to curl up in there.'

Whitefield gulped audibly, 'Good God! A kid stowaway! And on a voyage to *Callisto*!'

'And we can't turn back,' I reminded in a stricken voice, 'without wrecking ourselves. The Jovian satellite run is *poison.*'

'Look here,' Whitefield turned on the kid in a sudden belligerence. 'Who are you, you young nut, and what are you doing here?'

The kid flinched. 'I'm Stanley Fields,' he answered, a bit scared. 'I'm from New Chicago on Ganymede. I – I ran away to space, like they do in books.' He paused and then asked brightly, 'Do you think we'll have a fight with the pirates on this trip, mister?'

There was no doubt that the kid was filled to the brim with 'Dime Spacers.' I used to read them myself as a youngster.

'How about your parents?' asked Whitefield, grimly.

'Oh, all I got's an uncle. He won't care much, I guess.' He had gotten over his first uneasiness and stood grinning at us.

'Well, what's to be done?' said Whitefield, looking at me in complete helplessness.

I shrugged, 'Take him to the Captain. Let *him* worry.'

'And how will he take it?'

'Anyway he wants. It's not *our* fault. Besides, there's absolutely nothing to be done about the mess.'

And grabbing an arm apiece, we walked away, dragging the kid between us.

Captain Bartlett is a capable officer and one of the deadpan type that very rarely displays emotion. Consequently, on those few occasions when he does, it's like a Mercurian volcano in full eruption – and you haven't lived until you've seen one of those.

It was a case of the final straw. A satellite run is always wearing. The image of Callisto up ahead was harder on him than on any member of the crew. And now there was this kid stowaway.

It wasn't to be endured! For half an hour, the Captain shot off salvo after salvo of the very worst sort of profanity. He started with the sun and ran down the list of planets, satellites, asteroids, comets, to the very meteors themselves. He was starting on the nearer fixed stars, when he collapsed from sheer nervous exhaustion. He was so excited that he never thought to ask us what we were doing in the storeroom in the first place, and for that Whitefield and I were duly grateful.

But Captain Bartlett is no fool. Having purged his system of its nervous tension, he saw clearly that that which cannot be cured must be endured.

'Someone take him and wash him up,' he growled wearily, 'and keep him out of my sight for a while.' Then, softening a bit, he drew me towards him, 'Don't scare him by telling him where we're going. He's in a bad spot, the poor kid.'

When we left, the old soft-hearted fraud was sending through an emergency message to Ganymede trying to get in touch with the kid's uncle.

Of course, we didn't know it at the time, but that kid was a Godsend – a genuine stroke of Old Man Luck. He took our minds off Callisto. He gave us something else to think about. The tension, which at the end of four days had almost reached the breaking point, eased completely.

There was something refreshing in the kid's natural gayety; in his bright ingenuousness. He would meander about the ship asking the silliest kind of questions. He insisted on expecting pirates at any moment. And, most of all, he persisted in regarding each and every one of us as 'Dime Spacer' heroes.

That last flattered our egos, of course, and put us on our mettle. We vied with each other in chest-puffing and tale-telling, and old Mac Steeden, who in Stanley's eyes was a demigod, broke the all-time record for plain and fancy lying.

I remember, particularly, the talk-fest we had on the seventh day out. We were just past the midpoint of the trip and were set to begin a cautious deceleration. All of us (except Harrigan and Tuley, who were at the engines) were sitting in the control room. Whitefield, with half an eye on the Mathematico, led off, and, as usual, talked zoology.

'It's a little slug-like thing,' he was saying, 'found only on Europa. It's called the Carolus Europis but we always referred to it as the Magnet Worm. It's about six inches long and has a sort of a slate-gray color – most disgusting thing you could imagine.

'We spent six months studying that worm, though, and I never saw old Mornikoff so excited about anything before. You see, it killed by some sort of magnetic field. You put the Magnet Worm at one end of the room and a caterpillar, say, at the other. You wait about five minutes and the caterpillar just curls up and dies.

'And the funny thing is this. It won't touch a frog – too big; but if you take that frog and put some sort of iron band about it, that Magnet Worm kills it just like that. That's why we know it's some type of magnetic field that does it – the presence of iron more than quadruples its strength.'

His story made quite an impression on us. Joe Brock's deep bass voice sounded, 'I'm damn glad those things are only four inches long, if what you say is right.'

Mac Steeden stretched and then pulled at his gray mustachios with exaggerated indifference, 'You call *that* worm unusual. It isn't a patch on some of the things I've seen in my day –' He shook his head slowly and reminiscently, and we knew we were in for a long and gruesome tale. Someone groaned hollowly, but Stanley brightened up the minute he saw the old veteran was in a story-telling mood.

Steeden noticed the kid's sparkling eyes, and addressed himself to the little fellow, 'I was with Peewee Wilson when it happened – you've heard of Peewee Wilson, haven't you?'

'Oh, yes,' Stanley's eyes fairly exuded hero-worship. 'I've read books about him. He was the greatest spacer there ever was.'

'You bet all the radium on Titan he was, kid. He wasn't any taller than you, and didn't scale much more than a hundred pounds, but he was worth five times his weight in Venusian Devils in any fight. And me and him were just like that. He never went anyplace but what I was with him. When the going was toughest it was always me that he turned to.'

He sighed lugubriously, 'I was with him to the very end. It was only a broken leg that kept me from going with him on his last voyage –'

He choked off suddenly and a chilly silence swept over all of us. Whitefield's face went gray, the Captain's mouth twisted in a funny sort of way, and I felt my heart skid all the way down to the soles of my feet.

No one spoke, but there was only one thought among the six of us. Peewee Wilson's last trip had been to Callisto. He had been the second – and had never returned. We were the eighth.

Stanley stared from one to the other of us in astonishment, but we all avoided his eyes.

It was Captain Bartlett that recovered first.

'Say, Steeden, you've got an old spacesuit of Peewee Wilson's, haven't you?' His voice was calm and steady but I could see that it took a great deal of effort to keep it so.

Steeden brightened and looked up. He had been chewing at the tips of his mustachios (he always did when nervous) and now they hung downwards in a bedraggled fashion.

'Sure thing, Captain. He gave it to me with his own hand, he did. It was back in '23 when the new steel suits were just being put out. Peewee didn't have any more use for his old vitri-rubber contraption, so he let me have it – and I've kept it ever since. It's good luck for me.'

'Well, I was thinking that we might fix up that old suit for the boy here. No other suit'll fit him, and he needs one bad.'

The veteran's faded eyes hardened and he shook his head vigorously, 'No sir, Captain. No one touches that old suit. Peewee gave it to me himself. With his own hand! It's – it's *sacred*, that's what it is.'

The rest of us chimed in immediately upon the Captain's side but Steeden's obstinacy grew and hardened. Again and again he would repeat tonelessly, 'That old suit stays where it is.' And he would emphasize the statement with a blow of his gnarled fist.

We were about to give up, when Stanley, hitherto discreetly silent, took a hand.

'Please, Mr. Steeden,' there was just the suspicion of a quaver in his voice. 'Please let me have it. I'll take good care of it. I'll bet if Peewee Wilson were alive today he'd say I could have it.' His blue eyes misted up and his lower lip trembled a bit. The kid was a perfect actor.

Steeden looked irresolute and took to biting his mustachio again, 'Well – oh, hell, you've *all* got it in for me. The kid can have it but don't expect me to fix it up! The rest of you can lose sleep – I wash my hands of it.'

And so Captain Bartlett killed two birds with one stone. He took our minds off Callisto at a time when the morale of the crew hung in the balance and he gave us something to think about for the remainder of the trip – for renovating that ancient relic of a suit was almost a week's job.

We worked over that antique with a concentration out of all proportion to the importance of the job. In its pettiness, we forgot the steadily growing orb of Callisto. We soldered every last crack and blister in that venerable suit. We patched the inside with close-meshed aluminum wire. We refurbished the tiny heating unit and installed new tungsten oxygen-containers.

Even the Captain was not above giving us a hand with the suit, and Steeden, after the first day, in spite of his tirade at the beginning, threw himself into the job with a will.

We finished it the day before the scheduled landing, and Stanley, when he tried it on, glowed with pride, while Steeden stood by, grinning and twirling his mustachio.

And as the days passed, the pale blue circle that was Callisto grew upon the visiplate until it took up most of the sky. The last day was an uneasy one. We went about our tasks abstractedly, and studiously avoided the sight of the hard, emotionless satellite ahead.

We dived – in a long, gradually contracting spiral. By this maneuvre, the Captain had hoped to gain some preliminary knowledge of the nature of the planet and its inhabitants, but the information gained was almost entirely negative. The large percentage of carbon dioxide present in the thin, cold atmosphere was congenial to plant life, so that vegetation was plentiful and diversified. However, the three per cent oxygen content seemed to preclude the possibility of any animal life, other than the simplest and most sluggish species. Nor was there any evidence at all of cities or artificial structures of any kind.

Five times we circled Callisto before sighting a large lake, shaped something like a horse's head. It was towards that lake that we gently lowered ourselves, for the last message of the second expedition – Peewee Wilson's expedition – spoke of landing near such a lake.

We were still half a mile in the air, when we located the gleaming metal ovoid that was the *Phobos*, and when we finally thumped softly on to the green stubble of vegetation, we were scarcely five hundred yards from the unfortunate craft.

'Strange,' muttered the Captain, after we had all congregated in the control room, waiting for further orders, 'there seems to be no evidence of any violence at all.'

It was true! The *Phobos* lay quietly, seemingly unharmed. Its old-fashioned steel hull glistened brightly in the yellow light of a gibbous Jupiter, for the scant oxygen of the atmosphere could make no rusty inroads upon its resistant exterior.

The Captain came out of a brown study and turned to Charney at the radio.

'Ganymede has answered?'

'Yes, sir. They wish us luck.' He said it simply, but a cold shiver ran down my spine.

Not a muscle of the Captain's face flickered. 'Have you tried to communicate with the *Phobos*?'

'No answer, sir.'

'Three of us will investigate the *Phobos*. Some of the answers, at least, should be there.'

'Matchsticks!' grunted Brock, stolidly.

The Captain nodded gravely.

He palmed eight matches, breaking three in half, and extended his arm towards us, without saying a word.

Charney stepped forward and drew first. It was broken and he stepped quietly towards the space-suit rack. Tuley followed and after him Harrigan and Whitefield. Then I, and I drew the second broken match. I grinned and followed Charney, and in thirty seconds, old Steeden himself joined us.

'The ship will be backing you fellows,' said the Captain quietly, as he shook our hands. 'If anything dangerous turns up, run for it. No heroics now, for we can't afford to lose men.'

We inspected our pocket Lectronics and left. We didn't know exactly what to expect and weren't sure but that our first steps on Callistan soil might not be our last, but none of us hesitated an instant. In the 'Dime Spacers,' courage is a very cheap commodity, but it is rather more expensive in real life. And it is with considerable pride that I recall the firm steps with which we three left the protection of the *Ceres*.

I looked back only once and caught a glimpse of Stanley's face pressed white against the thick glass of the porthole. Even from a distance, his excitement was only too apparent. Poor kid! For the last two days he had been convinced we were on our way to clean up a pirate stronghold and was almost dying with impatience for the fighting to begin. Of course, none of us cared to disillusion him.

The outer hull of the *Phobos* rose before us and overshadowed us with its might. The giant vessel lay in the dark green stubble, silent as death. One of the seven that had attempted and failed. And we were the eighth.

Charney broke the uneasy silence, 'What are these white

smears on the hull?'

He put up a metal-encased finger and rubbed it along the steel plate. He withdrew it and gazed at the soft white pulp upon it. With an involuntary shudder of disgust, he scraped it off upon the coarse grass beneath.

'What do you think it is?'

The entire ship as far as we could see – except for that portion immediately next the ground – was besmeared by a thin layer of the pulpy substance. It looked like dried foam – like –

I said: 'It looks like slime left after a giant slug had come out of the lake and slithered over the ship.'

I wasn't serious in my statement, of course, but the other two cast hasty looks at the mirror-smooth lake in which Jupiter's image lay unruffled. Charney drew his hand Lec-tronic.

'Here!' cried Steeden, suddenly, his voice harsh and metallic as it came over the radio, 'that's no way to be talking. We've got to find some way of getting into the ship; there must be some break in its hull somewhere. You go around to the right, Charney, and you, Jenkins, to the left. I'll see if I can't get atop of this thing somehow.'

Eyeing the smoothly-round hull carefully, he drew back and jumped. On Callisto, of course, he weighed only twenty pounds or less, suit and all, so he rose upwards some thirty or forty feet. He slammed against the hull lightly, and as he started sliding downwards, he grabbed a rivet-head and scrambled to the top.

Waving a parting to Charney at this point, I left.

'Everything all right?' the Captain's voice sounded thinly in my ear.

'All O.K.,' I replied gruffly, 'so far.' And as I said so, the *Ceres* disappeared behind the convex bulge of the dead *Phobos* and I was entirely alone upon the mysterious moon.

I pursued my round silently thereafter. The spaceship's 'skin' was entirely unbroken except for the dark, staring port-holes, the lowest of which were still well above my head. Once or twice I thought I could see Steeden scrambling monkey-like on top of the smooth hulk, but perhaps that was only fancy.

I reached the prow at last which was bathed in the full light of Jupiter. There, the lowest row of portholes were low enough to see into and as I passed from one to the other, I felt as if I were gazing into a shipful of spectres, for in the ghostly light all objects appeared only as flickering shadows.

It was the last window in the line that proved to be of sudden, overpowering interest. In the yellow rectangle of Jupiter-light stamped upon the floor, there sprawled what remained of a man. His clothes were draped about him loosely and his shirt was ridged as if the ribs below had moulded it into position. In the space between the open shirt collar and the engineer's cap, there showed a grinning, eyeless skull. The cap, resting askew upon the smooth skull-case, seemed to add the last refinement of horror to the sight.

A shout in my ears caused my heart to leap. It was Steeden, exclaiming profanely somewhere above the ship. Almost at once, I caught sight of his ungainly steel-clad body slipping and sliding down the side of the ship.

We raced towards him in long, floating leaps and he waved us on, running ahead of us, towards the lake. At its very shores, he stopped and bent over some half-buried object. Two bounds brought us to him, and we saw that the object was a space-suited human, lying face downward. Over it was a thick layer of the same slimy smear that covered the *Phobos*.

'I caught sight of it from the heights of the ship,' said Steeden, somewhat breathlessly, as he turned the suited figure over.

What we saw caused all three of us to explode in a simultaneous cry. Through the glassy visor, there appeared a leprous countenance. The features were putrescent, fallen apart, as if decay had set in and ceased because of the limited air supply. Here and there a bit of gray bone showed through. It was the most repulsive sight I have ever witnessed, though I have seen many almost as bad.

'My God!' Charney's voice was half a sob. 'They simply die and decay.' I told Steeden of the clothed skeleton I had seen through the porthole.

'Damn it, it's a puzzle,' growled Steeden, 'and the answer *must* be inside the *Phobos*.' There was a momentary silence, 'I tell you what. One of us can go back and get the Captain to dismount the Disintegrator. It ought to be light enough to handle on Callisto, and at low power, we can draw it fine enough to cut a hole without blowing the entire ship to kingdom come. You go, Jenkins. Charney and I will see if we can't find any more of the poor devils.'

I set off for the *Ceres* without further urging, covering the ground in space-devouring leaps. Three-quarters of the distance had been covered when a loud shout, ringing metallically in my ear, brought me to a skidding halt. I wheeled in dismay and remained petrified at the sight before my eyes.

The surface of the lake was broken into boiling foam, and from it there reared the fore-parts of what appeared to be giant caterpillars. They squirmed out upon land, dirty-gray bodies dripping slime and water. They were some four feet long, about one foot in thickness, and their method of locomotion was the slowest of oxygen-conserving crawls. Except for one stalky growth upon their forward end, the tip of which glowed a faint red, they were absolutely featureless.

Even as I watched, their numbers increased, until the shore became one heaving mass of sickly gray flesh.

Charnley and Steeden were running towards the *Ceres*, but less than half the distance had been covered when they stumbled, their run slowing to a blind stagger. Even that ceased, and almost together they fell to their knees.

Charney's voice sounded faintly in my ear, 'Get help! My head is splitting. I can't move! I —' Both lay still now.

I started towards them automatically, but a sudden sharp pang just over my temples staggered me, and for a moment I stood confused.

Then I heard a sudden unearthly shout from Whitefield, 'Get back to the ship, Jenkins! Get back! Get back!'

I turned to obey, for the pain had increased into a continuous tearing pain. I weaved and reeled as I approached the yawning airlock, and I believe that I was at the point of collapse when I finally fell into it. After that, I can recall only a jumble for quite a period.

My next clear impression was of the control-room of the *Ceres*. Someone had dragged the suit off me, and I gazed about me in dismay at a scene of utmost confusion. My brain was still somewhat addled and Captain Bartlett as he leant over me appeared double.

'Do you know what those damnable creatures are?' He pointed outwards at the giant caterpillars.

I shook my head mutely.

'They're the great grand-daddies of the Magnet Worm Whitefield was telling us of once. Do you remember the Magnet Worm?'

I nodded, 'The one that kills by a magnetic field which is strengthened by surrounding iron.'

'Damn it, yes,' cried Whitefield, interrupting suddenly. 'I'll swear to it. If it wasn't for the lucky chance that our hull is beryl-tungsten and not steel – like the *Phobos* and the rest – every last one of us would be unconscious by now and dead before long.'

'Then *that's* the Callistan menace.' My voice rose in sudden dismay, 'But what of Charney and Steeden?'

'They're sunk,' muttered the Captain grimly. 'Unconscious – maybe dead. Those filthy worms are crawling towards them and there's nothing we can do about it.' He ticked off the points on his fingers. 'We can't go after them in a spacesuit without signing our own death warrant – spacesuits are steel. No one can last there and back without one. We have no weapons with a beam fine enough to blast the Worms without scorching Charney and Steeden as well. I've thought of maneuvering the *Ceres* nearer and making a dash for it, but one can't handle a spaceship on planetary surfaces like that – not without cracking up. We –'

'In short,' I interrupted hollowly, 'we've got to stand here and watch them die.' He nodded and I turned away bitterly.

I felt a slight twitch upon my sleeve, and when I turned, it was to find Stanley's wide blue eyes staring up at me. In the excitement, I had forgotten about him, and now I regarded him bad-temperedly.

'What is it?' I snapped.

'Mr. Jenkins,' his eyes were red, and I think he would have preferred pirates to Magnet Worms by a good deal, 'Mr. Jenkins, maybe *I* could go and get Mr. Charney and Mr. Steeden.'

I sighed, and turned away.

'But, Mr. Jenkins, I *could*. I heard what Mr. Whitefield said, and *my* spacesuit isn't steel. It's vitri-rubber.'

'The kid's right,' whispered Whitefield slowly, when Stanley repeated his offer to the assembled men. 'The unstrengthened field doesn't harm us, that's evident. He'd be safe in a vitri-rubber suit.'

'But it's a wreck, that suit!' objected the Captain. 'I never really intended having the kid use it.' He ended raggedly and his manner was evidently irresolute.

'We can't leave Neal and Mac out there without trying, Captain,' said Brock stolidly.

The Captain made up his mind suddenly and became a whirlwind of action. He dived into the space-suit rack for the battered relic himself, and helped Stanley into it.

'Get Steeden first,' said the Captain, as he clipped shut the last bolt. 'He's older and has less resistance to the field. – Good luck to you, kid, and if you can't make it, come back right away. Right away, do you hear me?'

Stanley sprawled at the first step, but life on Ganymede had inured him to below-normal gravities and he recovered quickly. There was no sign of hesitation, as he leaped towards the two prone figures, and we breathed easier. Evidently, the magnetic field was not affecting him yet.

He had one of the suited figures over his shoulders now and was proceeding back to the ship at an only slightly slower pace. As he dropped his burden inside the airlock, he waved an arm to us at the window and we waved back.

He had scarcely left, when we had Steeden inside. We ripped the spacesuit off him and laid him out, a gaunt pale figure, on the couch.

The Captain bent an ear to his chest and suddenly laughed aloud in sudden relief, 'The old geezer's still going strong.'

We crowded about happily at hearing that, all eager to place a finger upon his wrist and so assure ourselves of the life within him. His face twitched, and when a low, blurred voice suddenly whispered, 'So I said to Peewee, I said –' our last doubts were put to rest.

It was a sudden, sharp cry from Whitefield that drew us back to the window again, 'Something's wrong with the kid.'

Stanley was halfway back to the ship with his second burden, but he was staggering now – progressing erratically.

'It can't be,' whispered Whitefield, hoarsely, 'It can't be. The field *can't* be getting him!'

'God!' the Captain tore at his hair wildly, 'that damned antique has no radio. He can't tell us what's wrong.' He wrenched away suddenly. 'I'm going after him. Field or no field, I'm going to get him.'

'Hold on, Captain,' said Tuley, grabbing him by the arm, 'he may make it.'

Stanley was running again, but in a curious weaving fashion that made it quite plain, he didn't see where he was going. Two or three times he slipped and fell but each time he managed to scramble up again. He fell against the hull of the ship, at last, and felt wildly about for the yawning airlock. We shouted and prayed and sweated, but could help in no way.

And then he simply disappeared. He had come up against the lock and fallen inside.

We had them both inside in record time, and divested them of their suits. Charney was alive, we saw at a glance, and after that we deserted him unceremoniously for Stanley. The blue of his face, his swollen tongue, the line of fresh blood running from nose to chin told its own story.

'The suit sprung a leak,' said Harrigan.

'Get away from him,' ordered the Captain, 'give him air.'

We waited. Finally, a soft moan from the kid betokened

returning consciousness and we all grinned in concert.

'Spunky little kid,' said the Captain. 'He travelled that last hundred yards on nerve and nothing else.' Then, again. 'Spunky little kid. He's going to get a Naval Medal for this if I have to give him my own.'

Callisto was a shrinking blue ball on the televisor – an ordinary unmysterious world. Stanley Fields, honorary Captain of the good ship *Ceres*, thumbed his nose at it, protruding his tongue at the same time. An inelegant gesture, but the symbol of Man's triumph over a hostile Solar System.

THE END

As I reread the story now (it's the first time I've reread it since it was published) I am amused to see that my stowaway youngster's name is Stanley. That is the name of my younger brother, who was only nine when I wrote the story (the same younger brother who was the subject of my Boys' High essay, and who is now Assistant Publisher of the Long Island *Newsday*). Why it is necessary to use 'real names' I don't know, but almost every beginning writer does so, I suspect.

You will notice that there are no girls in the story. This is not really surprising. At eighteen I was busy finishing college and working in my father's candy store and handling a paper delivery route morning and evening, and I had actually never had time to have a date. I didn't know anything at all about girls (except for such biology as I got out of books and from other, more knowledgeable, boys).

I eventually had dates and I eventually introduced girls into my stories, but the early imprinting had its effect. To this very day, the romantic element in my stories is minor and the sexual element virtually nil.

On the other hand, I wonder if the above explanation for the lack of sex in my stories is not an oversimplification. After all, I am also a teetotaler and yet I notice that my characters drink Martian *jabra* water (whatever *that* is).

My knowledge of astronomy was quite respectable but I let myself be overinfluenced by the conventions common in the science fiction of that era. All worlds were Earthlike and inhabited in those days, so I gave Callisto an atmosphere containing a small quantity of free oxygen. I also gave it running water, and both plant and animal life. All of this is, of course, unlikely in the extreme, and what evidence we have seems to make of Callisto an airless, waterless world like our Moon (and, of course, I really knew this even back then).

Back to my third story, now –

On July 30, 1938, only eight days after Campbell's second rejection, I had finished my third story, 'Marooned off Vesta.' I did not think it politic to see Campbell oftener than once a month, however, since I suspected that I might easily wear out my welcome if I did. I put 'Marooned off Vesta' to one side, therefore, and began to write other stories. By the end of the month I had two more: 'This Irrational Planet' and 'Ring Around the Sun.'

My first three stories, including 'Marooned off Vesta,' had been typed on a very old, but completely serviceable Underwood No. 5 typewriter, which my father had obtained for me in 1936 for ten dollars. After I had submitted my second story to Campbell, however, my father decided that I was in earnest about a writing career, and feeling that my failure to sell was irrelevant and, in any case, temporary, he set about getting me a brand-new typewriter.

On August 10, 1938, a Smith-Corona portable entered the house and it was on the new typewriter that my fourth and fifth stories were written.

Of the three, I felt 'This Irrational Planet' to be the weakest, so I did *not* submit it to Campbell. I submitted it directly to *Thrilling Wonder Stories* on August 26, and it was not rejected till September 24. Campbell had spoiled me, and the four-week interval between submission and rejection appalled me. I even called during that interval to make an indignant inquiry – not knowing that a mere four-week wait was brief indeed for anyone but Campbell.

But at least the rejection, when it came, was typewritten and was not a printed form. What's more, it contained the sentence, 'Try us again, won't you?' That encouraged me. Perhaps I underestimated the story. Buoyantly I tried Campbell, and he rejected it in six days. Five other magazines rejected it afterward. I never did sell it, and 'This Irrational Planet' is also nonexistent now. I don't even remember the plot, except that I'm pretty certain that the planet of the title was Earth itself. (The only other information I have about it is that it was quite short, only three thousand words long. Actually, most of the stories of those early years that I never sold, and no longer exist, were short. The longest was the first, 'Cosmic Corkscrew.')

The other two stories written in the same month were reserved for a better fate, but it didn't seem so at first. On August 30, 1938, I visited Campbell for the third time and submitted both 'Marooned off Vesta' and 'Ring Around the Sun' – and both were returned to me on September 8.

The very next day I shipped off 'Marooned off Vesta,' which I felt to be the better of the two, to *Amazing Stories*. It took a month and a half to hear from them, but this time the wait was worth it. On October 21, 1938, there came a letter of acceptance from Raymond A. Palmer, who was then editor of *Amazing* and who has since achieved his greatest fame as a leading figure in the flying saucers craze and in other forms of occultism. To this day I have never met Mr. Palmer personally.

It was my first acceptance, four months to the day after my first visit to John Campbell. By that time I had written six stories and had collected nine rejections from various magazines. The check, for $64 (one cent a word), followed on October 31, and that was the first money I ever earned as a professional writer.*

For a number of years I kept that first acceptance letter, from Palmer, framed on my bedroom wall. But in the viscissitudes of life, it, too, has disappeared, and, yes, I'm sorry.

The story appeared in the March 1939 issue of *Amazing Stories*, which reached the newsstands on January 10, 1939, just eight days after my nineteenth birthday. It was the first occasion on which I ever appeared professionally, and I still have an intact copy of that issue of the magazine. I did not save one at the time (my sense of historical importance, as I have already explained, is deficient) but eventually removed my story for binding and discarded the rest. Ordinarily, I don't mind doing this and have done it ruthlessly through all the years (space is limited even in the best of apartments when one is as prolific as I have been), but the time came when I was sorry I hadn't saved that first one intact. The well-known science fiction fan Forrest J. Ackerman heard me express regret and kindly sent me a copy in excellent condition.

That copy, by the way, contains a little autobiographical squib in the rear, written by my teen-age self. On rereading, years later, it turned out to be exquisitely embarrassing.

* In this book, I am going to pay considerable attention to the money I received for my stories. This is not because I write primarily for money or regarded money as particularly important either then or now (my publishers will gladly bear witness to this). The money I received, however, was crucial in determining my career. It paid enough to put me through school and not so much as to lure me out of it. You'll see as we go along.

'Marooned off Vesta' is not included here, since it appeared in *Asimov's Mysteries.* (This doesn't mean it was a mystery. The reason for its inclusion in that particular collection is explained there. – Well, go ahead, buy the book and satisfy your curiosity.)

As for 'Ring Around the Sun,' it was rejected by *Thrilling Wonder Stories*, but then, on February 5, 1939, it was accepted by *Future Fiction*, one of the new science fiction magazines that were springing up.

It appeared in the second issue of that magazine, which did not, however, reach the stands until nearly a year after the sale. The payment (theoretically on publication, rather than on acceptance as was Campbell's more civilized procedure) was even more delayed. What's more, it was at the rate of only half a cent a word, so the check came to a mere twenty-five dollars. *Astonishing Stories* also paid only half a cent a word at that time, but 'The Callistan Menace' was the longer story – 6,500 words – so it netted me $32.50.

I didn't feel put upon, however. I well knew by that time that in the still earlier history of science fiction magazines, payment of a quarter of a cent a word was common, and that not on publication but (the saying went) on lawsuit. Besides, those were lean times, and twenty-five dollars represented something like five months' pocket money for me (no kidding).

The editor of *Future Fiction* was, at that time, Charles D. Hornig. I occasionally visited his office to inquire when a story might appear, or when a check might, but I don't recall ever having found him in. In fact, to this day I have never, to my knowledge, met him.

2: Ring Around the Sun

Jimmy Turner was humming merrily, if a bit raucously, when he entered the reception room.

'Is Old Sourpuss in?' he asked, accompanying the question with a wink at which the pretty secretary blushed gratefully. ·

'He is; and waiting for you.' She motioned him towards the door on which was written in fat, black letters, Frank Mc-Cutcheon, General Manager, United Space Mail.'

Jim entered. 'Hello Skipper, what now?'

'Oh, it's you, is it?' McCutcheon looked up from his desk, champing a foul-smelling stogie. 'Sit down.'

McCutcheon stared at him from under bushy gray eyebrows. 'Old Sourpuss,' as he was euphoniously known to all members of United Space Mail, had never been known to laugh within the memory of the oldest inmate, though rumor did have it that when a child he had smiled at the sight of his father falling out of an apple-tree. Right now his expression made the rumor appear exaggerated.

'Now, listen, Turner,' he barked, 'United Space Mail is in-augurating a new service and you're elected to blaze the trail.' Disregarding Jimmy's grimace, he continued, 'From now on the Venerian mail is on an all-year-round basis.'

'What! I've always thought that it was ruinous from a financial standpoint to deliver the Venerian mail except when it was this side of the Sun.'

'Sure,' admitted McCutcheon, 'if we follow the ordinary routes. But we might cut straight across the system if we could only get near enough to the sun. That's where you come in! They've put out a new ship equipped to approach within twenty million miles of the sun and which will be able to re-main at that distance indefinitely.'

Jimmy interrupted nervously, 'Wait a while, S – Mr. Mc-Cutcheon, I don't quite follow. What kind of a ship is this?'

'How do you expect me to know? I'm no fugitive from a laboratory. From what they tell me, it emits some kind of a field that bends the radiations of the sun around the ship. Get it? It's all deflected. No heat reaches you. You can stay there forever and be cooler than in New York.'

'Oh, is that so?' Jimmy was skeptical. 'Has it been tested, or

Future Fiction, March 1940
Copyright © 1940 by Double Action Magazines, Inc.

is that a little detail that has been left for me?'

'It's been tested, of course, but not under actual solar conditions.'

'Then it's out. I've done plenty for United, but this is the limit. I'm not crazy, *yet.*'

McCutcheon stiffened. 'Must I recall the oath you took upon entering the service, Turner? "Our flight through space –"'

' "– must ne'er be stopped by anything save death," ' finished Jimmy. 'I know that as well as you do and I also notice that it's very easy to quote that from a comfortable armchair. If you're that idealistic, you can do it yourself. It's still out, as far as I'm concerned. And if you want, you can kick me out. I can get other jobs just like that,' he snapped his fingers airily.

McCutcheon's voice dropped to a silky whisper. 'Now, now, Turner, don't be hasty. You haven't heard all I have to say yet. Roy Snead is to be your mate.'

'Huh! Snead! Why, that four-flusher wouldn't have the guts to take a job like this in a million years. Tell me some other fairy tale.'

'Well, as a matter of fact, he has already accepted. I thought you might accompany him, but I guess he was right. He insisted you'd back down. I thought at first you wouldn't.'

McCutcheon waved him away and bent his eyes unconcernedly on the report he had been scrutinizing at the time of Jimmy's entrance. Jimmy wheeled, hesitated, then returned.

'Wait a while, Mr. McCutcheon; do you mean to say that Roy is actually going?' McCutcheon nodded, still apparently absorbed in other matters, and Jimmy exploded, 'Why, that low-down, spindle-shanked, dish-faced mug! So he thinks I'm too yellow to go! Well, I'll show him. I'll take the job and I'll put up ten dollars to a Venerian nickel that *he* gets sick at the last minute.'

'Good!' McCutcheon rose and shook hands, 'I thought you'd see reason. Major Wade has all the details. I think you leave in about six weeks and as I'm leaving for Venus tomorrow, you'll probably meet me there.'

Jimmy left, still boiling, and McCutcheon buzzed for the secretary. 'Oh, Miss Wilson, get Roy Snead on the 'visor.'

A few minutes' pause and then the red signal-light shone. The 'visor was clicked on and the dark-haired, dapper Snead appeared on the visi-plate.

'Hello, Snead,' McCutcheon growled. 'You lose that bet, Turner accepted that job. I thought he'd laugh himself sick when I told him you said he wouldn't go. Send over the twenty dollars, please.'

'Wait a while, Mr. McCutcheon,' Snead's face was dark with fury, 'What's the idea of telling that punch-drunk imbecile I'm not going? You must have, you double-crosser. I'll be there all right, but you can put up another twenty and I'll bet he changes his mind *yet*. But *I'll* be there.' Roy Snead was still spluttering when McCutcheon clicked off.

The general Manager leaned back, threw away his mangled cigar, and lit a fresh one. His face remained sour, but there was a definite note of satisfaction in his tone when he said, 'Ha! I thought that would get them.'

It was a tired and sweaty pair that blasted the good ship *Helios* across Mercury's orbit. In spite of the perfunctory friendship enforced upon them by the weeks alone in space, Jimmy Turner and Roy Snead were scarcely on speaking terms. Add to this hidden hostility, the heat of the bloated sun and the torturing uncertainty of the final outcome of the trip and you have a miserable pair indeed.

Jimmy peered tiredly at the maze of dials confronting him, and, brushing a damp lock of hair from his eyes, grunted, 'What's the thermometer reading now, Roy?'

'One hundred twenty-five degrees Fahrenheit and still climbing,' was the growled response.

Jimmy cursed fluently, 'The cooling system is on at maximum, the ship's hull reflects ninety-five per cent of the solar radiation, and it's still in the hundred twenties.' He paused. 'The gravometer indicates that we're still some thirty-five million miles from the Sun. Fifteen million miles to go before the Deflection Field becomes effective. The temperature will probably scale 150 yet. That's a sweet prospect! Check the desiccators. If the air isn't kept absolutely dry, we're not going to last long.'

'Within Mercury's orbit, think of it!' Snead's voice was husky. 'No one has ever been this close to the sun before. And we're going closer yet.'

'There have been many this close and closer,' reminded Jimmy, 'but *they* were out of control and landed *in* the sun. Friedländer, Debuc, Anton –' His voice trailed into a brooding silence.

Roy stirred uneasily. 'How effective is this Deflection Field anyway, Jimmy? Your cheerful thoughts aren't very soothing, you know.'

'Well, it's been tested under the harshest conditions laboratory technicians could devise. I've watched them. It's been bathed in radiation approximating the sun's at a distance of twenty million. The Field worked like a charm. The light was bent about it so that the ship became invisible. The men inside the ship claimed that everything outside became invisible and that no heat reached them. A funny thing, though, the Field will work only under certain radiation strengths.'

'Well, I wish it were over one way or the other,' Roy glowered. 'If Old Sourpuss is thinking of making this my regular run –, well, he'll lose his ace pilot.'

'He'll lose his *two* ace pilots,' Jimmy corrected.

The two lapsed into silence and the *Helios* blasted on.

The temperature climbed: 130, 135, 140. Then, three days later, with the mercury quivering at 148, Roy announced that they were approaching the critical belt, the belt where the solar radiation reached sufficient intensity to energize the Field.

The two waited, minds at feverish concentration, pulses pounding.

'Will it happen suddenly?'

'I don't know. We'll have to wait.'

From the portholes, only the stars were visible. The sun, three times the size as seen from Earth, poured its blinding rays upon opaque metal, for on this specially designed ship, portholes closed automatically when struck by powerful radiation.

And then the stars began disappearing. Slowly, at first, the dimmest faded – then the brighter ones: Polaris, Regulus, Arcturus, Sirius. Space was uniformly black.

'It's working,' breathed Jimmy. The words were scarcely out of his mouth, when the sunward portholes clicked open. The sun was gone!

'Ha! I feel cooler already,' Jimmy Turner was jubilant. 'Boy, it worked like a charm. You know, if they could adjust this Deflection field to all radiation strengths, we would have perfected invisibility. It would make a convenient war weapon.' He lit a cigarette and leaned back luxuriously.

'But meanwhile we're flying blind,' Roy insisted.

Jimmy grinned patronizingly, 'You needn't worry about that, Dishface. I've taken care of everything. We're in an orbit about the sun. In two weeks, we'll be on the opposite side and then I'll let the rockets blast and out of this band we go, zooming towards Venus.' He was very self-satisfied indeed.

'Just leave it to Jimmy "Brains" Turner. I'll have us through in two months, instead of the regulation six. You're with United's ace pilot, now.'

Roy laughed nastily. 'To listen to you, you'd think you did

all the work. All you're doing is to run the ship on the course *I've* plotted. *You're* the mechanic; *I'm* the brains.'

'Oh, is that so? Any damn pilot-school rookie can plot a course. It takes a man to navigate one.'

'Well, that's your opinion. Who's paid more, though, the navigator or the course-plotter?'

Jimmy gulped on that one and Roy stalked triumphantly out of the pilot room. Unmindful of all this, the *Helios* blasted on.

For two days, all was serene; then, on the third day, Jimmy inspected the thermometer, scratched his head and looked worried. Roy entered, watched the proceedings and raised his eyebrows in surprise.

'Is anything wrong?' He bent over and read the height of the thin, red column. 'Just 100 degrees. That's nothing to look like a sick goat over. From your expression, I thought something had gone wrong with the Deflection Field and that it was rising again,' he turned away with an ostentatious yawn.

'Oh, shut up, you senseless ape,' Jimmy's foot lifted in a half-hearted attempt at a kick. 'I'd feel a lot better if the temperature were rising. This Deflection Field is working a lot too good for my liking.'

'Huh! What do you mean?'

'I'll explain, and if you listen carefully you *may* understand me. This ship is built like a vacuum bottle. It gains heat only with the greatest of difficulty and loses it likewise.' He paused and let his words sink in. 'At ordinary temperatures this ship is not supposed to lose more than two degrees a day if no outside sources of heat are supplied. Perhaps at the temperature at which we were, the loss might amount to five degrees a day. Do you get me?'

Roy's mouth was open wide and Jimmy continued. 'Now this blasted ship has lost fifty degrees in less than three days.'

'But that's impossible.'

'There it is.' Jimmy pointed ironically. 'I'll tell you what's wrong. It's that damn Field. It acts as a repulsive agent towards electromagnetic radiations and somehow is hastening the loss of heat of our ship.'

Roy sank into thought and did some rapid mental calculations. 'If what you say is true,' he said at length, 'we'll hit freezing point in five days and then spend a week in what amounts to winter weather.'

'That's right. Even allowing for the decrease in heat-loss as the temperature is lowered, we'll probably end up with the mercury anywhere between thirty and forty *below*.'

Roy gulped unhappily. 'And at twenty million miles away from the sun!'

'That isn't the worst,' Jimmy pointed out. 'This ship, like all others used for travel within the orbit of Mars, has no heating system. With the sun shining like fury and no way to lose heat except by ineffectual radiation, Mars and Venus space-ships have always specialized in cooling systems. We, for instance, have a very efficient refrigeration device.'

'We're in a devil of a fix, then. The same applies to our space suits.'

In spite of the still roasting temperature, the two were beginning to experience a few anticipatory chills.

'Say, I'm not going to stand this,' Roy burst out. 'I vote we get out of here right now and head for Earth. They can't expect more of us.'

'Go ahead! You're the pilot. Can you plot a course at this distance from the sun and guarantee that we won't fall *into* the sun?'

'Hell! I hadn't thought of that.'

The two were at their wits' end. Communication via radio had been impossible ever since they had passed Mercury's orbit. The sun was at sunspot maximum and static had drowned out all attempts.

So they settled down to wait.

The next few days were taken up entirely with thermometer watching, with a few minutes taken out here and there when one of the two happened to think of an unused malediction to hurl at the head of Mr. Frank McCutcheon. Eating and sleeping were indulged in, but not enjoyed.

And meanwhile, the *Helios*, entirely unconcerned in the plight of its occupants, blasted on.

As Roy had predicted, the temperature passed the red line marked 'Freezing' towards the end of their seventh day in the Deflection Belt. The two were remarkably unhappy when this happened even though they had expected it.

Jimmy had drawn off about a hundred gallons of water from the tank. With this he had filled almost every vessel on board.

'It might,' he pointed out, 'save the pipes from bursting when the water freezes. And if they do, as is probable, it is just as well that we supply ourselves with plenty of available water. We have to stay here another week, you know.'

And on the next day, the eighth, the water froze. There were the buckets, overflowing with ice, standing chill and bluecold. The two gazed at them forlornly. Jimmy broke one open.

'Frozen solid,' he said bleakly and wrapped another sheet about himself.

It was hard to think of anything but the increasing cold now. Roy and Jimmy had requisitioned every sheet and blanket on the ship, after having put on three or four shirts and a like number of pairs of pants.

They kept in bed for as long as they were able, and when forced to move out, they huddled near the small oil-burner for warmth. Even this doubtful pleasure was soon denied them, for, as Jimmy remarked, 'the oil supply is extremely limited and we will need the burner to thaw out the water and food.'

Tempers were short and clashes frequent, but the common misery kept them from actually jumping on each other's throats. It was on the tenth day, however, that the two, united by a common hatred, suddenly became friends.

The temperature was hovering down near the zero point, making up its mind to descend into the minus regions. Jimmy was huddled in a corner thinking of the times back in New York when he had complained of the August heat and wondered how he could have done so. Roy, meanwhile, had manipulated numb fingers long enough to calculate that they would have to endure the coldness for exactly 6354 minutes more.

He regarded the figures with distaste and read them off to Jimmy. The latter scowled and grunted, 'The way I feel, I'm not going to last 54 minutes, let alone 6354.' Then, impatiently. 'I wish you could manage to think of some way of getting us out of this.'

'If we weren't so near the sun,' suggested Roy, 'we might start the rear blasts and hurry us up.'

'Yes, and if we landed *in* the sun, we'd be nice and warm. You're a big help!'

'Well, you're the one that calls himself "Brains" Turner. *You* think of something. The way you talk, you'd think all this was my fault.'

'It certainly is, you donkey in human clothing! My better judgment told me all along not to go on this fool trip. When McCutcheon proposed it, I refused pointblank. I knew better.' Jimmy was very bitter. 'So what happened? Like the fool you are, you accept and rush in where sensible men fear to treat. And then, of course, I naturally *had* to tag along.

'Why, do you know what I should have done,' Jimmy's voice ascended the scale, 'I should have let you go alone and freeze and then sat down by a roaring fire all by myself and gloated. That is, if I had known what was going to happen.'

A hurt and surprised look appeared on Roy's face. 'Is that so? So that's how it is! Well, all I can say is that you certainly have a genius for twisting facts, if for nothing else. The fact of the matter is that *you* were unutterably stupid enough to accept and *I* the poor fellow raked in by the force of circumstances.'

Jimmy's expression was one of the utmost disdain. 'Evidently the cold has driven you batty, though I admit it wouldn't take much to knock the little sense you possess out of you.'

'Listen,' Roy answered hotly. 'On October 10th, McCutcheon called me up on the 'visor and told me you had accepted and laughed at me for a yellow-belly for refusing to go. Do you deny that?'

'Yes, I do, and unconditionally. On October 10, Sourpuss told *me* that *you* had decided to go and had bet him that –'

Jimmy's voice faded away very suddenly and a shocked look spread over his face. 'Say –, are you sure McCutcheon told you I had agreed to go?'

A chill, clammy feeling clutched at Roy's heart when he caught Jimmy's drift, a feeling that drowned out the numbness of the cold.

'Absolutely,' he answered, 'I'll swear to that. That's why I went.'

'But he told me you had accepted and that's why *I* went.' Jimmy felt very stupid all at once.

The two fell into a protracted and ominous silence which was broken at length by Roy, who spoke in a voice that quivered with emotion.

'Jimmy, we've been the victims of a contemptible, dirty, lowdown, doublecrossing trick.' His eyes dilated with fury. 'We've been cheated, robbed –' words failed him but he kept on uttering meaningless sounds, indicative mainly of devouring rage.

Jimmy was cooler, but none the less vindictive, 'You're right, Roy; McCutcheon has done us dirty. He has plumbed the depths of human iniquity. But we'll get even. When we get through in 6300 odd minutes, we will have a score to settle with Mr. McCutcheon.'

'What are we going to do?' Roy's eyes were filled with a blood-thirsty joy.

'On the spur of the moment, I suggest that we simply tear into him and rend him into tiny little pieces.'

'Not gruesome enough. How about boiling him in oil?'

'That's reasonable, yes; but it might take too long. Let's give him a good old-fashioned beating – with brass knuckles.'

Roy rubbed his hands. 'We'll have lots of time to think up some really adequate measures. The dirty, God-forsaken, yellow-livered, leprous –' The rest verged fluently into the unprintable.

And for four more days, the temperature dove. It was on the fourteenth and last day that the mercury froze, the solid red shaft pointed its congealed finger at forty below.

On this terrible last day, they had lit the oil-burner, using their entire scanty supply of oil. Shivering and more than half frozen, they crouched close, attempting to extract every last drop of heat.

Jimmy had found a pair of ear-muffs several days before in some obscure corner, and it now changed hands at the end of every hour. Both sat buried under a small mountain of blankets, chafing chilled hands and feet. With every passing minute, their conversation, concerning McCutcheon almost exclusively, grew more vitriolic.

'Always quoting that triply-damned slogan of the Space Mail: "Our flight through sp –"' Jimmy choked with impotent fury.

'Yes, and always rubbing holes in chairs instead of coming out here and doing something like a man's work, the rotten so-and-so,' agreed Roy.

'Well, we're due to pass out of the deflection zone in two hours. Then three weeks and we'll be on Venus,' said Jimmy, sneezing.

'That can't be too soon for me,' answered Snead, who had been sniffling for the last two days. 'I'm never taking another space trip except maybe the one that takes me back to Earth. After this, I make my living growing bananas in Central America. A fellow can be decently warm out there at least.'

'We might not get off Venus, after what we're going to do to McCutcheon.'

'No, you're right there. But that's all right. Venus is even warmer than Central America and that's all I care about.'

'We have no legal worries either,' Jimmy sneezed again. 'On Venus, life imprisonment's the limit for first-degree murder. A nice, warm, dry cell for the rest of my life. What could be sweeter?'

The second hand on the chronometer whirled at its even pace; the minutes ticked off. Roy's hands hovered lovingly over the lever that would set off the right rear blasts which would drive the *Helios* out away from the sun and from that terrible Deflection Zone.

And at last, 'Go!' shouted Jimmy eagerly. 'Let her blast!'

With a deep reverberating roar, the rockets fired. The *Helios* trembled from stem to stern. The pilots felt the acceleration press them back into their seats and were happy. In a matter of minutes, the sun would shine again and they would be warm, feel the blessed heat once more.

It happened before they were aware of it. There was a momentary flash of light and then a grinding and a click, as the sunward portholes closed.

'Look,' cried Roy, 'the stars! We're out of it! He cast an ecstatically happy glance at the thermometer. 'Well, old boy, from now on we go up again.' He pulled the blankets about him closer, for the cold still lingered.

There were two men in Frank McCutcheon's office at the Venus branch of the United Space Mail: McCutcheon himself and the elderly, white-haired Zebulon Smith, inventor of the Deflection Field. Smith was talking.

'But, Mr. McCutcheon, it is really of great importance that I learn exactly how my Deflection Field worked. Surely they have transmitted all possible information to you.'

McCutcheon's face was a study in dourness as he bit the edge off one of his two-for-five cigars and lit it.

'That, my dear Mr. Smith,' he said, 'is exactly what they did not do. Ever since they have receded far enough from the sun to render communication possible. I have been sending requests for information regarding the practicability of the Field. They just refuse to answer. They say it worked and that they're alive and that they'll give the details when they reach Venus. That's all!'

Zebulon Smith sighed in disappointment. 'Isn't that a bit unusual; insubordination, so to speak? I thought they were required to be complete in their reports and to give any requested details.'

'So they are. But these are my ace pilots and rather temperamental. We have to extend some leeway. Besides, I tricked them into going on this trip, a very hazardous one, as you know, and so am inclined to be lenient.'

'Well, then, I suppose I must wait.'

'Oh, it won't be for long,' McCutcheon assured him. 'They're due today, and I assure you that as soon as I get in touch with them, I shall send you the full details. After all, they survived for two weeks at a distance of twenty million miles from the sun, so your invention is a success. That should satisfy you.'

Smith had scarcely left when McCutcheon's secretary entered with a puzzled frown on her face.

'Something is wrong with the two pilots of the *Helios,* Mr. McCutcheon,' she informed him. 'I have just received a bulletin from Major Wade at Pallas City, where they landed. They have refused to attend the celebration prepared for them, but instead immediately chartered a rocket to come here, refusing to state the reason. When Major Wade tried to stop them, they became violent, he says.' She laid the communication down on his desk.

McCutcheon glanced at it perfunctorily. 'Hmm! They do seem confoundedly temperamental. Well, send them to me when they come. I'll snap them out of it.'

It was perhaps three hours later that the problem of the two misbehaving pilots again forced itself upon his mind, this time by a sudden commotion that had arisen in the reception room. He heard the deep angry tones of two men and then the shrill remonstrances of his secretary. Suddenly the door burst open and Jim Turner and Roy Snead strode in.

Roy coolly closed the door and planted his back against it.

'Don't let anyone disturb me until I'm through,' Jimmy told him.

'No one's getting through this door for a while,' Roy answered grimly, 'but remember, you promised to leave some for me.'

McCutcheon said nothing during all this, but when he saw Turner casually draw a pair of brass knuckles from his pocket and put them on with a determined air, he decided that it was time to call a halt to the comedy.

'Hello, boys,' he said, with a heartiness unusual in him. 'Glad to see you again. Take a seat.'

Jimmy ignored the offer. 'Have you anything to say, any last request, before I start operations?' He gritted his teeth with an unpleasant scraping noise.

'Well, if you put it that way,' said McCutcheon, 'I might ask exactly what this is all about – if I'm not being too unreasonable. Perhaps the Deflector was inefficient and you had a hot trip.'

The only answer to that was a loud snort from Roy and a cold stare on the part of Jimmy.

'First,' said the latter, 'what was the idea of that filthy, disgusting cheat you pulled on us?'

McCutcheon's eyebrows raised in surprise. 'Do you mean the little white lies I told you in order to get you to go? Why, that was nothing. Common business practice, that's all. Why, I pull worse things than that every day and people consider it just routine. Besides, what harm did it do you?'

'Tell him about our "pleasant trip," Jimmy,' urged Roy.

'That's exactly what I'm going to do,' was the response. He turned to McCutcheon and assumed a martyr-like air. 'First, on this blasted trip, we fried in a temperature that reached 150 but that was to be expected and we're not complaining; we were half Mercury's distance from the sun.

'But after that, we entered this zone where the light bends around us; incoming radiation sank to zero and we started losing heat and not just a degree a day the way we learned it in pilot school.' He paused to breathe a few novel curses he had just thought of, then continued.

'In three days, we were down to a hundred and in a week down to freezing. Then for one entire week, seven long days, we drove through our course at sub-freezing temperature. It was so cold the last day that the mercury froze.' Turner's voice rose till it cracked, and at the door, a fit of self-pity caused Roy to catch his breath with an audible gulp. McCutcheon remained inscrutable.

Jimmy continued. 'There we were without a heating system, in fact, no heat of any kind, not even any warm clothing. We froze, damn it; we had to thaw out our food and melt our water. We were stiff, couldn't move. It was hell, I tell you, in reverse temperature.' He paused, at a loss for words.

Roy Snead took up the burden. 'We were twenty million miles away from the sun and I had a case of frost-bitten ears. Frost-bitten, I say.' He shook his fist viciously under Mc-Cutcheon's nose. 'And it was your fault. You tricked us into it! While we were freezing we promised ourselves that we'd come back and get you and we're going to keep that promise.' He turned to Jimmy. 'Go ahead, start it, will you? We've wasted enough time.'

'Hold it, boys,' McCutcheon spoke at last. 'Let me get this straight. You mean to say that the Deflection Field worked so well that it kept all the radiation away and sucked out what heat there was in the ship in the first place?' Jimmy grunted a curt assent.

'And you froze for a week because of that?' McCutcheon continued.

Again the grunt.

And then a very strange and unusual thing happened. McCutcheon, 'Old Sourpuss,' the man without the 'risus' muscle, smiled. He actually bared his teeth in a grin. And what's more, the grin grew wider and wider until finally a rusty, long-unused chuckle was heard louder and louder, until it developed into a full-fledged laugh, and the laugh into a bellow. In one stentorian burst, McCutcheon made up for a lifetime of sour gloom.

The walls reverberated, the windowpanes rattled, and still the Homeric laughter continued. Roy and Jimmy stood open-mouthed, entirely non-plussed. A puzzled bookkeeper thrust his head inside the door in a fit of temerity and remained frozen in his tracks. Others crowded about the door, conversing in awed whispers. *McCutcheon had laughed!*

Gradually, the risibilities of the old General Manager subsided. He ended in a fit of choking and finally turned a purple face towards his ace pilots, whose surprise had long since given way to indignation.

'Boys,' he told them, 'that was the best joke I ever heard. You can consider your pay doubled, both of you.' He was still grinning away like clockwork and had developed a beautiful case of hiccoughs.

The two pilots were left cold at the handsome proposal. 'What's so killingly funny?' Jimmy wanted to know, 'I don't see anything to laugh at, myself.'

McCutcheon's voice dripped honey, 'Now, fellows, before I left I gave each of you several mimeographed sheets containing special instructions. What happened to them?'

There was sudden embarrassment in the air.

'I don't know. I must have mislaid mine,' gulped Roy.

'I never looked at mine; I forgot about it.' Jimmy was genuinely dismayed.

'You see,' exclaimed McCutcheon triumphantly, 'It was all the fault of your own stupidity.'

'How do you figure that out?' Jimmy wanted to know. 'Major Wade told us all we had to know about the ship, and besides, I guess there's nothing *you* could tell us about running one.'

'Oh, isn't there? Wade evidently forgot to inform you of one minor point which you would have found on my instructions. The strength of the Deflection Field was *adjustable*. It happened to be set at maximum strength when you started, that's all.' He was now beginning to chuckle faintly once more. 'Now, if you had taken the trouble to read the sheets, you would have known that a simple movement of a small lever,' he made the appropriate gesture with his thumb, 'would have weakened the Field any desired amount and allowed as much radiation to leak through as was wanted.'

And now the chuckle was becoming louder. 'And you froze

for a week because you didn't have the brains to pull a lever. And then you ace pilots come here and blame *me*. What a laugh!' and off he went again while a pair of very sheepish young men glanced askance at each other.

When McCutcheon came around to normal, Jimmy and Roy were gone.

Down in an alley adjoining the building, a little ten-year-old boy watched, with open mouth and intense absorption, two young men were engaged in the strange and rather startling occupation of kicking each other alternately. They were vicious kicks, too!

THE END

When I wrote 'Ring Around the Sun' I was much taken by the two protagonists, Turner and Snead. It was in my mind, I recall, to write other stories about the pair. This was a natural thought, for in the late 1930s there were a number of 'series' of stories about a given character or characters. Campbell himself had written some delightful stories featuring two men named Penton and Blake, and I longed to do a Penton–Blake imitation.

There was a practical value to writing a 'series.' For one thing, you had a definite background that was carried on from story to story, so that half your work was done for you. Secondly, if the 'series' became popular, it would be difficult to reject new stories that fit into it.

I didn't make it with Turner and Snead. In fact, I never tried. The time was to come, two years later, when I was to have a pair of very similar characters, Powell and Donovan, who were to be in four stories and who were to be part of a very successful 'series' indeed.

By the end of August 1938, then, I had written five stories, of which three were eventually published. Not bad!

However, there followed a dry spell. I was finishing my third year of college and was trying, without success, to get admission into medical school. The situation in Europe was disturbing. It was the time of the surrender at Munich, and for a Jewish teen-ager there was something unsettling about the rapid, sure-fire victories of Hitler.

The next three stories took not one month, as had the previous three, but three months. And all were clearly well below the limits of salability even in the most permissive market.

49

They were 'The Weapon,' 'Paths of Destiny,' and 'Knossos in Its Glory.'' Campbell rejected each one in very short order, and all made the rounds without luck. There came a time, nearly three years later, when *Astonishing* seemed interested in 'The Weapon,' but that fell through and the other two didn't even come that close.

All three stories are now gone forever. I remember nothing at all about two of them, but 'Knossos in Its Glory' was an ambitious attempt to retell the Theseus myth in science fiction terms. The minotaur was an extraterrestrial who landed in ancient Crete with only the kindliest of intentions, and I remember writing terribly stilted prose in an attempt to make my Cretans sound as I imagined characters in Homer ought to sound. Campbell, always kind, said in rejecting it that my work 'was definitely improving, especially where I was not straining for effect.'

By the time I was writing 'Knossos in Its Glory' I had just received my check for 'Marooned off Vesta' and I was a *professional*. My spirits rose accordingly, and towards the end of November I wrote 'Ammonium,' which was another attempt (like 'Ring Around the Sun') at humor.

I had a pretty good notion that Campbell wouldn't like it, however, and I never showed it to him. I sent it to *Thrilling Wonder Stories* instead. When they rejected it, I lost heart and retired it. It was only after *Future Fiction* had taken 'Ring Around the Sun' that I thought I would chance this other one, too.

On August 23, 1939, I sent it in to *Future Fiction*, which took it, altering its name to 'The Magnificent Possession.'

3 : The Magnificent Possession

Walter Sills reflected now, as he had reflected often before, that life was hard and joyless. He surveyed his dingy chemical laboratory and grinned cynically—working in a dirty hole of a place, living on occasional ore analyses that barely paid for absolutely indispensable equipment, while others, not half his worth perhaps, were working for big industrial concerns and taking life easy.

He looked out the window at the Hudson River, ruddied in the flame of the dying sun, and wondered moodily whether these last experiments would finally bring him the fame and success he was after, or if they were merely some more false alarms.

The unlocked door creaked open a crack and the cheerful face of Eugene Taylor burst into view. Sills waved and Taylor's body followed his head and entered the laboratory.

'Hello, old soak,' came the loud and carefree hail. 'How go things?'

Sills shook his head at the other's exuberance. 'I wish I had your foolish outlook on life, Gene. For your information, things are bad. I need money, and the more I need it, the less I have.'

'Well, I haven't any money either, have I?' demanded Taylor. 'But why worry about it? You're fifty, and worry hasn't got you anything except a bald head. I'm thirty, and I want to keep my beautiful brown hair.'

The chemist grinned. 'I'll get my money yet, Gene. Just leave it to me.'

'Your new ideas shaping out well?'

'Are they? I haven't told you much about it, have I? Well, come here and I'll show you what progress I've made.'

Taylor followed Sills to a small table, on which stood a rack of test-tubes, in one of which was about half an inch of a shiny metallic substance.

'Sodium-mercury mixture, or sodium amalgam, as it is called,' explained Sills pointing to it.

He took a bottle labeled 'Ammonium Chloride Sol.' from the shelf and poured a little into the tube. Immediately the sodium amalgam began changing into a loosely-packed, spongy sub-

Future Fiction, July 1940
Copyright © 1940 by Double Action Magazines, Inc.

stance.

'That,' observed Sills, 'is ammonium amalgam. The ammonium radical (NH_4) acts as a metal here and combines with mercury.' He waited for the action to go to completion and then poured off the supernatant liquid.

'Ammonium amalgam isn't very stable,' he informed Taylor, 'so I'll have to work fast.' He grasped a flask of straw-colored, pleasant-smelling liquid and filled the test-tube with it. Upon shaking, the loosely-packed ammonium amalgam vanished and in its stead a small drop of metallic liquid rolled about the bottom.

Taylor gazed at the test-tube, open-mouthed. 'What happened?'

'This liquid is a complex derivative of hydrazine which I've discovered and named Ammonaline. I haven't worked out its formula yet, but that doesn't matter. The point about it is that it has the property of dissolving the ammonium out of the amalgam. Those few drops at the bottom are pure mercury; the ammonium is in solution.'

Taylor remained unresponsive and Sills waxed enthusiastic. 'Don't you see the implications? I've gone half way towards isolating pure ammonium, a thing which has never been done before! Once accomplished it means fame, success, the Nobel Prize, and who knows what else.'

'Wow!' Taylor's gaze became more respectful. 'That yellow stuff doesn't look so important to me.' He snatched for it, but Sills withheld it.

'I haven't finished, by any means, Gene. I've got to get it in its free metallic state, and I can't do that so far. Every time I try to evaporate the Ammonaline, the ammonium breaks down to everlasting ammonia and hydrogen. . . . But I'll get it – I'll get it!'

Two weeks later, the epilogue to the previous scene was enacted. Taylor received a hurried and emphatic call from his chemist friend and appeared at the laboratory in a flurry of anticipation.

'You've got it?'

'I've got it—and it's bigger than I thought! There's millions in it, really,' Sills' eyes shone with rapture.

'I've been working from the wrong angle up to now,' he explained. 'Heating the solvent always broke down the dissolved ammonium, so I separated it out by freezing. It works the same way as brine, which, when frozen slowly, freezes into fresh ice, the salt crystallizing out. Luckily, the Ammonaline freezes at 18 degrees Centigrade and doesn't require much cooling.'

He pointed dramatically to a small beaker, inside a glass-walled case. The beaker contained pale, straw-colored, needle-like crystals and, covering the top of this, a thin layer of a dullish, yellow substance.

'Why the case?' asked Taylor.

'I've got it filled with argon to keep the ammonium (which is the yellow substance on top of the Ammonaline) pure. It is so active that it will react with anything else but a helium-type gas.'

Taylor marveled and pounded his complacently-smiling friend on the back.

'Wait, Gene, the best is yet to come.'

Taylor was led to the other end of the room and Sills' trembling finger pointed out another airtight case containing a lump of metal of a gleaming, yellow that sparkled and glistened.

'That, my friend, is ammonium oxide (NH_4O_2), formed by passing *absolutely dry* air over free ammonium metal. It is perfectly inert (the sealed case contains quite a bit of chlorine, for instance, and yet there is no reaction). It can be made as cheaply as aluminum, if not more so, and yet it looks more like gold than gold does itself. Do you see the possibilities?'

'Do I?' exploded Taylor. 'It will sweep the country. You can have ammonium jewelry, and ammonium-plated table-ware, and a million other things. Then again, who knows how many countless industrial applications it may have? You're rich, Walt—you're rich!'

'*We're* rich,' corrected Sills gently. He moved towards the telephone, 'The newspapers are going to hear of this. I'm going to begin to cash in on fame right now.'

Taylor frowned, 'Maybe you'd better keep it a secret, Walt.'

'Oh, I'm not breathing a hint as to the process. I'll just give them the general idea. Besides, we're safe; the patent application is in Washington right now.'

But Sills was wrong! The article in the paper ushered in a very, very hectic two days for the two of them.

J. Throgmorton Bankhead is what is commonly known as a 'captain of industry.' As head of the Acme Chromium and Silver Plating Corporation he no doubt deserved the title; but to his patient and long-suffering wife, he was merely a dyspeptic and grouchy husband, especially at the breakfast table ... and he was at the breakfast table now.

Rustling his morning paper angrily, he sputtered between

bites of buttered toast, 'This man is ruining the country.' He pointed aghast at big, black headlines. 'I said before and I'll say again that the man is as crazy as a bedbug. He won't be satisfied...'

'Joseph, please,' pleaded his wife, 'you're getting purple in the face. Remember your high blood pressure. You know the doctor told you to stop reading the news from Washington if it annoys you so. Now, listen dear, about the cook. She's...'

'The doctor's a damn fool, and so are you,' shouted J. Throgmorton Bankhead. 'I'll read all the news I please and get purple in the face too, if I want to.'

He raised the cup of coffee to his mouth and took a critical sip. While he did so, his eyes fell upon a more insignificant headline towards the bottom of the page: 'Savant Discovers Gold Substitute.' The coffee cup remained in the air while he scanned the article quickly. 'This new metal,' it ran in part, 'is claimed by its discoverer to be far superior to chromium, nickel, or silver for cheap and beautiful jewelry. "The twenty-dollar-a-week clerk," said Professor Sills, "will eat off ammonium plate more impressive in appearance than the gold plate of the Indian Nabob." There is no...'

But J. Throgmorton Bankhead had stopped reading. Visions of a ruined Acme Chromium and Silver Plating Corporation danced before his eyes; and as they danced, the cup of coffee dropped from his hand, and splashed hot liquid over his trousers.

His wife rose to her feet in alarm, 'What is it, Joseph; what is it?'

'Nothing,' Bankhead shouted. 'Nothing. For God's sake, go away, will you?'

He strode angrily out of the room, leaving his wife to search the paper for anything that could have disturbed him.

'Bob's Tavern' on Fifteenth Street is usually pretty well filled at all times, but on the morning we are speaking of, it was empty except for four or five rather poorly-dressed men who clustered about the portly and dignified form of Peter Q. Hornswoggle, eminent ex-Congressman.

Peter Q. Hornswoggle was, as usual, speaking fluently. His subject, again as usual, concerned the life of a Congressman.

'I remember a case in point,' he was saying, 'when that same argument was brought up in the House, and which I answered as follows: "The eminent gentleman from Nevada in his statements overlooks one very important aspect of the problem. He does not realize that it is to the interest of the entire nation that the apple-parers of this country be attended to promptly; for, gentlemen, on the welfare of the apple-parers depends the future of the entire fruit industry and on the fruit-industry is based the entire economy of this great and glorious nation, the United States of America." '

Hornswoggle paused, swallowed half a pint of beer at once, and then smiled in triumph, 'I have no hesitation in saying, gentlemen, that at that statement, the entire House burst into wild and tumultuous applause.'

One of the assembled listeners shook his head slowly and marvelled. 'It must be great to be able to spiel like that, Senator. You musta been a sensation.'

'Yeah,' agreed the bartender, 'it's a dirty shame you were beat last election.'

The ex-Congressman winced and in a very dignified tone began, 'I have been reliably informed that the use of bribery in that campaign reached unprecedented prop . . .' His voice died away suddenly as he caught sight of a certain article in the newspaper of one of his listeners. He snatched at it and read it through in silence and thereupon his eyes gleamed with a sudden idea.

'My friends,' he said turning to them again, 'I find I must leave you. There is pressing work that must be done immediately at City Hall.' He leant over to whisper to the bar-keeper, 'You haven't got twenty-five cents, have you? I find I left my wallet in the Mayor's office by mistake. I will surely repay you tomorrow.'

Clutching the quarter, reluctantly given, Peter Q. Hornswoggle left.

In a small and dimly lit room somewhere in the lower reaches of First Avenue, Michael Maguire, known to the police by the far more euphonious name of Mike the Slug, cleaned his trusty revolver and hummed a tuneless song. The door opened a crack and Mike looked up.

'That you, Slappy?'

'Yeh,' a short, wizened person sidled in, 'I brung ya de evenin' sheet. De cops are still tinkin' Bragoni pulled de job.'

'Yeh? That's good.' He bent unconcernedly over the revolver. 'Anything else doing?'

'Naw! Some dippy dame killed herself, but dat's all.'

He tossed the newspaper to Mike and left. Mike leaned back and flipped the pages in a bored manner.

A headline attracted his eye and he read the short article that followed. Having finished, he threw aside the paper, lit a cigarette, and did some heavy thinking. Then he opened the door.

'Hey, Slappy, c'mere. There's a job that's got to be done.'

Walter Sills was happy, deliriously so. He walked about his laboratory king of all he surveyed, strutting like a peacock, basking in his new-found glory. Eugene Taylor sat and watched him, scarcely less happy himself.

'How does it feel to be famous?' Taylor wanted to know.

'Like a million dollars; and that's what I'm going to sell the secret of ammonium metal for. It's the fat of the land for me from now on.'

'You leave the practical details to me, Walt. I'm getting in touch with Staples of Eagle Steel today. You'll get a decent price from him.'

The bell rang, and Sills jumped. He ran to open the door.

'Is this the home of Walter Sills?' The large, scowling visitor gazed about him superciliously.

'Yes, I'm Sills. Do you wish to see me?'

'Yes. My name is J. Throgmorton Bankhead and I represent the Acme Chromium and Silver Plating Corporation. I would like to have a moment's discussion with you.'

'Come right in. Come right in! This is Eugene Taylor, my associate. You may speak freely before him.'

'Very well.' Bankhead seated himself heavily. 'I suppose you surmise the reason for my visit.'

'I take it that you have read of the new ammonium metal in the papers.'

'That's right. I have come to see whether there is any truth in the story and to buy your process if there is.'

'You can see for yourself, sir,' Sills led the magnate to where the argon-filled container of the few grams of pure ammonium were. 'That is the metal. Over here to the right, I've got the oxide, an oxide which is more metallic than the metal itself, strangely enough. It is the oxide that is what the papers call "substitute gold."'

Bankhead's face showed not an atom of the sinking feeling within him as he viewed the oxide with dismay. 'Take it out in the open,' he said, 'and let's see it.'

Sills shook his head. 'I can't, Mr. Bankhead. Those are the first samples of ammonium and ammonium-oxide that ever existed. They're museum pieces. I can easily make more for you, if you wish.'

'You'll have to, if you expect me to sink my money in it. You satisfy me and I'll be willing to buy your patent for as much as – oh, say a thousand dollars.'

'A thousand dollars!' exclaimed Sills and Taylor together.

'A very fair price, gentlemen.'

'A million would be more like it,' shouted Taylor in an outraged tone. 'This discovery is a goldmine.'

'A million, indeed! You are dreaming, gentlemen. The fact of the matter is that my company has been on the track of ammonium for years now, and we are just at the point of solving the problem. Unfortunately you beat us by a week or so, and so I wish to buy up your patent in order to save my company a great deal of annoyance. You realize, of course, that if you refuse my price, I could just go ahead and manufacture the metal, using my own process.'

'We'll sue if you do,' said Taylor.

'Have you got the money for a long, protracted – and expensive – lawsuit?' Bankhead smiled nastily. 'I have, you know. To prove, however, that I am not unreasonable, I will make the price two thousand.'

'You've heard our price,' answered Taylor stonily, 'and we have nothing further to say.'

'All right, gentlemen,' Bankhead walked towards the door, 'think it over. You'll see it my way, I'm sure.'

He opened the door and revealed the symmetrical form of Peter Q. Hornswoggle bent in rapt concentration at the keyhole. Bankhead sneered audibly and the ex-Congressman jumped to his feet in consternation, bowing rapidly two or three times, for want of anything better to do.

The financier passed by disdainfully and Hornswoggle entered, slammed the door behind him, and faced the two bewildered friends.

'That man, my dear sirs, is a malefactor of great wealth, an economic royalist. He is the type of predatory interest that is the ruination of this country. You did quite right in refusing his offer.' He placed his hand on his ample chest and smiled at them benignantly.

'Who the devil are you?' rasped Taylor, suddenly recovering from his initial surprise.

'I?' Hornswoggle was taken aback. 'Why – er I am Peter Quintus Hornswoggle. Surely you know me. I was in the House of Representatives last year.'

'Never heard of you. What do you want?'

'Why, bless me! I read in the papers of your wonderful discovery and have come to place my services at your feet.'

'What services?'

'Well, after all, you two are not men of the world. With your new invention, you are prey for every self-seeking unscrupulous person that comes along – like Bankhead, for instance. Now, a practical man of affairs, such as I, one with experience of the world, would be of inestimable use to you. I could handle your affairs, attend to details, see that –'

'All for nothing, of course, eh?' Taylor asked, sardonically.

Hornswoggle coughed convulsively. 'Well, naturally, I thought that a small interest in your discovery might fittingly be assigned to me.'

Sills, who had remained silent during all this, rose to his feet suddenly. 'Get out of here! Did you hear me? Get out, before I call the police.'

'Now, Professor Sills, pray don't get excited,' Hornswoggle retreated towards the door which Taylor held open for him. He passed out, still protesting, and swore softly to himself when the door slammed in his face.

Sills sank wearily into the nearest chair. 'What are we to do, Gene? He offers only two thousand. A week ago that would have been beyond anything I could have hoped for, but now –'

'Forget it. The fellow was only bluffing. Listen, I'm going right now to call on Staples. We'll sell to him for what we can get (it ought to be plenty) and then if there's any trouble with Bankhead – well, that's Staples' worry.' He patted the other on the shoulder. 'Our troubles are practically over.'

Unfortunately, however, Taylor was wrong; their troubles were only beginning.

Across the street, a furtive figure, with beady eyes peering from upturned coat-collar, surveyed the house carefully. A curious policeman might have identified him as 'Slappy' Egan if he had bothered to look, but no one did and 'Slappy' remained unmolested.

'Cripes,' he muttered to himself, 'dis is gonna be a cinch. De whole woiks on the bottom floor, back window can be jimmied wid a toot'pick, no alarms, no nuttin'.' He chuckled and walked away.

Nor was 'Slappy' alone with his ideas. Peter Q. Hornswoggle, as he walked away, found strange thoughts wandering through his massive cranium – thoughts which involved a certain amount of unorthodox action.

And J. Throgmorton Bankhead was likewise active. Belonging to that virile class known as 'go-getters' and being not at all scrupulous as to how he 'go-got,' and certainly not intending to pay a million dollars for the secret of Ammonium, he found it necessary to call on a certain one of his acquaintances.

This acquaintance, while a very useful one, was a bit unsavory, and Bankhead found it advisable to be very careful and cautious while visiting him. However, the conversation that ensued ended in a pleasing manner for both of them.

Walter Sills snapped out of an uneasy sleep with startled suddenness. He listened anxiously for a while and then leaned over and nudged Taylor. He was rewarded by a few incoherent snuffles.

'Gene, Gene, wake up! Come on, get up!'

'Eh? What is it? What are you bothering –'

'Shut up! Listen, do you hear it?'

'I don't hear anything. Leave me alone, will you?'

Sills put his finger on his lips, and the other quieted. There was a distinct shuffling noise down below, in the laboratory.

Taylor's eyes widened and sleep left them entirely. 'Burglars!' he whispered.

The two crept out of bed, donned bathrobes and slippers, and tiptoed to the door. Taylor had a revolver and took the lead in descending the stairs.

They had traversed perhaps half the flight, when there was a sudden, surprised shout from below, followed by a series of loud, threshing noises. This continued for a few moments and then there was a loud crash of glassware.

'My ammonium!' cried Sills in a stricken voice and rushed headlong down the stairs evading Taylor's clutching arms.

The chemist burst into the laboratory, followed closely by his cursing associate, and clicked the lights on. Two struggling figures blinked owlishly in the sudden illumination, and separated.

Taylor's gun covered them. 'Well, isn't this nice,' he said.

One of the two lurched to his feet from amid a tangle of broken beakers and flasks, and, nursing a cut on his wrist, bent his portly body in a still dignified bow. It was Peter Q. Hornswoggle.

'No doubt,' he said, eyeing the unwavering firearm nervously, 'the circumstances seem suspicious, but I can explain very easily. You see, in spite of the very rough treatment I received after having made my reasonable proposal, I still felt a great deal of kindly interest in you two.

'Therefore, being a man of the world, and knowing the iniquities of mankind, I just decided to keep an eye on your house tonight, for I saw you had neglected to take precautions against housebreakers. Judge my surprise to see this dastardly creature,' he pointed to the flat-nosed, plug-ugly, who still remained on the floor in a daze, 'creeping in at the back window.

'Immediately, I risked life and limb in following the criminal, attempting desperately to save your great discovery. I really feel I deserve great credit for what I have done. I'm sure you will feel that I am a valuable person to deal with and reconsider your answers to my earlier proposals.'

Taylor listened to all this with a cynical smile. 'You can certainly lie fluently, can't you P.Q.?'

He would have continued at greater length and with greater forcefulness had not the other burglar suddenly raised his voice in loud protest. 'Cripes, boss, dis fat slob here is only tryin' to get me in bad. I'm just followin' orders, boss. A fellow hired me to come in here and rifle the safe and I'm just oinin' a bit o' honest money. Just plain safe-crackin', boss, I ain't out to hurt no one.

'Den, just as I was gettin' down to de job – warming up, so to say – in crawls dis little guy wid a chisel and blowtorch and makes for de safe. Well, naturally, I don't like no competition, so I lays for him and then –'

But Hornswoggle had drawn himself up in icy hauteur. 'It remains to be seen whether the word of a gangster is to be taken before the word of one, who, I may truthfully say, was, in his time, one of the most eminent members of the great –'

'Quiet, both of you,' shouted Taylor, waving the gun threateningly. 'I'm calling the police and you can annoy *them* with your stories. Say, Walt, is everything all right?'

'I think so!' Sills returned from his inspection of the laboratory. 'They only knocked over empty glassware. Everything else is unharmed.'

'That's good,' Taylor began, and then choked in dismay.

From the hallway, a cool individual, hat drawn well over his eyes, entered. A revolver, expertly handled, changed the situation considerably.

'O.K.,' he grunted at Taylor, 'drop the gat!' The other's weapon slipped from reluctant fingers and hit the floor with a clank.

The new menace surveyed the four others with a sardonic glance. 'Well!' So there were two others trying to beat me to it. This seems to be a very popular place.'

Sills and Taylor stared stupidly, while Hornswoggle's teeth chattered energetically. The first mobster moved back uneasily, muttering as he did so, 'For Pete's sake, it's Mike the Slug.'

'Yeah,' Mike rasped, 'Mike the Slug. There's lots of guys who know me and who know I ain't afraid to pull the trigger anytime I feel like. Come on, Baldy, hand over the works. You know – the stuff about your fake gold. Come on, before I count five.'

Sills moved slowly towards the old safe in the corner. Mike stepped back carelessly to give him room, and in so doing, his coat sleeve brushed against a shelf. A small vial of sodium sulplate solution tottered and fell.

With sudden inspiration, Sills yelled, 'My God, watch out! It's nitroglycerine!'

The vial hit the floor with a smashing tinkle of broken glass, and involuntarily, Mike yelled and jumped in wild dismay. And as he did so, Taylor crashed into him with a beautiful flying tackle. At the same time, Sills lunged for Taylor's weapon to cover the other two. For this, however, there was no longer need. At the very beginning of the confusion, both had faded hurriedly into the night from whence they came.

Taylor and Mike the Slug rolled round and round the laboratory floor, locked in a desperate struggle while Sills hopped over and about them, praying for a moment of comparative quiet that he might bring the revolver into sharp and sudden contact with the gangster's skull.

But no such moment came. Suddenly Mike lunged, caught Taylor stunningly under the chin, and jerked free. Sills yelled in consternation and pulled the trigger at the fleeing figure. The shot was wild and Mike escaped unharmed. Sills made no attempt to follow.

A sluicing stream of cold water brought Taylor back to his senses. He shook his head dazedly as he surveyed the surrounding shambles.

'Whew!' he said, 'What a night!'

Sills groaned, 'What are we going to do now, Gene? Our very lives are in danger. I never thought of the possibility of thieves, or I would never have told of the discovery to the newspapers.'

'Oh, well, the harm's done; no use weeping over it. Now, listen, the first thing we have to do now is to get back to sleep. They won't bother us again tonight. Tomorrow you'll go to the bank and put the papers outlining the details of the process in the vault (which you should have done long ago). Staples will be here at 3 p.m.; we'll close the deal, and then, at last, we'll live happily ever after.'

The chemist shook his head dolefully. 'Ammonium has certainly proved to be very upsetting so far. I almost wish I had never heard of it. I'd almost rather be back doing ore analysis.'

As Walter Sills rattled cross-town towards his bank, he found no reason to change his wish. Even the comforting and homely jiggling of his ancient and battered automobile failed to cheer him. From a life characterized by peaceful monotony, he had entered a period of bedlam, and he was not at all satisfied with the change.

'Riches, like poverty, has its own peculiar problems,' he remarked sententiously to himself as he braked the car before the two-story, marble edifice that was the bank. He stepped out carefully, stretched his cramped legs, and headed for the revolving door.

He didn't get there right away, though. Two husky specimens of the human race stepped up, one at each side, and Sills felt a very hard object pressing with painful intensity against his ribs. He opened his mouth involuntarily, and was rewarded by an icy voice in his ears, 'Quiet, Baldy, or you'll get what you deserve for the damn trick you pulled on me last night.'

Sills shivered and subsided. He recognized Mike the Slug's voice very easily.

'Where's the details?' asked Mike, 'and make it quick.'

'Inside jacket pocket,' croaked Sills tremulously.

Mike's companion passed his hand dexterously into the indicated pocket and flicked out three or four folded sheets of foolscap.

'Dat it, Mike?'

A hasty appraisal and a nod, 'Yeh, we got it. All right, Baldy, on your way!' A sudden shove and the two gangsters jumped into their car and drove away rapidly, while the chemist sprawled on the sidewalk. Kindly hands raised him up.

'It's all right,' he managed to gasp. 'I just tripped, that's all. I'm not hurt.' He found himself alone again, passed into the bank, and dropped into the nearest bench, in near-collapse. There was no doubt about it; the new life was not for him.

But he should have been prepared for it. Taylor had foreseen a possibility of this sort of thing happening. He, himself, had thought a car had been trailing him. Yet, in his surprise and fright, he had almost ruined everything.

He shrugged his thin shoulders and, taking off his hat, abstracted a few folded sheets of paper from the sweatband. It was the work of five minutes to deposit them in a vault, and see the immensely strong steel door swing shut. He felt relieved.

'I wonder what they'll do,' he muttered to himself on the

way home, 'when they try to follow the instructions on the paper they *did* get.' He pursed his lips and shook his head. 'If they do, there's going to be one heck of an explosion.'

Sills arrived home to find three policemen pacing leisurely up and down the sidewalk in front of the house.

'Police guard,' explained Taylor shortly, 'so that we have no more trouble like last night.'

The chemist related the events at the bank and Taylor nodded grimly. 'Well, it's checkmate for them now. Staples will be here in two hours, and until then the police will take care of things. Afterwards,' he shrugged, 'it will be Staples' affair.'

'Listen, Gene,' the chemist put in suddenly, 'I'm worried about the ammonium. I haven't tested its plating abilities and those are the most important things, you know. What if Staples comes, and we find that all we have is pigeon milk.'

'Hmm,' Taylor stroked his chin, 'You're right there. But I'll tell you what we can do. Before Staples comes, let's plate something – a spoon, suppose – for our own satisfaction.'

'It's really very annoying,' Sills complained fretfully. 'If it weren't for these troublesome hooligans, we wouldn't have to proceed in this slipshod and unscientific manner.'

'Well, let's eat dinner first.'

After the mid-day meal, they began. The apparatus was set up in feverish haste. In a cubic vat, a foot each way, a saturated solution of Ammonaline was poured. An old, battered spoon was the cathode and a mass of ammonium amalgam (separated from the rest of the solution by a perforated glass partition) was the anode. Three batteries in series provided the current.

Sills explained animatedly, 'It works on the same principle as ordinary copper plating. The ammonium ion, once the electric current is run through, is attracted to the cathode, which is in the spoon. Ordinarily it would break up, being unstable, but this is not the case when it is dissolved in Ammonaline. This Ammonaline is itself very slightly ionized and oxygen is given off at the anode.

'This much I know from theory. Let us see what happens in practice.'

He closed the key while Taylor watched with breathless interest. For a moment, no effect was visible. Taylor looked disappointed.

Then Sills grasped his sleeve. 'See!' he hissed. 'Watch the anode!'

Sure enough, bubbles of gas were slowly forming upon the spongy ammonium amalgam. They shifted their attention to the spoon.

Gradually, they noticed a change. The metallic appearance became dulled, the silver color slowly losing its whiteness. A layor of distinct, if dull, yellow was being built up. For fifteen minutes, the current ran and then Sills broke the circuit with a contented sigh.

'It plates perfectly,' he said.

'Good! Take it out! Let's see it!'

'What?' Sills was aghast. 'Take it out! Why that's pure ammonium. If I were to expose it to ordinary air, the water vapor would dissolve it to NH_4OH in no time. We can't do that.'

He dragged a rather bulky piece of apparatus to the table. 'This,' he said, 'is a compressed-air container. I run it through calcium chloride dryers and then bubble the perfectly dry oxygen (safely diluted with four times its own volume of nitrogen) directly into the solvent.'

He introduced the nozzle into the solution just beneath the spoon and turned on a slow stream of air. It worked like magic. With almost lightning speed, the yellow coating began to glitter and gleam, to shine with almost ethereal beauty.

The two men watched it with beating heart and panting breath. Sills shut the air off, and for a while they watched the wonderful spoon and said nothing.

Then Taylor whispered hoarsely, 'Take it out. Let me feel it! My God! – it's beautiful!'

With reverent awe, Sills approached the spoon, grasped it with forceps, and withdrew it from the surrounding liquid.

What followed immediately after that can never be fully described. Later on, when excited newspaper reporters pressed them unmercifully, neither Taylor nor Sills had the least recollection of the happenings of the next few minutes.

What happened was that the moment the ammonium-plated spoon was exposed to open air, the most horrible odor ever conceived assailed their nostrils! – an odor that cannot be described, a terrible broth of Hell that plunged the room into sheer, horrible nightmare.

With one strangled gasp, Sills dropped the spoon. Both were coughing and retching, tearing wildly at their throats and mouths, yelling, weeping, sneezing!

Taylor pounced upon the spoon and looked about wildly. The odor grew steadily more powerful and their wild exertions to escape it had already succeeded in wrecking the laboratory and had upset the vat of Ammonaline. There was only one thing to do, and Sills did it. The spoon went flying out the open window in the middle of Twelfth Avenue. It hit the sidewalk right at the feet of one of the policemen, but Taylor didn't care.

'Take off your clothes. We'll have to burn them,' Sills was gasping. 'Then spray something over the laboratory – anything with a strong smell. Burn sulphur. Get some liquid Bromine.'

Both were tearing at their clothes in distraction when they realized that someone had walked in through the unlocked door. The bell had rung, but neither had heard it. It was Staples, six-foot, lion-maned Steel King.

One step into the hall ruined his dignity utterly. He collapsed in one tearing sob and Twelfth Avenue was treated to the spectacle of an elderly, richly-dressed gentleman tearing uptown as fast as his feet would carry him, shedding as much of his clothes as he dared while doing so.

The spoon continued its deadly work. The three policemen had long since retired in abject rout, and now to the numbed and tortured senses of the two innocent and suffering causes of the entire mess came a roaring and confused shouting from the street.

Men and women were pouring out of the neighboring houses, horses were bolting. Fire engines clanged down the street, only to be abandoned by their riders. Squadrons of police came – and left.

Sills and Taylor finally gave up, and clad only in trousers, ran pell-mell for the Hudson. They did not stop until they found themselves neck-deep in water, with blessed, pure air above them.

Taylor turned bewildered eyes to Sills. 'But how could it emit that horrible odor? You said it was stable and stable solids have no odors. It takes vapor for that, doesn't it?'

'Have you ever smelled musk?' groaned Sills. 'It will give off an aroma for an indefinite period without losing any appreciable weight. We've come up against something like that.'

The two ruminated in silence for a while, wincing whenever the wind brought a vagrant waft of Ammonium vapor to them, and then Taylor said in a low voice, 'When they finally trace the trouble to the spoon, and find out who made it, I'm afraid we'll be sued – or maybe thrown in jail.'

Sills' face lengthened. 'I wish I'd never seen the damned stuff! It's brought nothing but trouble.' His tortured spirit gave way and he sobbed loudly.

Taylor patted him on the back mournfully. 'It's not as bad as all that, of course. The discovery will make you famous and you'll be able to demand your own price, working at any industrial lab in the country. Then, too, you're a cinch to win the Nobel Prize.

'That's right,' Sills smiled again, 'and I may find a way to counteract the odor, too. I hope so.'

'I hope so, too,' said Taylor feelingly. 'Let's go back. I think they've managed to remove the spoon by now.'

THE END

It should be quite obvious to anyone reading 'The Magnificent Possession' that I was majoring in chemistry in college at the time. As supposed humor, it is much more embarrassing on rereading than 'Ring Around the Sun' is. Imagine having a Congressman named 'Hornswoggle' and having gangsters speak in a ridiculous, misspelled version of Brooklyn slang.

'The Magnificent Possession' was the only one of the first nine stories I wrote that Campbell never saw, and I'm glad of that.

In early December I wrote a story I called 'Ad Astra,' and on December 21, 1938 (my father's forty-second birthday, though I don't recall thinking of it as an omen one way or the other), I went in to submit it to Campbell. It was my seventh visit to his office, for I had not yet missed a month, and it was the ninth story I submitted to him.

'Ad Astra' is the first story I wrote for which I remember, even after all this time, the exact circumstances of the initiating inspiration. That fall, I applied for and received a National Youth Administration (NYA) job designed to help me through college. I received fifteen dollars a month, if memory serves me, in return for a few hours of typing. The typing I did was for a sociologist who was writing a book on the subject of social resistance to technological innovation. This included everything from the resistance of the early Mesopotamian priesthood to the dissemination of the knowledge of reading and writing among the general population, down to objections to the airplane by those who said heavier-than-air flight was impossible.

Naturally it occurred to me that a story might be written in which social resistance to space flight might play a small part. It was because of that that I used 'Ad Astra' as the title. This was from the Latin proverb 'Per aspera ad astra' ('Through difficulties to the stars').

For the first time, Campbell did more than simply send a

rejection. On December 29, I received a letter from him asking me to come in for a conference to discuss the story in detail.

On January 5, 1939, I went to see Campbell for the eighth time – and for the first time at his specific request. It turned out that what he liked in the story was the social resistance to space flight – the space flight itself was of course, run of the mill.

Rather daunted, for I had never before had to revise a story to meet editorial specification, I went to work. I brought in the revised story on January 24, and on January 31 I discovered the system used by Campbell in accepting stories. Though his rejections were usually accompanied by long and useful letters, his acceptances consisted of a check only, without a single accompanying word. It was his feeling that the check was eloquent enough. In this case it was for sixty-nine dollars, since the story was 6,900 words long and Campbell paid one cent a word in those days.

It was my first sale to Campbell, after seven months of trying and after eight consecutive rejections. The story appeared half a year later, and I then found that Campbell had changed the title (on the whole justifiably, I think) to 'Trends.'

John Harman was sitting at his desk, brooding, when I entered the office that day. It had become a common sight, by then, to see him staring out at the Hudson, head in hand, a scowl contorting his face – all too common. It seemed unfair for the little bantam to be eating his heart out like that day after day, when by rights he should have been receiving the praise and adulation of the world.

I flopped down into a chair. 'Did you see the editorial in today's *Clarion,* boss?'

He turned weary, bloodshot eyes to me. 'No, I haven't. What do they say? Are they calling the vengeance of God down upon me again?' His voice dripped with bitter sarcasm.

'They're going a little farther *now* boss,' I answered. 'Listen to this:

' "Tomorrow is the day of John Harman's attempt at profaning the heavens. Tomorrow, in defiance of world opinion and world conscience, this man will defy God.

' "It is not given to man to go wheresoever ambition and desire lead him. There are things forever denied him, and aspiring to the stars is one of these. Like Eve, John Harman wishes to eat of the forbidden fruit, and like Eve he will suffer due punishment therefor.

' "But it is not enough, this mere talk. If we allow him thus to brook the vengeance of God, the trespass is mankind's and not Harman's alone. In allowing him to carry out his evil designs, we make ourselves accessory to the crime, and Divine vengeance will fall on all alike.

' "It is, therefore, essential that immediate steps be taken to prevent Harman from taking off in his so-called rocketship tomorrow. The government in refusing to take such steps may force violent action. If it will make no move to confiscate the rocketship, or to imprison Harman, our enraged citizenry may have to take matters into their own hands –" '

Harman sprang from his seat in a rage and, snatching the paper from my hands, threw it into the corner furiously. 'It's an open call to a lynching,' he raved. 'Look at this!'

He cast five or six envelopes in my direction. One glance sufficed to tell what they were.

Astounding Science Fiction, July 1939
Copyright © 1939 by Street & Smith Publications, Inc.
Copyright renewed © 1966 by Isaac Asimov

'More death threats?' I asked.

'Yes, exactly that. I've had to arrange for another increase in the police patrol outside the building and for a motor cycle police escort when I cross the river to the testing ground to-morrow.'

He marched up and down the room with agitated stride. 'I don't know what to do, Clifford. I've worked on the *Prometheus* almost ten years. I've slaved, spent a fortune of money, given up all that makes life worth while – and for what? So that a bunch of fool revivalists can whip up public sentiment against me until my very life isn't safe.'

'You're in advance of the times, boss,' I shrugged my shoulders in a resigned gesture which made him whirl upon me in a fury.

'What do you mean "in advance of the times"? This is 1973. The world has been ready for space travel for half a century now. Fifty years ago, people were talking, dreaming of the day when man could free himself of Earth and plumb the depths of space. For fifty years, science has inched toward this goal, and now ... now I finally have it, and behold! you say the world is not ready for me.'

'The '20s and '30s were years of anarchy, decadence, and misrule, if you remember your history,' I reminded him gently. 'You cannot accept them as criteria.'

'I know, I know. You're going to tell me of the First War of 1914, and the Second of 1940. It's an old story to me; my father fought in the Second and my grandfather in the First. Nevertheless, those were the days when science *flourished*. Men were not afraid then; somehow they dreamed and dared. There was no such thing as conservatism when it came to matters mechanical and scientific. No theory was too radical to advance, no discovery too revolutionary to publish. Today, dry rot has seized the world when a great vision, such as space travel, is hailed as "defiance of God." '

His head sank slowly down, and he turned away to hide his trembling lips and the tears in his eyes. Then he suddenly straightened again, eyes blazing: 'But I'll show them. I'm going through with it, in spite of Hell, Heaven, and Earth. I've put too much into it to quit now.'

'Take it easy, boss,' I advised. 'This isn't going to do you any good tomorrow, when you get into that ship. Your chances of coming out alive aren't too good now, so what will they be if you start out worn to pieces with excitement and worry?'

'You're right. Let's not think of it any more. Where's Shelton?'

'Over at the Institute arranging for the special photographic plates to be sent us.'

'He's been gone a long time, hasn't he?'

'Not especially; but listen, boss, there's something wrong with him. I don't like him.'

'Poppycock! He's been with me two years, and I have no complaints.'

'All right.' I spread my hands in resignation. 'If you won't listen to me, you won't. Just the same I caught him reading one of those infernal pamphlets Otis Eldredge puts out. You know the kind: "Beware, O mankind, for judgment draws near. Punishment for your sins is at hand. Repent and be saved." And all the rest of the time-honoured junk.'

Harman snorted in disgust. 'Cheap tub-thumping revivalist! I suppose the world will never outgrow his type – not while sufficient morons exist. Still you can't condemn Shelton just because he reads it. I've read them myself on occasion.'

'He *says* he picked it up on the sidewalk and read it in "idle curiosity," but I'm pretty sure that I saw him take it out of his wallet. Besides, he goes to church every Sunday.'

'Is *that* a crime? Everyone does, nowadays!'

'Yes, but not to the Twentieth Century Evangelical Society. That's Eldredge's.'

That jolted Harman. Evidently, it was the first he had heard of it. 'Say, that *is* something isn't it? We'll have to keep an eye on him, then.'

But after that, things started to happen, and we forgot all about Shelton – until it was too late.

There was nothing much left to do that last day before the test, and I wandered into the next room, where I went over Harman's final report to the Institute. It was my job to correct any errors or mistakes that crept in, but I'm afraid I wasn't very thorough. To tell the truth, I couldn't concentrate. Every few minutes, I'd fall into a brown study.

It seemed queer, all this fuss over a space travel. When Harman had first announced the approaching perfection of the *Prometheus*, some six months before, scientific circles had been jubilant. Of course, they were cautious in their statements and qualified everything they said, but there was real enthusiasm.

However, the masses didn't take it that way. It seems strange, perhaps, to you of the twenty-first century, but perhaps we should have expected it in those days of '73. People weren't very progressive then. For years there had been a swing toward religion, and when the churches came out un-animously against Harman's rocket – well, there you were.

At first, the opposition confined itself *to* the churches and we thought it might play itself out. But it didn't. The papers got hold of it, and literally spread the gospel. Poor Harman became an anathema to the world in a remarkably short time, and then his troubles began.

He received death threats, and warnings of divine vengeance every day. He couldn't walk the streets in safety. Dozens of sects, to none of which he belonged – he was one of the very rare free-thinkers of the day, which was another count against him – excommunicated him and placed him under special interdict. And, worst of all, Otis Eldredge and his Evangelical Society began stirring up the populace.

Eldredge was a queer character – one of those geniuses, in their way, that arise every so often. Gifted with a golden tongue and a sulphurous vocabulary, he could fairly hypnotize a crowd. Twenty thousand people were so much putty in his hands, could he only bring them within earshot. And for four months, he thundered against Harman; for four months, a pouring stream of denunciation rolled forth in oratorical frenzy. And for four months, the temper of the world rose.

But Harman was not to be daunted. In his tiny, five-foot-two body, he had enough spirit for five six-footers. The more the wolves howled, the firmer he held his ground. With almost divine – his enemies said, diabolical – obstinacy, he refused to yield an inch. Yet his outward firmness was to me, who knew him, but an imperfect concealment of the great sorrow and bitter disappointment within.

The ring of the doorbell interrupted my thoughts at that point and brought me to my feet in surprise. Visitors were very few those days.

I looked out the window and saw a tall, portly figure talking with Police Sergeant Cassidy. I recognized him at once as Howard Winstead, head of the Institute. Harman was hurrying out to greet him, and after a short exchange of phrases, the two entered the office. I followed them in, being rather curious as to what could have brought Winstead, who was more politician than scientist, here.

Winstead didn't seem very comfortable, at first; not his usual suave self. He avoided Harman's eyes in an embarrassed manner and mumbled a few conventionalities concerning the weather. Then he came to the point with direct, undiplomatic bluntness.

'John,' he said, 'How about postponing the trial for a time?'

'You really mean abandoning it altogether, don't you? Well, I won't, and that's final.'

Winstead lifted his hand. 'Wait now, John, don't get excited. Let me state my case. I know the Institute agreed to give you a free hand, and I know that you paid at least half the expenses out of your own pocket, but – you can't go through with it.'

'Oh, can't I, though?' Harman snorted derisively.

'Now listen, John, you know your science, but you don't know your human nature, and I do. This is not the world of the "Mad Decades," whether you realize it or not. There have been profound changes since 1940.' He swung into what was evidently a carefully prepared speech.

'After the First World War, you know, the world as a whole swung away from religion and toward freedom from convention. People were disgusted and disillusioned, cynical and sophisticated. Eldredge calls them "wicked and sinful." In spite of that, science flourished – some say it always fares best in such an unconventional period. From *its* standpoint it was a "Golden Age."

'However, you know the political and economic history of the period. It was a time of political chaos and international anarchy; a suicidal, brainless, insane period – and it culminated in the Second World War. And just as the First War led to a period of sophistication, so the Second initiated a return to religion.

'People were disgusted with the "Mad Decades." They had had enough of it, and feared, beyond all else, a return to it. To remove that possibility, they put the ways of those decades behind them. Their motives, you see, were understandable and laudable. All the freedom, all the sophistication, all the lack of convention were gone – swept away clean. We are living now in a second Victorian age; and naturally so, because human history goes by swings of the pendulum and this is the swing toward religion and convention.

'One thing only is left over since those days of half a century ago. That one thing is the respect of humanity for science. We have prohibition; smoking for women is outlawed; cosmetics are forbidden; low dresses and short skirts are unheard of; divorce is frowned upon. But science has not been confined – *as yet*.

'It behoves science, then, to be circumspect, to refrain from arousing the people. It will be very easy to make them believe – and Otis Eldredge has come perilously close to doing it in some of his speeches – that it was science that brought about the horrors of the Second World War. Science outstripped culture, they will say, technology outstripped sociology, and it was that unbalance that came so near to destroying the world. Somehow, I am inclined to believe they are not so far wrong, at that.

'But do you know what would happen, if it ever *did* come to that? Scientific research may be forbidden; or, if they don't go that far, it will certainly be so strictly regulated as to stifle in its own decay. It will be a calamity from which humanity would not recover for a millennium.

'And it is your trial flight that may precipitate all this. You are arousing the public to a stage where it will be difficult to calm them. I warn you, John. The consequences will be on your head.'

There was absolute silence for a moment and then Harman forced a smile. 'Come, Howard, you're letting yourself be frightened by shadows on the wall. Are you trying to tell me that it is your serious belief that the world as a whole is ready to plunge into a second Dark Ages? After all, the intelligent men are on the side of science, aren't they?'

'If they are, there aren't many of them left from what I see.' Winstead drew a pipe from his pocket and filled it slowly with tobacco as he continued: 'Eldredge formed a League of the Righteous two months ago – they call it the L. R. – and it has grown unbelievably. *Twenty million is its membership in the United States alone.* Eldredge boasts that after the next election Congress will be his; and there seems to be more truth than bluff in that. Already there has been strenuous lobbying in favour of a bill outlawing rocket experiments, and laws of that type have been enacted in Poland, Portugal, and Rumania. Yes, John, we are perilously close to open persecution of science.' He was smoking now in rapid, nervous puffs.

'But if I succeed, Howard, if I succeed! What then?'

'Bah! You know the chances for that. Your own estimate gives you only one chance in ten of coming out alive.'

'What does that signify? The next experimenter will learn by my mistakes, and the odds will improve. That's the scientific method.'

'The mob doesn't know anything about the scientific method; and they don't want to know. Well, what do you say? Will you call it off?'

Harman sprang to his feet, his chair tumbling over with a crash. 'Do you know what you ask? Do you want me to give up my life's work, my dream, just like that? Do you think I'm going to sit back and wait for your *dear* public to become benevolent? Do you think they'll change in *my* lifetime?

'Here's my answer: I have an inalienable right to pursue knowledge. Science has an inalienable right to progress and develop without interference. The world, in interfering with me, is wrong; I am right. And it shall go hard; but I *will not* abandon my rights.'

Winstead shook his head sorrowfully. 'You're wrong, John, when you speak of "inalienable" rights. What you call a "right" is merely a *privilege, generally agreed upon.* What society accepts, is right; what it does not, is wrong.'

'Would your friend, Eldredge, agree to such a definition of his "righteousness"?' questioned Harman bitterly.

'No, he would not, but that's irrelevant. Take the case of those African tribes who used to be cannibals. They were brought up as cannibals, have the long tradition of cannibalism, and their society accepts the practice. To *them*, cannibalism is *right*, and why shouldn't it be? So you see how relative the whole notion is, and how inane your conception of "inalienable" rights to perform experiments is.'

'You know, Howard, you missed your calling when you didn't become a lawyer.' Harman was really growing angry. 'You've been bringing out every moth-eaten argument you can think of. For God's sake, man, are you trying to pretend that it is a crime to refuse to run with the crowd? Do you stand for absolute uniformity, ordinariness, orthodoxy, commonplaceness? Science would die far sooner under the programme you outline than under governmental prohibition.'

Harman stood up and pointed an accusing finger at the other. 'You're betraying science and the tradition of those glorious rebels: Galileo, Darwin, Einstein, and their kind. My rocket leaves tomorrow on schedule in spite of you and every other stuffed shirt in the United States. That's that, and I refuse to listen to you any longer. So you can just get out.'

The head of the Institute, red in the face, turned to me. 'You're my witness, young man, that I warned this obstinate nitwit, this ... this hare-brained fanatic.' He spluttered a bit, and then strode out, the picture of fiery indignation.

Harman turned to me when he had gone: 'Well, what do *you* think? I suppose you agree with him.'

There was only one possible answer and I made it: 'You're not paying me to do anything else but follow orders, boss. I'm sticking with you.'

Just then Shelton came in and Harman packed us both off to go over the calculations of the orbit of flight for the umpteenth time, while he himself went off to bed.

The next day, July 15th, dawned in matchless splendour, and Harman, Shelton, and myself were in an almost gay mood as we crossed the Hudson to where the *Prometheus* – surrounded by an adequate police guard – lay in gleaming grandeur.

Around it, roped off at an apparently safe distance, rolled a crowd of gigantic proportions. Most of them were hostile, raucously so. In fact, for one fleeting moment, as our motorcycle police escort parted the crowds for us, the shouts and imprecations that reached our ears almost convinced me that we should have listened to Winstead.

But Harman paid no attention to them at all, after one supercilious sneer at a shout of: 'There goes John Harman, son of Belial.' Calmly, he directed us about our task of inspection. I tested the foot-thick outer walls and the airlocks for leaks, then made sure the air purifier worked. Shelton checked up on the repellent screen and the fuel tanks. Finally, Harman tried on the clumsy spacesuit, found it suitable, and announced himself ready.

The crowd stirred. Upon a hastily erected platform of wooden planks piled in confusion by some in the mob, there rose up a striking figure. Tall and lean; with thin, ascetic countenance; deep-set, burning eyes, peering and half closed; a thick, white mane crowning all – it was Otis Eldredge. The crowd recognized him at once and many cheered. Enthusiasm waxed and soon the entire turbulent mass of people shouted themselves hoarse over him.

He raised a hand for silence, turned to Harman, who regarded him with surprise and distaste, and pointed a long, bony finger at him:

'John Harman, son of the devil, spawn of Satan, you are here for an evil purpose. You are about to set out upon a blasphemous attempt to pierce the veil beyond which man is forbidden to go. You are tasting of the forbidden fruit of Eden and beware that you taste not of the fruits of sin.'

The crowd cheered him to the echo and he continued: 'The finger of God is upon you, John Harman. He shall not allow His works to be defiled. You die today, John Harman.' His voice rose in intensity and his last words were uttered in truly prophetlike fervour.

Harman turned away in disdain. In a loud, clear voice, he addressed the police sergeant: 'Is there any way, officer, of removing these spectators. The trial flight may be attended by some destruction because of the rocket blasts, and they're crowding too close.'

The policeman answered in a crisp, unfriendly tone: 'If you're afraid of being mobbed, say so, Mr. Harman. You don't have to worry, though, we'll hold them back. And as for danger – from *that* contraption –' He sniffed loudly in the direction of the *Prometheus,* evoking a torrent of jeers and yells.

Harman said nothing further, but climbed into the ship in silence. And when he did so, a queer sort of stillness fell over the mob; a palpable tension. There was no attempt at rushing the ship, an attempt I had thought inevitable. On the contrary, Otis Eldredge himself shouted to everyone to move back.

'Leave the sinner to his sins,' he shouted. ' "Vengeance is mine," saith the Lord.'

As the moment approached, Shelton nudged me. 'Let's get out of here,' he whispered in a strained voice. 'Those rocket blasts are poison.' Saying this, he broke into a run, beckoning anxiously for me to follow.

We had not yet reached the fringes of the crowd when there was a terrific roar behind me. A wave of heated air swept over me. There was the frightening hiss of some speeding object past my ear, and I was thrown violently to the ground. For a few moments I lay dazed, my ears ringing and my head reeling.

When I staggered drunkenly to my feet again, it was to view a dreadful sight. Evidently, the entire fuel supply of the *Prometheus* had exploded at once, and where it had lain a moment ago there was now only a yawning hole. The ground was strewn with wreckage. The cries of the hurt were heart-rending, and the mangled bodies – but I won't try to describe those.

A weak groan at my feet attracted my attention. One look, and I gasped in horror, for it was Shelton, the back of his head a bloody mass.

'I did it.' His voice was hoarse and triumphant but withal so low that I could scarcely hear it. 'I did it. I broke open the liquid-oxygen compartments and when the spark went through the acetylide mixture the whole cursed thing exploded.' He gasped a bit and tried to move but failed. 'A piece of wreckage must have hit me, but I don't care. I'll die knowing that –'

His voice was nothing more than a rasping rattle, and on his face was the ecstatic look of martyr. He died then, and I could not find it in my heart to condemn him.

It was then I first thought of Harman. Ambulances from

Manhattan and from Jersey City were on the scene, and one had sped to a wooden patch some five hundred yards distant, where, caught in the treetops, lay a splintered fragment of the *Prometheus*' forward compartment. I limped there as fast as I could, but they had dragged out Harman and clanged away long before I could reach them.

After that, I didn't stay. The disorganized crowd had no thought but for the dead and wounded *now*, but when they recovered, and bent their thoughts to revenge, my life would not be worth a straw. I followed the dictates of the better part of valour and quietly disappeared.

The next week was a hectic one for me. During that time, I lay in hiding at the home of a friend, for it would have been more than my life was worth to allow myself to be seen and recognized. Harman, himself, lay in a Jersey City hospital, with nothing more than superficial cuts and bruises – thanks to the backward force of the explosion and the saving clump of trees which cushioned the fall of the *Prometheus*. It was on him that the brunt of the world's wrath fell.

New York, and the rest of the world also, just about went crazy. Every last paper in the city came out with gigantic headlines, '28 Killed, 73 Wounded – the Price of Sin,' printed in blood-red letters. The editorials howled for Harman's life, demanding he be arrested and tried for first-degree murder.

The dreaded cry of 'Lynch him!' was raised throughout the five boroughs, and milling thousands crossed the river and converged on Jersey City. At their head was Otis Eldredge, both legs in splints, addressing the crowd from an open automobile as they marched. It was a veritable army.

Mayor Carson of Jersey City called out every available policeman and phoned frantically to Trenton for the State militia. New York clamped down on every bridge and tunnel leaving the city – but not till after many thousands had left.

There were pitched battles on the Jersey coast that sixteenth of July. The vastly outnumbered police clubbed indiscriminately but were gradually pushed back and back. Mounties rode down upon the mob relentlessly, but were swallowed up and pulled down by sheer force of numbers. Not until tear gas was used, did the crowd halt – and even then they did not retreat.

The next day martial law was declared, and the State Militia entered Jersey City. That was the end for the lynchers. Eldredge was called to confer with the mayor, and after the conference ordered his followers to disperse.

In a statement to the newspapers, Mayor Carson said: 'John Harman must needs suffer for his crime, but it is essential that he do so legally. Justice must take its course, and the State of New Jersey will take all necessary measures.'

By the end of the week, normality of a sort had returned and Harman slipped out of the public spotlight. Two more weeks and there was scarcely a word about him in the newspapers, excepting such casual references to him in the discussion of the new Zittman antirocketry bill that had just passed both houses of Congress by unanimous votes.

Yet he remained in the hospital still. No legal action had been taken against him, but it began to appear that a sort of indefinite imprisonment 'for his own protection' might be his eventual fate. Therefore, I bestirred myself to action.

Temple Hospital is situated in a lonely and outlying district of Jersey City, and on a dark, moonless night I experienced no difficulty at all in invading the grounds unobserved. With a facility that surprised me, I sneaked in through a basement window, slugged a sleepy interne into insensibility and proceeded to Room 15E, which was listed in the books as Harman's.

'Who's there?' Harman's surprised shout was music in my ears.

'Sh! Quiet! It's I, Cliff McKenny.'

'You! What are you doing here?'

'Trying to get you out. If I don't, you're liable to stay here the rest of your life. Come on, let's go.'

I was hustling him into his clothes while we were speaking, and in no time at all we were sneaking down the corridor. We were out safely and into my waiting car before Harman collected his scattered wits sufficiently to begin asking questions.

'What's happened since that day?' was the first question. 'I don't remember a thing after starting the rocket blasts until I woke up in the hospital.'

'Didn't they tell you anything?'

'Not a damn thing,' he swore. 'I asked until I was hoarse.'

So I told him the whole story from the explosion on. His eyes were wide with shocked surprise when I told of the dead and wounded, and filled with wild rage when he heard of Shelton's treachery. The story of the riots and attempted lynching evoked a muffled curse from between set lips.

'Of course, the papers howled "murder," ' I concluded, 'but they couldn't pin *that* on you. They tried manslaughter, but there were too many eye-witnesses that had heard your request for the removal of the crowd and the police sergeant's absolute refusal to do so. That, of course, absolved you from all blame.

The police sergeant himself died in the explosion, and they couldn't make him the goat.

'Still, with Eldredge yelling for your hide, you're never safe. It would be best to leave while able.'

Harman nodded his head in agreement. 'Eldredge survived the explosion, did he?'

'Yes, worse luck. He broke both legs, but it takes more than that to shut his mouth.'

Another week had passed before I reached our future haven – my uncle's farm in Minnesota. There, in a lonely and out-of-the-way rural community, we stayed while the hullabaloo over Harman's disappearance gradually died down and the perfunctory search for us faded away. The search, by the way, was short indeed, for the authorities seemed more relieved than concerned over the disappearance.

Peace and quiet did wonders with Harman. In six months he seemed a new man – quite ready to consider a second attempt at space travel. Not all the misfortunes in the world could stop him, it seemed, once he had his heart set on something.

'My mistake the first time,' he told me one winter's day, 'lay in announcing the experiment. I should have taken the temper of the people into account, as Winstead said. This time, however' – he rubbed his hands and gazed thoughtfully into the distance – 'I'll steal a march on them. The experiment will be performed in secrecy – absolute secrecy.'

I laughed grimly, 'It would have to be. Do you know that all future experiment in rocketry, even entirely theoretical research is a crime punishable by death?'

'Are you afraid, then?'

'Of course not, boss. I'm merely stating a fact. And here's another plain fact. We two can't build a ship all by ourselves, you know.'

'I've thought of that and figured a way out, Cliff. What's more, I can take care of the money angle, too. You'll have to do some travelling, though.

'First, you'll have to go to Chicago and look up the firm of Roberts & Scranton and withdraw everything that's left of my father's inheritance, which,' he added in a rueful aside, 'is more than half gone on the first ship. Then, locate as many of the old crowd as you can: Harry Jenkins, Joe O'Brien, Neil Stanton – all of them. And get back as quickly as you can. I am tired of delay.'

Two days later, I left for Chicago. Obtaining my uncle's consent to the entire business was a simple affair. 'Might as well be strung up for a herd of sheep as for a lamb,' he grunted, 'so go ahead. I'm in enough of a mess now and can afford a bit more, I guess.'

It took quite a bit of travelling and even more smooth talk and persuasion before I managed to get four men to come: the three mentioned by Harman and one other, a Saul Simonoff. With that skeleton force and with the half million still left Harman out of the reputed millions left him by his father, we began work.

The building of the *New Prometheus* is a story in itself – a long story of five years of discouragement and insecurity. Little by little, buying girders in Chicago, beryl-steel plates in New York, a vanadium cell in San Francisco, miscellaneous items in scattered corners of the nation, we constructed the sister ship to the illfated *Prometheus*.

The difficulties in the way were all but insuperable. To prevent drawing suspicion down upon us, we had to spread our purchases over periods of time, and to see to it, as well, that the orders were made out to various places. For this we required the co-operation of various friends, who, to be sure, did not know at the time for exactly what purpose the purchases were being used.

We had to synthesize our own fuel, ten tons of it, and that was perhaps the hardest job of all; certainly it took the most time. And finally, as Harman's money dwindled, we came up against our biggest problem – the necessity of economizing. From the beginning we had known that we could never make the *New Prometheus* as large or as elaborate as the first ship had been, but it soon developed that we would have to reduce its equipment to a point perilously close to the danger line. The repulsion screen was barely satisfactory and all attempts at radio communication were perforce abandoned.

And as we labored through the years, there in the backwoods of northern Minnesota, the world moved on, and Winstead's prophecies proved to have hit amazingly near the mark.

The events of those five years – from 1973 to 1978 – are well known to the schoolboys of today, the period being the climax of what we now call the 'Neo-Victorian Age.' The happenings of those years seem well-nigh unbelievable as we look back upon them now.

The outlawing of all research on space travel came in the very beginning, but was a bare start compared to the antiscientific measures taken in the ensuing years. The next congressional elections, those of 1974, resulted in a Congress in which

Eldredge controlled the House and held the balance of power in the Senate.

Hence, no time was lost. All the first session of the ninety-third Congress, the famous Stonely–Carter Bill was passed. It established the Federal Scientific Research Investigatory Bureau – the FSRIB – which was given full power to pass on the legality of all research in the country. Every laboratory, industrial or scholastic, was required to file information, in advance, on all projected research before this new bureau, which could, and did, ban absolutely all such as it disapproved of.

The inevitable appeal to the supreme court came on November 9, 1974, in the case of Westly vs. Simmons in which Joseph Westly of Stanford upheld his right to continue his investigations on atomic power on the grounds that the Stonely–Carter act was unconstitutional.

How we five, isolated amid the snowdrifts of the Middle West, followed that case! We had all the Minneapolis and St. Paul papers sent to us – always reaching us two days late – and devoured every word of print concerning it. For the two months of suspense work ceased entirely on the *New Prometheus*.

It was rumoured at first that the court would declare the act unconstitutional, and monster parades were held in every large town against this eventuality. The League of the Righteous brought its powerful influence to bear – and even the supreme court submitted. It was five to four for constitutionality. *Science strangled by the vote of one man.*

And it was strangled beyond a doubt. The members of the bureau were Eldredge men, heart and soul, and nothing that would not have immediate industrial use was passed.

'Science has gone too far,' said Eldredge in a famous speech at about that time. 'We must halt it indefinitely, and allow the world to catch up. Only through that and trust in God may we hope to achieve universal and permanent prosperity.'

But this was one of Eldridge's last statements. He had never fully recovered from the broken legs he received that fateful day in July of '73, and his strenuous life since then had strained his constitution past the breaking point. On February 2, 1976, he passed away amid a burst of mourning unequalled since Lincoln's assassination.

His death had no immediate effect on the course of events. The rules of the FSRIB grew, in fact, in stringency as the years passed. So starved and choked did science become, that once more colleges found themselves forced to reinstate philosophy and the classics as the chief studies – and at that the student body fell to the lowest point since the beginning of the twentieth century.

These conditions prevailed more or less throughout the civilized world, reaching even lower depths in England, and perhaps least depressing in Germany, which was the last to fall under the 'Neo-Victorian' influence.

The nadir of science came in the spring of 1978, a bare month before the completion of the *New Prometheus*, with the passing of the 'Easter Edict' – it was issued the day before Easter. By it, *all* independent research or experimentation was absolutely forbidden. The FSRIB thereafter reserved the right to allow only such research as it *specifically requested*.

John Harman and I stood before the gleaming metal of the *New Prometheus* that Easter Sunday; I in the deepest gloom, and he in an almost jovial mood.

'Well, Clifford, my boy,' said he, 'the last ton of fuel, a few polishing touches, and I am ready for my second attempt. This time there will be no Sheltons among us.' He hummed a hymn. That was all the radio played in those days, and even we rebels sang them from sheer frequency of repetition.

I grunted sourly: 'It's no use, boss. Ten to one, you end up somewhere in space, and even if you come back, you'll most likely be hung by the neck. We can't win.' My head shook dolefully from side to side.

'Bah! This state of affairs can't last, Cliff.'

'I think it will. Winstead was right that time. The pendulum swings, and since 1945 it's been swinging against us. We're ahead of the times – or behind them.'

'Don't speak of that fool, Winstead. You're making the same mistake he did. Trends are things of centuries and millenniums, not years or decades. For five hundred years we have been moving toward science. You can't reverse that in thirty years.'

'Then what are we doing?' I asked sarcastically.

'We're going through a momentary reaction following a period of too-rapid advance in the Mad Decades. Just such a reaction took place in the Romantic Age – the first Victorian Period – following the too-rapid advance of the eighteenth-century Age of Reason.'

'Do you really think so?' I was shaken by his evident self-assurance.

'Of course. This period has a perfect analogy in the spasmodic "revivals" that used to hit the small towns in America's

Bible Belt a century or so ago. For a week, perhaps everyone would get religion, and virtue would reign triumphant. Then, one by one, they would backslide and the Devil would resume his sway.

'In fact, there are symptoms of backsliding even now. The L.R. has indulged in one squabble after another since Eldredge's death. There have been half a dozen schisms already. The very extremities to which those in power are going are helping us, for the country is rapidly tiring of it.'

And that ended the argument – I in total defeat, as usual.

A month later, the *New Prometheus* was complete. It was nowhere near as glittering and as beautiful as the original, and bore many a trace of makeshift workmanship, but we were proud of it – proud and triumphant.

'I'm going to try again, men' – Harman's voice was husky, and his little frame vibrant with happiness – 'and I may not make it, but for that I don't care.' His eyes shone in anticipation. 'I'll be shooting through the void at last, and the dream of mankind will come true. Out around the Moon and back; the first to see the other side. It's worth the chance.'

'You won't have fuel enough to land on the Moon, boss, which is a pity,' I said.

At that a pessimistic whisper ran through the little group surrounding him, to which he paid no attention.

'Good-bye,' he said. 'I'll be seeing you.' And with a cheerful grin he climbed into the ship.

Fifteen minutes later, the five of us sat about the living-room table, frowning, lost in thought, eyes gazing out of the building at the spot where a burned section of soil marked the spot where a few minutes earlier the *New Prometheus* had lain.

Simonoff voiced the thought that was in the mind of each one of us: 'Maybe it would be better for him *not* to come back. He won't be treated very well if he does, I think.' And we all nodded in gloomy assent.

How foolish that prediction seems to me now from the hindsight of three decades.

The rest of the story is really not mine, for I did not see Harman again until a month after his eventful trip ended in a safe landing.

It was almost thirty-six hours after the take-off that a screaming projectile shot its way over Washington and buried itself in the mud just across the Potomac.

Investigators were at the scene of the landing within fifteen minutes, and in another fifteen minutes the police were there, for it was found the projectile was a *rocketship*. They stared in involuntary awe at the tired, dishevelled man who staggered out in near-collapse.

There was utter silence while he shook his fist at the staring spectators and shouted: 'Go ahead, hang me, fools. But I've reached the Moon, and you can't hang *that*. Get the FSRIB. Maybe they'll declare the flight illegal and, therefore, nonexistent.' He laughed weakly and suddenly collapsed.

Someone shouted: 'Take him to a hospital. He's sick.' In stiff unconsciousness Harman was bundled into a police car and carried away, while the police formed a guard about the rocketship.

Government officials arrived and investigated the ship, read the log, inspected the drawings and photographs he had taken of the Moon, and finally departed in silence. The crowd grew and the word spread that a man had reached the Moon.

Curiously enough, there was little resentment of the fact. Men were impressed and awed; the crowd whispered and cast inquisitive glances at the dim crescent of Luna, scarcely seen in the bright sunlight. Over all, an uneasy pall of silence, the silence of indecision, lay.

Then, at the hospital, Harman revealed his identity, and the fickle world went wild. Even Harman himself was stunned in surprise at the rapid change in the world's temper. It seemed almost incredible, and yet it was true. Secret discontent, combined with a heroic tale of man against overwhelming odds – the sort of tale that had stirred man's soul since the beginning of time – served to sweep everyone into an ever-swelling current of anti-Victorianism. And Eldredge was dead – no other could replace him.

I saw Harman at the hospital shortly after that. He was propped up and still half buried with papers, telegrams, and letters. He grinned at me and nodded. 'Well, Cliff,' he whispered, 'the pendulum swung back again.'

THE END

Actually, though 'Trends' was the second story I sold, it was the third to be published. Ahead of it was not only 'Marooned off Vesta,' but another story (to be mentioned shortly) that was written and sold after 'Trends' but was rushed into print sooner. Both earlier stories were, however, published in *Amazing* and, somehow, I find it difficult to count them. To me, the first story I sold to Campbell and published in *Astounding* is my first *significant* published story. This is rather ungrateful of me toward *Amazing*, but I can't help it.

The July 1939 issue of *Astounding* is sometimes considered by later fans to mark the beginning of science fiction's so-called Golden Age, a period of stretching through most of the 1940s. In that period, Campbell's views were in full force in the magazine, and the authors he trained and developed were writing with the full ardor of youth. I wish I could say that 'Trends' was what marked the beginning of that Golden Age, but I can't. Its appearance in that issue was pure coincidence.

What really counted was that the lead novelette in the July 1939 issue was 'Black Destroyer,' by A. E. van Vogt, a first story by a new author, while in the next issue, August 1939, was a short story, 'Lifeline,' by Robert A. Heinlein, another first story by a new author.

In time to come, Van Vogt, Heinlein, and I would be universally listed among the top authors of the Golden Age, but Van Vogt and Heinlein were that from the very beginning. Each blazed forth as a first magazine star at the moment his first story appeared, and their status never flagged throughout the remainder of the Golden Age. I, on the other hand (and this is not false modesty), came up only gradually. I was very little noticed for a while and came to be considered a major author by such gradual steps that despite the healthy helping of vanity with which I am blessed, I myself was the last to notice.

'Trends' is an amusing story in some respects. It sets the initial space flights to the Moon in the 1970s. I thought at the time I was being daring indeed, but it has turned out that I was behind the eventual reality by a full decade, since what I described was done, and with immensely greater sophistication, in the 1960s. My description of the first attempts at space flight was, of course, incredibly naïve, in hindsight.

In one respect, however, the story is unusual. In recent years Phil Klass (a science fiction writer who publishes under the pseudonym 'William Tenn') pointed out to me that this was the first story in history that predicted resistance of any kind to the notion of space exploration. In all other stories, the general public was either indifferent or enthusiastic. This makes me sound enormously and uniquely perceptive, but having explained the nature of the book I was doing my NYA work on, I can't take credit for brilliance. (Heck!)

Notice also the reference to the 'Second [World War] of 1940.' The story, remember, was written two months after Munich. I did not believe at the time that this meant 'peace in our time,' as Neville Chamberlain had maintained. I estimated that there would be a war in a year and a half, and again I was too conservative.

'Trends,' incidentally, is one of the few stories I have written in the first person, and the narrator is named Clifford Mc-Kenny. (Why my penchant for Irish last names in those days I haven't been able to figure out.) Behind the first name, though, lies a story.

After my May 1938 scare concerning the demise of *Astounding*, I began sending monthly letters to the magazine, carefully rating the stories. (I stopped after I began selling stories myself.) These were all published, and, in fact, I had sent a letter to *Astounding*, which was published, back in 1935. Two established science fiction writers wrote me personally in response to remarks I made concerning their stories. These were Russell R. Winterbotham and Clifford D. Simak.

With both, I maintained a correspondence, quite regular at first, and with long dry intervals in later years. The friendship that resulted, though long distance, was enduring. I met Russ Winterbotham in person only once, and that was at the World Science Fiction Convention in Cleveland in 1966. He died in 1971. I have met Cliff Simak three times, the most recent occasion being at the World Science Fiction Convention in Boston in 1971, where he was guest of honor.

Simak's first letter to me was in response to a letter of mine printed in *Astounding* that had given a low rating to his story 'Rule 18,' in the July 1938 issue. Simak wrote to ask details so that he might consider my criticisms and perhaps profit from them. (Would that I could react so gently and rationally to adverse criticism!)

I reread the story in order to be able to answer properly and found, to my surprise, that there was nothing wrong with it at all. What he had done was to write the story in separate scenes with no explicit transition passages between. I wasn't used to that technique, so the story seemed choppy and incoherent. The second time around, I recognized what he was doing and realized that not only was the story not in the least incoherent but it moved with a slick speed that would have been impossible if all the dull, bread-and-butter transitions had been inserted.

I wrote Simak to explain, and adopted the same device in my own stories. What's more, I attempted, as far as possible, to make use of something similar to Simak's cool and unadorned style.

I have sometimes heard science fiction writers speak of the influence upon their style of such high-prestige literary figures as Kafka, Proust, and Joyce. This may be pose or it may be reality, but, for myself, I make no such claim. I learned how to write science fiction by the attentive reading of science fiction, and among the major influences on my style was Clifford Simak.

Simak was particularly encouraging in those anxious months during which I was trying to sell a story. On the day I made my first sale, I had a letter, all sealed and addressed and stamped, waiting to be mailed to him. I tore it open to add the news, and destroying a stamped envelope, which represented a clear loss of several cents, was not something I did lightly in those days.

It has always pleased me, therefore, that my first sale to Campbell had, as its first-person narrator, a character named in Clifford Simak's honor.

One more point about 'Trends' –

In my early sessions with Campbell, he had occasionally pointed out the value of having a name that wasn't odd and hard to pronounce, and suggested the use of a common Anglo-Saxon name as a pseudonym. On this point, I clearly expressed intransigence. My name was my name and it would go on my stories.

When 'Trends' was sold, I steeled myself for what I thought might be a struggle with Campbell thut might even cost me my precious sale. – It never happened. Perhaps it was because my name had already appeared on two stories in *Amazing*, or perhaps Campbell recognized I would not agree to a pseudonym, but he never raised the point.

As it happened, my disinclination for a pseudonym was lucky indeed, for the name Isaac Asimov proved highly visible. No one could see the name for the first time without smiling at its oddness; and anyone seeing it the second time would instantly remember the first time. I'm convinced that at least part of my eventual popularity came about because the readers recognized the name quickly and became aware of my stories as a group.

Indeed, matters came full circle. In later years, I frequently met readers who were convinced the name was a pseudonym *designed* to achieve visibility and that my real name must be something like John Smith. It was sometimes hard to disabuse them.

While I was revising 'Trends' for Campbell, I was also working on another story, 'The Weapon Too Dreadful to Use.' That one I did *not* submit to Campbell. Either I did not wish to push him too hard immediately after I had made a sale to him, or I suspected the story wasn't good enough for him and didn't want to spoil the impression 'Trends' might have made. In either case (and I don't really remember the motive) I decided to try it on *Amazing* first. It was also a one cent market, after all, and perhaps I thought I owed them another chance, now that I had made my Campbell sale.

I mailed 'The Weapon Too Dreadful to Use' to *Amazing* on February 6, 1939, and on February 20 received notice of acceptance. *Amazing* may have bought it because it needed a story in a hurry, for it appeared in the May issue, which reached the newsstands only three weeks after the sale. That made it my second published story, for it appeared two months before 'Trends.'

5: The Weapon Too Dreadful to Use

Karl Frantor found the prospect a terribly dismal one. From low-hanging clouds, fell eternal misty rain; squat, rubbery vegetation with its dull, reddish-brown colour stretched away in all directions. Now and then a Hop-scotch Bird fluttered wildly above them, emitting plaintive squawks as it went.

Karl turned his head to gaze at the tiny dome of *Aphrodopolis*, largest city on Venus.

'God,' he muttered, 'even the dome is better than this awful world out here.' He pulled the rubberized fabric of his coat closer about him. 'I'll be glad to get back to Earth again.'

He turned to the slight figure of Antil, the Venusian, 'When are we coming to the ruins, Antil?'

There was no answer and Karl noticed the tear that rolled down the Venusian's green, puckered cheeks. Another glistened in the large, lemur-like eyes; soft, incredibly beautiful eyes.

The Earthman's voice softened. 'Sorry, Antil, I didn't mean to say anything against Venus.'

Antil turned his green face toward Karl, 'It was not that, my friend. Naturally, you would not find much to admire in an alien world. I, however, love Venus, and I weep because I am overcome with its beauty.' The words came fluently but with the inevitable distortion caused by vocal cords unfitted for harsh languages.

'I know it seems incomprehensible to you,' Antil continued, 'but to me Venus is a paradise, a golden land – I cannot express my feelings for it properly.'

'Yet there are some that say only Earthmen can love.' Karl's sympathy was strong and sincere.

The Venusian shook his head sadly. 'There is much besides the capacity to feel emotion that your people deny us.'

Karl changed the subject hurriedly. 'Tell me, Antil, doesn't Venus present a dull aspect even to you? You've been to Earth and should know. How can this eternity of brown and grey compare to the living, warm colours of Earth?'

'It is far more beautiful to me. You forget that my colour

Amazing Stories, May 1939
Copyright © 1939 by Ziff-Davis Publishing Company
Copyright renewed © 1966 by Isaac Asimov

sense is so enormously different from yours.* How can I explain the beauties, the wealth of colour in which this landscape abounds?' He fell silent, lost in the wonders he spoke of, while to the Terrestrial the deadly, melancholy grey remained unchanged.

'Someday,' Antil's voice came as from a person in a dream, 'Venus will once more belong to the Venusians. The Earthlings shall no longer rule us, and the glory of our ancestors shall return to us.'

Karl laughed. 'Come, now, Antil, you speak like a member of the Green Bands, that are giving the government so much trouble. I thought you didn't believe in violence.'

'I don't, Karl,' Antil's eyes were grave and rather frightened, 'but the extremists are gaining power, and I fear the worst. And if – if open rebellion against Earth breaks out, I *must* join them.'

'But you disagree with them.'

'Yes, of course,' he shrugged his shoulders, a gesture he had learned from Earthmen, 'we can gain nothing by violence. There are five billion of you and scarcely a hundred million of us. You have resources and weapons while we have none. It would be a fool's venture and even should we win, we might leave such a heritage of hatred that there could never be peace among our two planets.'

'Then why join them?'

'Because I am a Venusian.'

The Earthman burst into laughter again. 'Patriotism, it seems, is as irrational on Venus as on Earth. But come, let us proceed to the ruins of your ancient city. Are we nearly there?'

'Yes,' answered Antil, 'it's a matter of little more than an Earth mile now. Remember, however, that you are to disturb nothing. The ruins of *Ash-taz-zor* are sacred to us, as the sole existing remnant of the time when we, too, were a great race, rather than the degenerate remains of one.'

They walked on in silence, slogging through the soft earth beneath, dodging the writhing roots of the Snaketree, and giving the occasional Tumbling Vines they passed a wide berth.

It was Antil who resumed the conversation.

'Poor Venus.' His quiet, wistful voice was sad. 'Fifty years ago the Earthman came with promise of peace and plenty – and we believed. We showed them the emerald mines and the

* The Venusian eye can distinguish between two tints, the wavelengths of which differ by as little as five Angstrom units. They see thousands of colours to which Earthmen are blind. – Author.

juju weed and their eyes glittered with desire. More and more came, and their arrogance grew. And now –'

'It's too bad, Antil,' Karl said, 'but you really feel too strongly about it.'

'Too strongly! Are we allowed to vote? Have we any representation at all in the Venusian Provincial Congress? Aren't there laws against Venusians riding in the same stratocars as Earthlings, or eating in the same hotel, or living in the same house? Are not all colleges closed to us? Aren't the best and most fertile parts of the planet pre-empted by Earthlings? Are there any rights *at all* that Terrestrials allow us upon our *own* planet?'

'What you say is perfectly true, and I deplore it. But similar conditions once existed on Earth with regard to certain so-called 'inferior races,' and in time, all those disabilities were removed until today total equality reigns. Remember, too, that the intelligent people of Earth are on your side. Have I, for instance, ever displayed any prejudice against a Venusian?'

'No, Karl, you know you haven't. But how many intelligent men are there? On Earth, it took long and weary millennia, filled with war and suffering, before equality was established. What if Venus refuses to wait those millennia?'

Karl frowned, 'You're right, of course, but you must wait. What else can you do?'

'I don't know – I don't know,' Antil's voice trailed into silence.

Suddenly, Karl wished he hadn't started on this trip to the ruins of mysterious *Ash-taz-zor*. The maddeningly monotonous terrain, the just grievances of Antil had served to depress him greatly. He was about to call the whole thing off when the Venusian raised his webbed fingers to point out a mound of earth ahead.

'That's the entrance,' he said; '*Ash-taz-zor* has been buried under the soil for uncounted thousands of years, and only Venusians know of it. You're the first Earthman ever to see it.'

'I shall keep it absolutely secret, Antil. I have promised.'

'Come, then.'

Antil brushed aside the lush vegetation to reveal a narrow entrance between two boulders and beckoned to Karl to follow. Into a narrow, damp corridor they crept. Antil drew from his pouch a small Atomite lamp, which cast its pearly white glow upon walls of dripping stone.

'These corridors and burrows,' he said, 'were dug three centuries ago by our ancestors who considered the city a holy place. Of late, however, we have neglected it. I was the first to visit it in a long, long time. Perhaps that is another sign of our degeneracy.'

For over a hundred yards they walked on straight ahead; then the corridors flared out into a lofty dome. Karl gasped at the view before him. There were the remains of buildings, architectural marvels unrivalled on Earth since the days of Periclean Athens. But all lay in shattered ruins, so that only a hint of the city's magnificence remained.

Antil led the way across the open space and plunged into another burrow that twisted its way for half a mile through soil and rock. Here and there, side-corridors branched off, and once or twice Karl caught glimpses of ruined structures. He would have investigated had not Antil kept him on the path.

Again they emerged, this time before a low, sprawling building constructed of a smooth, green stone. Its right wing was utterly smashed, but the rest seemed scarcely touched.

The Venusian's eyes shone; his slight form straightened with pride. 'This is what corresponds to a modern museum of arts and sciences. In this you shall see the past greatness and culture of Venus.'

With high excitement, Karl entered – the first Earthman ever to see these ancient achievements. The interior, he found, was divided into a series of deep alcoves, branching out from the long central colonnade. The ceiling was one great painting that showed dimly in the light of the Atomite lamp.

Lost in wonder, the Earthman wandered through the alcoves. There was an extraordinary sense of strangeness to the sculptures and paintings about him, an unearthliness that doubled their beauty.

Karl realized that he missed something vital in Venusian art simply because of the lack of common ground between his own culture and theirs, but he could appreciate the technical excellence of the work. Especially, did he admire the colour-work of the paintings which went far beyond anything he had ever seen on Earth. Cracked, faded, and scaling though they were, there was a blending and a harmony about them that was superb.

'What wouldn't Michelangelo have given,' he said to Antil, 'to have the marvellous colour perception of the Venusian eye.'

Antil inflated his chest with happiness. 'Every race has its own attributes. I have often wished *my* ears could distinguish the slight tones and pitches of sound the way it is said Earthmen can. Perhaps I would then be able to understand what it is that is so pleasing about your Terrestrial music. As it is, its noise is dreadfully monotonous to me.'

They passed on, and every minute Karl's opinion of Venusian culture mounted higher. There were long, narrow strips of thin metal, bound together, covered with the lines and ovals of Venusian script – thousands upon thousands of them. In them, Karl knew, might lie such secrets as the scientists of Earth would give half their lives to know.

Then, when Antil pointed out a tiny, six-inch-high affair, and said that, according to the inscription, it was some type of atomic converter with an efficiency several times any of the current Terrestrial models, Karl exploded.

'Why don't you reveal these secrets to Earth? If they only knew your accomplishments in ages past, Venusians would occupy a far higher place than they do now.'

'They would make use of our knowledge of former days, yes,' Antil replied bitterly, 'but they would never release their stranglehold on Venus and its people. I hope you are not forgetting your promise of absolute secrecy.'

'No, I'll keep quiet, but I think you're making a mistake.'

'I think not,' Antil turned to leave the alcove, but Karl called to him to wait.

'Aren't we going into this little room here?' he asked.

Antil whirled, eyes staring, 'Room? What room are you talking about? There's no room here.'

Karl's eyebrows shot up in surprise, as he mutely pointed out the narrow crack that extended halfway up the rear wall.

The Venusian muttered something beneath his breath and fell to his knees, delicate fingers probing the crack.

'Help me, Karl. This door was never meant to be opened, I think. At least there is no record of its being here, and I know the ruins of *Ash-taz-zor* perhaps better than any other of my people.'

The two pushed against the section of the wall, which gave backward with groaning reluctance for a short distance, then yielded suddenly so as to catapult them into the tiny, almost empty cubicle beyond. They regained their feet and stared about.

The Earthman pointed out broken, ragged rust-streaks on the floor, and along the line where door joined wall. 'Your people seem to have sealed this room up pretty effectively. Only the rust of eons broke the bonds. You'd think they had some sort of secret stored here.'

Antil shook his green head. 'There was no evidence of a door last time I was here. However –' he raised the Atomite lamp up high and surveyed the room rapidly, 'there doesn't seem to be anything here, anyway.'

He was right. Aside from a nondescript oblong chest that squatted on six stubby legs, the place contained only unbelievable quantities of dust and the musty, almost suffocating smell of long-shut-up tombs.

Karl approached the chest, tried to move it from the corner where it stood. It didn't budge, but the cover slipped under his pressing fingers.

'The cover's removable, Antil. Look!' He pointed to a shallow compartment within, which contained a square slab of some glassy substance and five six-inch-long cylinders resembling fountain-pens.

Antil shrieked with delight when he saw these objects and for the first time since Karl knew him, lapsed into sibilant Venusian gibberish. He removed the glassy slab and inspected it closely. Karl, his curiosity aroused, did likewise. It was covered with closely-spaced, vari-coloured dots, but there seemed no reason for Antil's extreme glee.

'What is it, Antil?'

'It is a complete document in our ancient ceremonial language. Up to now we have never had more than disjointed fragments. This is a great find.'

'Can you decipher it?' Karl regarded the object with more respect.

'I think I can. It is a dead language and I know little more than a smattering. You see, it is a colour language. Each word is designated by a combination of two, and sometimes three, coloured dots. The colours are finely differentiated, though, and a Terrestrial, even if he had the key to the language, would have to use a spectroscope to read it.'

'Can you work on it now?'

'I think so, Karl. The Atomite lamp approximates normal daylight very closely, and I ought to have no trouble with it. However, it may take me quite a time; so perhaps you'd better continue your investigation. There's no danger of your getting lost, provided you remain inside this building.'

Karl left, taking a second Atomite lamp with him, left Antil, the Venusian, bent over the ancient manuscript, deciphering it slowly and painfully.

Two hours passed before the Earthman returned; but when he did, Antil had scarcely changed his position. Yet, now, there was a look of horror on the Venusian's face that had not been there before. The 'colour' message lay at his feet, disregarded. The noisy entrance of the Earthman made no impression upon him. As if ossified, he sat in unmoving, staring fright.

Karl jumped to his side. 'Antil, Antil, what's wrong?'

Antil's head turned slowly, as though moving through viscous liquid, and his eyes gazed unseeingly at his friend. Karl grasped the other's thin shoulders and shook him unmercifully.

The Venusian came to his senses. Writhing out of Karl's grasp he sprang to his feet. From the desk in the corner he removed the five cylindrical objects, handling them with a queer sort of reluctance, placing them in his pouch. There, likewise did he put the slab he had deciphered.

Having done this, he replaced the cover on the chest and motioned Karl out of the room. 'We must go now. Already we have stayed too long.' His voice had an odd, frightened tone about it that made the Earthman uncomfortable.

Silently, they retraced their steps until once more they stood upon the soaked surface of Venus. It was still day, but twilight was near. Karl felt a growing hunger. They would need to hurry if they expected to reach *Aphrodopolis* before the coming of night. Karl turned up the collar of his slicker, pulled his rubberized cap low over his forehead, and set out.

Mile after mile passed by and the domed city once more rose upon the grey horizon. The Earthman chewed at damp ham sandwiches, wished fervently for the comfortable dryness of *Aphrodopolis*. Through it all, the normally friendly Venusian maintained a stony silence, vouchsafing not so much as a glance upon his companion.

Karl accepted this philosophically. He had a far higher regard for Venusians than the great majority of Earthmen, but even he experienced a faint disdain for the ultra-emotional character of Antil and his kind. This brooding silence was but a manifestation of feelings that in Karl would perhaps have resulted in no more than a sigh or a frown. Realizing this, Antil's mood scarcely affected him.

Yet the memory of the haunting fright in Antil's eyes aroused a faint unease. It had come after the translation of that queer slab. What secret could have been revealed in that message by those scientific progenitors of the Venusians?

It was with some diffidence that Karl finally persuaded himself to ask, 'What did the slab say, Antil? It must be interesting, I judge, considering that you've taken it with you.'

Antil's reply was simply a sign to hurry, and the Venusian thereupon plunged into the gathering darkness with redoubled speed. Karl was puzzled and rather hurt. He made no further attempt at conversation for the duration of the trip.

When they reached *Aphrodopolis,* however, the Venusian broke his silence. His puckered face, drawn and haggard, turned to Karl with the expression of one who has come to a painful decision.

'Karl,' he said, 'we have been friends, so I wish to give you a bit of friendly advice. You are going to leave for Earth next week. I know your father is high in the councils of the Planetary President. You yourself will probably be a personage of importance in the not-too-distant future. Since this is so, I beg you earnestly to use every atom of your influence to a moderation of Earth's attitude toward Venus. I, in my turn, being a hereditary noble of the largest tribe on Venus, shall do my utmost to repress all attempts at violence.'

The other frowned. 'There seems to be something behind all this. I don't get it at all. What are you trying to say?'

'Just this. Unless conditions are bettered – and soon – Venus will rise in revolt. In that case, I will have no choice but to place my services at her feet, and then Venus will no longer be defenceless.'

These words served only to amuse the Earthman. 'Come, Antil, your patriotism is admirable, and your grievances justified, but melodrama and chauvinism don't go with me. I am, above all, a realist.'

There was a terrible earnestness in the Venusian's voice. 'Believe me, Karl, when I say nothing is more real than what I tell you now. In case of a Venusian revolt, I cannot vouch for Earth's safety.'

'Earth's safety!' The enormity of this stunned Karl.

'Yes,' continued Antil, 'for I may be forced to destroy Earth. There you have it.' With this, he wheeled and plunged into the underbrush on the way back to the little Venusian village outside the great dome.

Five years passed – years of turbulent unrest, and Venus stirred in its sleep like an awakening volcano. The short-sighted Terrestrial masters of *Aphrodopolis, Venusia,* and other domed cities cheerfully disregarded all danger signals. When they thought of the little green Venusians at all, it was with a disdainful grimace as if to say, 'Oh, THOSE things!'

But 'those things' were finally pushed beyond endurance, and the nationalistic Green Bands became increasingly vociferous with every passing day. Then, on one grey day, not unlike the grey days preceding, crowds of natives swarmed upon the cities in organized rebellion.

The smaller domes, caught by surprise, succumbed. In rapid succession *New Washington*, *Mount Vulcan*, and *St. Denis* were taken, together with the entire eastern continent. Before the reeling Terrestrials realized what was happening, half of Venus was no longer theirs.

Earth, shocked and stunned by this sudden emergency – which, of course, should have been foreseen – sent arms and supplies to the inhabitants of the remaining beleaguered towns and began to equip a great space fleet for the recovery of the lost territory.

Earth was annoyed but not frightened, knowing that ground lost by surprise could easily be regained at leisure, and that ground not now lost would never be lost. Or such, at least, was the belief.

Imagine, then, the stupefaction of Earth's leaders as no pause came in the Venusian advance. *Venusia City* had been amply stocked with weapons and food; her outer defences were up, the men at their posts. A tiny army of naked, unarmed natives approached and demanded unconditional surrender. *Venusia* refused haughtily, and the messages to Earth were mirthful in their references to the unarmed natives who had become so recklessly flushed with success.

Then, suddenly, no more messages were received, and the natives took over *Venusia*.

The events at *Venusia* were duplicated, over and over again, at what should have been impregnable fortresses. Even *Aphrodopolis* itself, with half a million population, fell to a pitiful five hundred Venusians. This, in spite of the fact that every weapon known to Earth was available to the defenders.

The Terrestrial Government suppressed the facts, and Earth itself remained unsuspecting of the strange events on Venus; but in the inner councils, statesmen frowned as they listened to the strange words of Karl Frantor, son of the Minister of Education.

Jan Heersen, Minister of War, rose in anger at the conclusion of the report.

'Do you wish us to take seriously the random statement of a half-mad Greenie and make our peace with Venus on its own terms? That is definitely and absolutely impossible. What those damned beasts need is the mailed fist. Our fleet will blast them out of the Universe, and it is time that it were done.'

'The blasting may not be so simple, Heersen,' said the grey-haired elder Frantor, rushing to his son's defence. 'There are many of us who have claimed that the Government policy toward the Venusians was all wrong. Who knows what means of attack they have found and what, in revenge, they will do with it?'

'Fairy tales!' exclaimed Heersen. 'You treat the Greenies as if they were people. They're animals and should be thankful for the benefits of civilization we brought them. Remember, we're treating them much better than some of our own Earth races were treated in our early history, the Red Indians for example.'

Karl Frantor burst in once more in an agitated voice. 'We must investigate, sirs! Antil's threat is too serious to disregard, no matter how silly it sounds – and in the light of the Venusian conquests, it sounds anything but silly. I propose that you send me with Admiral von Blumdorff, as a sort of envoy. Let me get to the bottom of this before we attack them.'

The saturnine Earth President, Jules Debuc, spoke now for the first time. 'Frantor's proposal is reasonable, at least. It shall be done. Are there any objections?'

There were none, though Heersen scowled and snorted angrily. Thus, a week later, Karl Frantor accompanied the space armada of Earth when it set off for the inner planet.

It was a strange Venus that greeted Karl after his five years' absence. It was still, its old soaking self, its old dreary, monotony of white and grey, its scattering of domed cities – and yet how different.

Where before the haughty Terrestrials had moved in disdainful splendour among the cowering Venusians, now the natives maintained undisputed sway. *Aphrodopolis* was a native city entirely, and in the office of the former governor sat – Antil.

Karl eyed him doubtfully, scarcely knowing what to say. 'I rather thought you might be king-pin,' he managed at length. 'You – the pacifist.'

'The choice was not mine. It was that of circumstance,' Antil replied. 'But you! I did not expect *you* to be your planet's spokesman.'

'It was to me that you made your silly threats years ago, and so it is I who was most pessimistic concerning your rebellion. I come, you see, but not unaccompanied.' His hand motioned vaguely upward, where spaceships lazed motionless and threatening.

'You come to menace me?'

'No! To hear your aims and your terms.'

'That is easily accomplished. Venus demands its independence and we promise friendship, together with free and unrestricted trade.'

'And you expect us to accept all that without a struggle.'

'I hope you do – for Earth's own sake.'

Karl scowled and threw himself back in his chair in annoyance, 'For God's sake, Antil, the time for mysterious hints and bogies has passed. Show your hand. How did you overcome *Aphrodopolis* and the other cities so easily?'

'We were forced to it, Karl. We did not desire it.' Antil's voice was shrill with agitation. 'They would not accept our fair terms of surrender and began to shoot their Tonite guns. We – we had to use the – the weapon. We had to kill most of them afterward – out of mercy.'

'I don't follow. What weapon are you talking about?'

'Do you remember that time in the ruins of *Ash-taz-zor*, Karl? The hidden room; the ancient inscription; the five little rods.'

Karl nodded sombrely. 'I thought so, but I wasn't sure.'

'It was a horrible weapon, Karl.' Antil hurried on as if the mere thought of it were not to be endured. 'The ancients discovered it – but never used it. They hid it instead, and why they did not destroy it, I can't imagine. I wish they had destroyed it; I really do. But they didn't and I found it and I must use it – for the good of Venus.'

His voice sank to a whisper, but with a manifest effort he nerved himself to the task of explanation. 'The little harmless rods you saw then, Karl, were capable of producing a force field of some unknown nature (the ancients wisely refused to be explicit there) which has the power of disconnecting brain from mind.'

'What?' Karl stared in open-mouthed surprise. 'What *are* you talking about?'

'Why, you must know that the brain is merely the *seat* of the mind, and not the mind itself. The nature of "mind" is a mystery, unknown even to our ancients; but whatever it is, it uses the brain as its intermediary to the world of matter.'

'I see. And your weapon divorces mind from brain – renders mind helpless – a space-pilot without his controls.'

Antil nodded solemnly. 'Have you ever seen a decerebrated animal?' he asked suddenly.

'Why, yes, a dog – in my bio course back in college.'
'Come, then, I will show you a decerebrated human.'

Karl followed the Venusian to an elevator. As he shot downward to the lowest level – the prison level – his mind was in a turmoil. Torn between horror and fury, he had alternate impulses of unreasoning desire to escape and almost insuperable yearnings to slay the Venusian at his side. In a daze, he left the cubicle and followed Antil down a gloomy corridor, winding its way between rows of tiny, barred cells.

'There.' Antil's voice roused Karl as would a sudden stream of cold water. He followed the pointing webbed hand and stared in fascinated revulsion at the human figure revealed.

It was human, undoubtedly, in a form – but inhuman, nevertheless. It (Karl could not imagine it as 'he') sat dumbly on the floor, large staring eyes never leaving the blank wall before him. Eyes that were empty of soul, loose lips from which saliva drooled, fingers that moved aimlessly. Nauseated, Karl turned his head hastily.

'He is not exactly decerebrated.' Antil's voice was low. 'Organically, his brain is perfect and unharmed. It is merely – disconnected.'

'How does it live, Antil? Why doesn't it die?'

'Because the autonomic system is untouched. Stand him up and he will remain balanced. Push him and he will regain his balance. His heart beats. He breathes. If you put food in his mouth, he will swallow, though he would die of starvation before performing the voluntary act of eating food that has been placed before him. It is life – of a sort; but it were better dead, for the disconnection is permanent.'

'It is horrible – horrible.'

'It is worse than you think. I feel convinced that somewhere within the shell of humanity, the mind, unharmed, still exists. Imprisoned helplessly in a body it cannot control, what must be that mind's torture?'

Karl stiffened suddenly. 'You shan't overcome Earth by sheer unspeakable brutality. It is an unbelievably cruel weapon but no more deadly than any of a dozen of ours. You shall pay for this.'

'Please, Karl, you have no conception of one-millionth of the deadliness of the "Disconnection Field." The Field is independent of space, and perhaps of time, too, so that its range can be extended almost indefinitely. Do you know that it required merely one discharge of the weapon to render every warm-blooded creature in *Aphrodopolis* helpless?' Antil's voice rose tensely. 'Do you know that I am able to bathe ALL

EARTH in the Field – to render all your teeming billions the duplicate of that dead–alive hulk in there AT ONE STROKE'.

Karl did not recognize his own voice as he rasped, 'Fiend! Are you the only one who knows the secret of this damnable Field?'

Antil burst into a hollow laugh, 'Yes, Karl, the blame rests on me, alone. Yet killing me will not help. If I die, there are others who know where to find the inscription, others who have not my sympathy for Earth. I am perfectly safe from you, Karl, for my death would be the end of your world.'

The Earthman was broken – utterly. Not a fragment of doubt as to the Venusian's power was left within him. 'I yield,' he muttered, 'I yield. What shall I tell my people?'

'Tell them of my terms, and of what I could do if I wished.'

Karl shrank from the Venusian as if his very touch was death, 'I will tell them that.'

'Tell them also, that Venus is not vindictive. We do not wish to use our weapon, for it is too dreadful to use. If they will give us our independence on our own terms, and allow us certain wise precautions against future re-enslavement, we will hurl each of our five guns and the explanatory inscription explaining it into the sun.'

The Terrestrial's voice did not change from its toneless whisper. 'I will tell them that.'

Admiral von Blumdorff was as Prussian as his name, and his military code was the simple one of brute force. So it was quite natural that his reactions to Karl's report were explosive in their sarcastic derision.

'You forsaken fool,' he raved at the young man. 'This is what comes of talk, of words, of tomfoolery. You *dare* to come back to me with this old-wives' tale of mysterious weapons of untold force. Without any proof at all, you accept all that this damned Greenie tells you at absolute face value, and surrender abjectly. Couldn't *you* threaten, couldn't *you* bluff, couldn't *you* lie?'

'He didn't threaten, bluff, or lie,' Karl answered warmly. 'What he said was the gospel truth. If you had seen the decerebrated man –'

'Bah! That is the most inexcusable part of the whole cursed business. To exhibit a lunatic to you, some perfectly normal mental defective, and to say, "This is our weapon!" and for you to accept that without question! Did they do anything but talk? Did they demonstrate the weapon? Did they even show it to you?'

'Naturally not. The weapon is deadly. They're not going to kill a Venusian to satisfy me. As for showing me the weapon – well, would *you* show your ace-in-the-hole to the enemy? Now you answer *me* a few questions. Why is Antil so cocksure of himself? How did he conquer all Venus so easily?'

'I can't explain it I admit, but does that prove that *theirs* is the correct explanation? Anyhow, I'm sick of this talk. We're attacking now, and to hell with theories. I'll face them with Tonite projectiles and you can watch their bluff backfire in their ugly faces.'

'But, Admiral, you *must* communicate my report to the President.'

'I will – after I blow *Aphrodopolis* into kingdom come.'

He turned on the central broadcasting unit. 'Attention, all ships! Battle formation! We dive at *Aphrodopolis* with all Tonites blasting in fifteen minutes.' Then he turned to the orderly. 'Have Captain Larsen inform *Aphrodopolis* that they have fifteen minutes to hoist the white flag.'

The minutes that ticked by after that were tense and nerve-wracking for Karl Frantor. He sat in bent silence, head buried in his hands and the faint click of the chronometer at the end of every minute sounded like a thunder-clap in his ears. He counted those clicks in a mumbling whisper – 8 – 9 – 10. God!

Only five minutes to certain death! Or *was* it certain death? Was von Blumdorff right? Were the Venusians putting over a daring bluff?

An orderly catapulted into the room and saluted. 'The Greenies have just answered, sir.'

'Well,' von Blumdorff leaned forward eagerly.

'They say, "Urgently request fleet not to attack. If done, we shall not be responsible for the consequences." '

'Is that all?' came the outraged shout.

'Yes, sir.'

The Admiral burst into a sulphurous stream of profanity. 'Why, the infernal gall of them,' he shouted. 'They dare bluff to the very end.'

And as he finished, the fifteenth minute clicked off, and the mighty armada burst into motion. In streaking, orderly flight they shot down toward the cloudy shroud of the second planet. Von Blumdorff grinned in a grisly appreciation of the awesome view spread over the televisor – until the mathematically precise battle formation suddenly broke.

The Admiral stared and rubbed his eyes. The entire further

half of the fleet had suddenly gone crazy. First, the ships wavered; then they veered and shot off at mad angles.

Then calls came in from the sane half of the fleet – reports that the left wing had ceased to respond to radio.

The attack on *Aphrodopolis* was immediately disrupted as the order went out to capture the ships that had run amok. Von Blumdorff stamped up and down and tore his hair. Karl Frantor cried out dully, 'It is their weapon,' and lapsed back into his former silence.

From *Aphrodopolis* came no word at all.

For two solid hours the remnant of the Terrestrial fleet battled their own ships. Following the aimless courses of the stricken vessels, they approached and grappled. Bound together then by rigid force, rocket blasts were applied until the insane flight of the others had been balanced and stopped. Fully twenty of the fleet were never caught; some continuing on some orbit about the sun, some shooting off into unknown space, a few crashing down to Venus.

While the remaining ships of the left wing were boarded, the unsuspecting boarding parties stopped short in horror. *Seventy-five staring witless shells of humanity in each ship.* Not a single *human* being left.

Some of the first to enter screamed in horror and fled in a panic. Others merely retched and turned away their eyes. One officer took in the situation at a glance, calmly drew his Atomo-pistol and rayed every decerebrate in sight.

Admiral von Blumdorff was a stricken man; a pitiful, limp wreck of his former proud and blustering self, when he heard the worst. One of the decerebrates was brought to him, and he reeled back.

Karl Frantor gazed at him with red-rimmed eyes, 'Well, Admiral, are you satisfied?'

But the Admiral made no answer. He drew his gun, and before anyone could stop him, shot himself through the head.

Once again Karl Frantor stood before a meeting of the President and his Cabinet, before a dispirited, frightened group of men. His report was definite and left no doubt as to the course that must now be followed.

President Debuc stared at the decerebrate brought in as an exhibit. 'We are finished,' he said. 'We must surrender unconditionally, throw ourselves upon their mercy. But someday –' his eyes kindled in retribution.

'No, Mr. President!' Karl's voice rang out, 'There shall be no someday. We must give the Venusians their simple due –

liberty and independence. Bygones must be bygones – our dead have but paid for the half-century of Venusian slavery. After this, there must be a new order in the Solar System – the birth of a new day.'

The President lowered his head in thought and then raised it again. 'You are right,' he answered with decision; 'there shall be no thought of revenge.'

Two months later the peace treaty was signed and Venus became what it has remained ever since – an independent and sovereign power. And with the signing of the treaty, a whirling speck shot out toward the sun. It was – the weapon too dreadful to use.

THE END

Amazing Stories was, at that time, heavily slanted toward adventure and action and disapproved of too much scientific exposition in the course of the story. I, of course, even then was writing the kind of science fiction that involved scientific extrapolation that was specifically described. What Raymond Palmer did in this case was to omit some of my scientific discussion and to place in footnotes a condensed version of passages that he could not omit without damaging the plot. This was an extraordinarily inept device, at which I chafed at the time. I took the only retaliation available to me. I placed *Amazing* at the bottom of the list, as far as the order in which to submit stories was concerned.

What I remember most clearly about the story, though, is Fred Pohl's remark concerning it. The story ends with Earth and Venus at peace, with Earth promising to respect Venus' independence and Venus destroying its weapon. Fred said, upon reading the published story, 'And after the weapon was destroyed, Earth wiped the Venusians off the face of their planet.'

He was quite right. I was naïve enough then to suppose that words and good intentions are sufficient. (Fred also remarked that the weapon that was too dreadful to be used *was*, in fact, used. He was right in that case, too, and that helped sour me on titles that were too long and elaborate. I have tended toward shorter titles since, even one-word titles, something Campbell consistently encouraged perhaps because short titles fit better on the cover and on the title page of a magazine.)

If I thought that my sale to Campbell had made me an

expert in knowing what he wanted and in being ably to supply that want, I was quite wrong. In February 1939 I wrote a story called 'The Decline and Fall.' I submitted it to Campbell on February 21 and it was back in my lap, quite promptly, on the twenty-fifth. It made the rounds thereafter without results and was never published. It no longer exists and I remember nothing at all about it.

On March 4, 1939, I began my most ambitious writing project to that date. It was a novelette (in which I named an important character after Russell Winterbotham) that was intended to be at least twice as long as any of my previous stories. I called the story 'Pilgrimage.' It was my first attempt to write 'future history'; that is, a tale about a far future time written as though it were a historical novel. It was also my first attempt to write a story on a galactic scale.

I was very excited while working at it and felt somehow that it was an 'epic.' (I remember, though that Winterbotham was rather dubious about it when I described the plot to him in a letter.) I brought it in to Campbell on March 21, 1939, with high hopes, but it was back on the twenty-fourth with a letter that said, 'You have a basic idea which might be made into an interesting yarn, but as it is, it is not strong enough.'

This time I would not let go. I was in to see Campbell again on the twenty-seventh and talked him into letting me revise it in order to strengthen the weaknesses he found in it. I brought in the second version on April 25, and it, too, was found wanting, but this time it was Campbell who asked for a revision. I tried again and the third version was submitted on May 9 and rejected on the seventeenth. Campbell admitted that there was still the possibility of saving it, but, after three tries, he said, I should put it to one side for some months and then look at it from a fresh viewpoint.

I did as he said and waited two months (the minimum time I could interpret as 'some months') and brought in the fourth version on August 8.

This time, Campbell hesitated over it till September 6, and then rejected it permanently on the ground that Robert A. Heinlein had just submitted an important short novel (later published as 'If This Goes On –') that had a religious theme. Since 'Pilgrimage' also had a religious theme, John couldn't use it. Two stories on so sensitive a subject in rapid succession were one too many.

I had written the story four times, but I saw Campbell's point. Campbell said Heinlein's story was the better of the two and I could see that an editor could scarcely be expected to take the worse and reject the better simply because writing the worse had been such hard work.

There was nothing, however, to prevent me from trying to sell it elsewhere. I kept trying for two years, during which time I rewrote it twice more and retitled it 'Galactic Crusade.'

Eventually I sold it to another of the magazines that were springing up in the wake of Campbell's success with *Astounding*. This was *Planet Stories*, which during the 1940s was to make its mark as a home for the 'space opera,' the blood-and-thunder tale of interplanetary war. My story was of this type, and the editor of *Planet*, Malcolm Reiss, was attracted.

The religious angle worried him, too, however. Would I go through the story, he asked during luncheon on August 18, 1941, and remove any direct reference to religion. Would I, in particular, refrain from referring to any of my characters as 'priests.' Sighing, I agreed, and the story was revised for a sixth time. On October 7, 1941, he accepted it and, after two and a half years that included ten rejections, the story was finally placed.

But, having put me to the trouble of that particular remove-the-religion revision, what did Reiss do? Why, he retitled it (without consulting me, of course) and called the story 'Black Friar of the Flame.'

I might mention two points about this story before presenting it.

First, it was the only story I ever sold to *Planet*.

Second, it was illustrated by Frank R. Paul. Paul was the most prominent of all the science fiction illustrators of the pre-Campbell era, and, to the best of my knowledge, this is the only time our paths crossed professionally.

I did see him once from a distance, though. On July 2, 1939, I attended the First World Science Fiction Convention, which was held in Manhattan. Frank Paul was guest of honor. It was the first occasion on which I was publicly recognized as a professional, rather than as merely a fan. With three published stories under my belt ('Trends' had just appeared) I was pushed up to the platform to take a bow. Campbell was sitting in an aisle seat and he waved me toward the platform delightedly, I remember.

I said a few words, referring to myself as the 'worst science fiction writer unlynched.' I didn't mean it, of course, and I doubt that anyone thought for a moment that I did.

6 : Black Friar of the Flame.

Russell Tymball's eyes were filled with gloomy satisfaction as they gazed at the blackened ruins of what had been a cruiser of the Lhasinuic Fleet a few hours before. The twisted girders, scattered in all directions, were ample witness of the terriffic force of the crash.

The pudgy Earthman re-entered his own sleek Strato-rocket and waited. Fingers twisted a long cigar aimlessly for minutes before lighting it. Through the up-drifting smoke, his eyes narrowed and he remained lost in thought.

He came to his feet at the sound of a cautious hail. Two men darted in with one last fugitive glance behind them. The door closed softly, and one stepped immediately to the controls. The desolate desert landscape was far beneath them almost at once, and the silver prow of the Strato-rocket pointed for the ancient metropolis of New York.

Minutes passed before Tymball spoke, 'All clear?'

The man at the controls nodded. 'Not a tyrant ship about. It's quite evident the "Grahul" had not been able to radio for help.'

'You have the dispatch?' the other asked eagerly.

'We found it easily enough. It is unharmed.'

'We also found,' said the second man bitterly, 'one other thing – the last report of Sidi Peller.'

For a moment, Tymball's round face softened and something almost like pain entered his expression. And then it hardened again, 'He died! But it was for Earth, and so it was not death. It was martyrdom!'

Silence, and then sadly, 'Let me see the report, Petri.'

He took the single, folded sheet handed him and held it before him. Slowly, he read aloud:

'On September 4, made successful entry into "Grahul" cruiser of the tyrant fleet. Maintained self in hiding during passage from Pluto to Earth. On September 5, located dispatch in question and assumed possession. Have just shorted rocket jets. Am sealing this report in with dispatch. Long live Earth!'

Tymball's voice was strangely moved as he read the last word. 'The Lhasinuic tyrants have never martyrized a greater man than Sidi Peller. But we'll be repaid, and with interest.

Planet Stories, spring 1942
Copyright © 1942 by Love Romances Publishing Co.
Copyright renewed © 1969 by Isaac Asimov

The Human Race is not quite decadent yet.'

Petri stared out the window. 'How did Peller do it all? One man – to stow away successfully upon a cruiser of the fleet and in the face of the entire crew to steal the dispatch and wreck the fleet. How was it done? And we'll never know; except for the bare facts in his report.'

'He had his orders,' said Willums, as he locked controls and turned about. 'I carried them to him on Pluto myself. Get the dispatch! Wreck the "Grahul" in the Gobi! He did it! That's all!' He shrugged his shoulders wearily.

The atmosphere of depression deepened until Tymball himself broke it with a growl. 'Forget it. Did you take care of everything at the wreck?'

The other two nodded in unison. Petri's voice was businesslike, 'All traces of Peller were removed and de-atomized. They will never detect the presence of a Human among the wreckage. The document itself was replaced by the prepared copy, and carefully burnt beyond recognition. It was even impregnated with silver salts to the exact amount contained in the official seal of the Tyrant Emperor. I'll stake my head that no Lhasinu will suspect that the crash was no accident or that the dispatch was not destroyed by it.'

'Good! They won't locate the wreck for twenty-four hours at least. It's an airtight job. Let me have the dispatch now.'

He fondled the metalloid container almost with reverence. It was blackened and twisted, still faintly warm. And then with a savage twist of the wrist, he tore off the lid.

The document that he lifted out unrolled with a rustling sound. At the lower left hand corner was the huge silver seal of the Lhasinuic Emperor himself – the tyrant, who from Vega, ruled one third of the Galaxy. It was addressed to the Viceroy of Sol.

The three Earthmen regarded the fine print solemnly. The harshly angular Lhasinuic script glinted redly in the rays of the setting sun.

'Was I right?' whispered Tymball.

'As always,' assented Petri.

Night did not really fall. The sky's black-purple deepened ever so slightly and the stars brightened imperceptibly, but aside from that the stratosphere did not differentiate between the absence and the presence of the sun.

'Have you decided upon the next step?' asked Willums, hesitantly.

'Yes – long ago. I'm going to visit Paul Kane tomorrow,

with this,' and he indicated the dispatch.

'*Loara* Paul Kane!' cried Petri.

'That – that *Loarist*!' came simultaneously from Willums.

'The Loarist,' agreed Tymball. 'He is our man!'

'Say rather that he is the lackey of the Lhasinu,' ground out Willums. 'Kane – the head of Laorism – consequently the head of the traitor Humans who preach submission to the Lhasinu.'

'That's right,' Petri was pale but more calm. 'The Lhasinu are our known enemies and are to be met in fair fight – but the Loarists are vermin. Great Space! I would rather throw myself on the mercy of the tyrant Viceroy himself than have anything to do with those snuffling students of ancient history, who praise the ancient glory of Earth and encompass its present degradation.'

'You judge too harshly.' There was the trace of a smile about Tymball's lips. 'I have had dealings with this leader of Loarism before. Oh –' he checked the cries of startled dismay that rose, 'I was quite discreet about it. Even you two didn't know, and, as you see, Kane has not yet betrayed me. I failed in those dealings, but I learned a little bit. Listen to me!'

Petri and Willums edged nearer, and Tymball continued in crisp, matter-of-fact tones, 'The first Galactic Drive of the Lhasinu ended two thousand years ago just after the capture of Earth. Since then, the aggression has not been resumed, and the independent Human Planets of the Galaxy are quite satisfied at the maintenance of the status quo. They are too divided among themselves to welcome a return of the struggle. Loarism itself is only interested in its own survival against the encroachments of newer ways of thought, and it is no great moment to them whether Lhasinu or Human rules Earth as long as Loarism itself prospers. As a matter of fact, we – the Nationalists – are perhaps a greater danger to them in that respect than the Lhasinu.'

Willums smiled grimly, 'I'll say we are.'

'Then, granting that, it is natural that Loarism assume the role of appeasement. Yet, if it were to their interests, they would join us at a second's notice. And this,' he slapped the document before him, 'is what will convince them where their interests lie.'

The other two were silent.

Tymball continued, 'Our time is short. Not more than three years, perhaps not more than two. And yet you know what the chances of success for a rebellion today are.'

'We'd do it,' snarled Petri, and then in a muffled tone, 'if the only Lhasinu we had to deal with were those of Earth.'

'Exactly. But they can call upon Vega for help, and we can call upon no one. No one of the Human Planets would stir in our defense, any more than they did five hundred years ago. And that's why we must have Loarism on our side.'

'And what did Loarism do five hundred years ago during the Bloody Rebellion?' asked Willums, bitter hatred in his voice. 'They abandoned us to save their own precious hides.'

'We are in no position to remember that,' said Tymball. 'We will have their help now – and then, when all is over, our reckoning with them –'

Willums returned to the controls, 'New York in fifteen minutes!' And then, 'But I still don't like it. What can those filthy Loarists *do*? Dried out husks fit for nothing but treason and platitudes!'

'They are the last unifying force of Humanity,' answered Tymball. 'Weak enough now and helpless enough, but Earth's only chance.'

They were slanting downwards now into the thicker, lower atmosphere, and the whistling of the air as it streamed past them became shriller in pitch. Willums fired the braking rockets as they pierced a gray layer of clouds. There upon the horizon was the great diffuse glow of New York City.

'See that our passes are in perfect order for the Lhasinuic inspection and hide the document. They won't search us, anyway.'

Loara Paul Kane leaned back in his ornate chair. The slender fingers of one hand played with the ivory paperweight upon his desk. His eyes avoided those of the smaller, rounder man before him, and his voice, as he spoke, took on solemn inflections.

'I cannot risk shielding you longer, Tymball. I have done so until now because of the bond of common Humanity between us, but –' his voice trailed away.

'But?' prompted Tymball.

Kane's fingers turned his paperweight over and over. 'The Lhasinu are growing harsher this past year. They are almost arrogant.' He looked up suddenly. 'I am not quite a free agent, you know, and haven't the influence and power you seem to think I have.'

His eyes dropped again, and a troubled note entered his voice, 'The Lhasinu suspect. They are beginning to detect the workings of a tightly-knit conspiracy underground, and we cannot afford to become entangled in it.'

'I know. If necessary, you are quite willing to sacrifice us as your predecessor sacrificed the patriots five centuries ago. Once again, Loarism shall play its noble part.'

'What good are your rebellions?' came the weary reply. 'Are the Lhasinu so much more terrible than the oligarchy of Humans that rules Santanni or the dictator that rules Trantor? If the Lhasinu are not Human, they are at least intelligent. Loarism must live at peace with the rulers.'

And now Tymball smiled. There was no humor in it – rather mocking irony, and from his sleeve, he drew forth a small card.

'You think so, do you? Here, read this. It is a reduced photostat of – no, don't touch it – read it as *I* hold it, and –'

His further remarks were drowned in the sudden hoarse cry from the other. Kane's face twisted alarmingly into a mask of horror, as he snatched desperately at the reproduction held out to him.

'Where did you get this?' He scarcely recognized his own voice.

'What odds? I have it, haven't I? And yet it cost the life of a brave man, and a ship of His Reptilian Eminence's navy. I believe you can see that there is no doubt as to the genuineness of this.'

'No – no!' Kane put a shaking hand to his forehead. 'That is the Emperor's signature and seal. It is impossible to forge them.'

'You see, Excellency,' there was sarcasm in the title, 'the renewal of the Galactic Drive is a matter of two years – or three – in the future. The first step in the drive comes within the year – and it is concerning that first step,' his voice took on a poisonous sweetness, 'that this order has been issued to the Viceroy.'

'Let me think a second. Let me think.' Kane dropped into his chair.

'Is there the necessity?' cried Tymball, remorselessly. 'This is nothing but the fulfillment of my prediction of six months ago, to which you would not listen. Earth, as a Human world, is to be destroyed; its population scattered in groups throughout the Lhasinuic portions of the Galaxy; every trace of Human occupancy destroyed.'

'But Earth! Earth, the home of the Human Race; the beginning of our civilization.'

'Exactly! Loarism is dying and destruction of the Earth will kill it. And with Loarism gone, the last unifying force is destroyed, and the human planets, invincible when united, shall be wiped out, one by one, in the Second Galactic Drive. Unless –'

The other's voice was toneless.

'I know what you're going to say.'

'No more than I said before. Humanity must unite, and can do so only about Loarism. It must have a Cause for which to fight, and that Cause must be the liberation of Earth. *I* shall fire the spark here on Earth and *you* must convert the Human portion of the Galaxy into a powder-keg.'

'You wish a Total War – a Galactic Crusade,' Kane spoke in a whisper, 'yet who should know better than I that a Total War has been impossible for these thousand years.' He laughed suddenly, harshly, 'Do you know how weak Loarism is to-day?'

'Nothing is so weak that it cannot be strengthened. Although Loarism has weakened since its great days during the First Galactic Drive, you still have your organization and your discipline; the best in the Galaxy. And your leaders are, as a whole, capable men, I must say that for you. A thoroughly centralized group of capable men, working desperately, can do much. It *must* do much, for it has no choice.'

'Leave me,' said Kane, brokenly, 'I can do no more now. I must think.' His voice trailed away, but one finger pointed toward the door.

'What good are thoughts?' cried Tymball, irritably. 'We need deeds!' And with that, he left.

The night had been a horrible one for Kane. His face was pale and drawn; his eyes hollow and feverishly brilliant. Yet he spoke loudly and firmly.

'We are allies, Tymball.'

Tymball smiled bleakly, took Kane's outstretched hand for a moment, and dropped it, 'By necessity, Excellency, only. I am not your friend.'

'Nor I yours. Yet we may work together. My initial orders have gone out and the Central Council will ratify them. In that direction, at least, I anticipate no trouble.'

'How quickly may I expect results?'

'Who knows? Loarism still has its facilities for propaganda. There are still those who will listen from respect and others from fear, and still others from the mere force of the propaganda itself. But who can say? Humanity has slept, and Loarism as well. There is little anti-Lhasinuic feeling, and it will be hard to drum it up out of nothing.'

'Hate is never hard to drum up,' and Tymball's moon-face seemed oddly harsh. 'Emotionalism! Propaganda! Frank and unscrupulous opportunism! And even in its weakened state,

Loarism is rich. The masses may be corrupted by words, but those in high places, the important ones, will require a bit of the yellow metal.'

Kane waved a weary hand, 'You preach nothing new. That line of dishonor was Human policy far back in the misty dawn of history when only this poor Earth was human and even *it* split into warring segments.' Then, bitterly, 'To think that we must return to the tactics of that barbarous age.'

The conspirator shrugged his shoulders cynically, 'Do you know any better?'

'And even so, with all that foulness, we may yet fail.'

'Not if our plans are well-laid.'

Loara Paul Kane rose to his feet and his hands clenched before him, 'Fool! You and your plans! Your subtle, secret, snaky, tortuous plans! Do you think that conspiracy is rebellion, or rebellion, victory? What can you do? You can ferret out information and dig quietly at the roots, but you can't lead a rebellion. I can organize and prepare, but I can't lead a rebellion.'

Tymball winced, 'Preparation – perfect preparation –'

'– is nothing, I tell you. You can have every chemical ingredient necessary, and all the proper conditions, and yet there may be no reaction. In psychology – particularly mob psychology – as in chemistry, one must have a catalyst.'

'What in space do you mean?'

'Can *you* lead a rebellion?' cried Kane. 'A crusade is a war of emotion. Can *you* control the emotions? Why, you conspirator, you could not stand the light of open warfare an instant. Can I lead the rebellion? I, old and a man of peace? Then who is to be the leader, the psychological catalyst, that can take the dull worthless clay of your precious "preparation" and breathe life into it?'

Russell Tymball's jaw muscles quivered. 'Defeatism! So soon?'

The answer was harsh, 'No! Realism!'

There was angry silence and Tymball turned on his heel and left.

It was midnight, ship time, and the evening's festivities were reaching their high point. The grand salon of the superliner *Flaming Nova* was filled with whirling, laughing, glittering figures, growing more convivial as the night wore on.

'This reminds me of the triply-damned affairs my wife makes me attend back on Lacto,' muttered Sammel Maronni to his companion. 'I thought I'd be getting away from some of it, at least out here in hyperspace, but evidently I didn't.' He groaned softly and gazed at the assemblage with a faintly disapproving stare.

Maronni was dressed in the peak of fashion, from purple head-sash to sky-blue sandals, and looked exceedingly uncomfortable. His portly figure was crammed into a brilliantly red and terribly tight tunic and the occasional jerks at his wide belt showed that he was only too conscious of its ill fit.

His companion, taller and slimmer, bore his spotless white uniform with an ease born of long experience, and his imposing figure contrasted strongly with the slightly ridiculous appearance of Sammel Maronni.

The Lactonian exporter was conscious of this fact. 'Blast it, Drake, you've got one fine job here. You dress like a nob and do nothing but look pleasant and answer salutes. How much do you get paid, anyway?'

'Not enough.' Captain Drake lifted one gray eyebrow and stared quizzically at the Lactonian. 'I wish *you* had my job for a week or so. You'd sing mighty small after that. If you think taking care of fat dowager damsels and curly-headed society snobs is a bed of roses, you're welcome to it.' He muttered viciously to himself for a moment and then bowed politely to a bejeweled harridan who simpered past. 'It's what's grayed my hair and furrowed my brow, by Rigel.'

Maronni drew a long *Karen* smoke out of his waist-pouch and lit up luxuriously. He blew a cloud of apple-green smoke into the Captain's face and smiled impishly.

'I've never heard the man yet who didn't knock his own job, even when it was the pushover yours is, you hoary old fraud. Ah, if I'm not mistaken, the gorgeous Ylen Surat is bearing down upon us.'

'Oh, pink devils of Sirius! I'm afraid to look. Is that old hag actually moving in our direction?'

'She certainly is – and aren't you the lucky one! She's one of the richest women on Santanni and a widow, too. The uniform gets them, I suppose. What a pity I'm married.'

Captain Drake twisted his face into a most frightful grimace, 'I hope a chandelier falls on her.'

And with that he turned, his expression metamorphosed into one of bland delight in an instant, 'Why, Madam Surat, I thought I'd never get the chance to see you tonight.'

Ylen Surat, for whom the age of sixty was past experience, giggled girlishly, 'Be still, you old flirt, or you'll make me forget that I've come here to scold you.'

'Nothing is wrong, I hope?' Drake felt a sinking of the

heart. He had had previous experience with Madam Surat's complaints. Things usually *were* wrong.

'A great deal is wrong. I've just been told that in fifty hours, we shall land on Earth – if that's the way you pronounce the word.'

'Perfectly correct,' answered Captain Drake, a bit more at ease.

'But it wasn't listed as a stop when we boarded.'

'No, it wasn't. But then, you see, it's quite a routine affair. We leave ten hours after landing.'

'But this is insupportable. It will delay me an entire day. It is necessary for me to reach Santanni within the week, and days are precious. Now, I've never heard of Earth. My guide book,' she extracted a leather-covered volume from her reticule and flipped it pages angrily, 'doesn't even mention the place. No one, I feel sure, has any interest in a halt there. If you persist in wasting the passengers' time in a perfectly useless stop, I shall take it up with the president of the line. I'll remind you that I have some little influence back home.'

Captain Drake sighed inaudibly. It had not been the first time he had been reminded of Ylen Surat's 'little influence.'

'My dear madam, you are right, entirely right, perfectly right – but I can do nothing. All ships on the Sirius, Alpha Centauri, and 61 Cygni lines must stop at Earth. It is by interstellar agreement, and even the president of the line, no matter how stimulated he may be by your argument, could do nothing.'

'Besides,' interrupted Maronni, who thought it time to come to the aid of the beleaguered captain, 'I believe that we have two passengers who are actually headed for Earth.'

'That's right. I had forgotten.' Captain Drake's face brightened a bit. 'There! We have concrete reason for the stop as well.'

'Two passengers out of over fifteen hundred! Reason, indeed!'

'You are unfair,' said Maronni, lightly. 'After all, it was on Earth that the Human race originated. You know that, I suppose?'

Ylen Surat lifted patently false eyebrows, 'Did we?'

The blank look on her face twisted to one of disdain, 'Oh, well, that was all thousands and thousands of years ago. It doesn't matter any more.'

'It does to the Loarists and the two who wish to land are Loarists.'

'Do you mean to say,' sneered the widow, 'that there are still people in this enlightened age who go about studying "our ancient culture." Isn't that what they're always talking about?'

'That's what Filip Sanat is always talking about,' laughed Maronni. 'He gave me a long sermon only a few days ago on that very subject. And it was interesting, too. There was a lot to what he said.'

He nodded lightly and continued, 'He's got a good head on him, that Filip Sanat. He might have made a good scientist or businessman.'

'Speak of meteors and hear them whizz,' said the Captain, suddenly, and nodded his head to the right.

'Well!' gasped Maronni. 'There he is. But – but what in space is he doing *here*?'

Filip Sanat *did* make a rather incongruous picture as he stood framed in the far doorway. His long, dark purple tunic – mark of the Loarist – was a sombre splotch upon an otherwise gay scene. His grave eyes turned toward Maronni and he lifted his hand in immediate recognition.

Astonished dancers made way automatically as he passed, staring at him long and curiously afterwards. One could hear the wake of whispering that he left in his path. Filip Sanat, however, took no notice of this. Eyes fixed stonily ahead of him and expression stolidly immobile, he reached Captain Drake, Sammel Maronni, and Ylen Surat.

Filip Sanat greeted the two men warmly and then, in response to an introduction, bowed gravely to the widow, who regarded him with surprise and open disdain.

'Pardon me for disturbing you, Captain Drake,' said the young man in a low tone. 'I only want to know at what time we are leaving hyper-space.'

The captain yanked out a corpulent pocket-chromo. 'An hour from now. Not more.'

'And we shall then be –?'

'Just outside the orbit of Planet IX.'

'That would be Pluto. Sol will then be in sight as we enter normal space?'

'If you're looking in the right direction, it will be – toward the prow of the ship.'

'Thank you,' Filip Sanat made as if to depart, but Maronni detained him.

'Hold on there, Filip, you're not going to leave us, are you? I'm sure Madam Surat here is fairly dying to ask you several questions. She has displayed great interest in Loarism.' There was more than the suspicion of a twinkle in the Lactonian's eye.

Filip Sanat turned politely to the widow, who, taken aback for the moment, remained speechless, and then recovered.

'Tell me, young man,' she burst forth, 'are there really still people like you left? – Loarists, I mean.'

Filip Sanat started and stared quite rudely at his questioner, but did not lose his tongue. With calm distinctness, he said, 'There are still people left who try to maintain the culture and way of life of ancient Earth.'

Captain Drake could not forbear a tiny bit if irony, 'Even down to the culture of the Lhasinuic masters?'

Ylen Surat uttered a stifled scream, 'Do you mean to say Earth is a Lhasinuic world? Is it? Is it?' Her voice rose to a frightened squeak.

'Why, certainly,' answered the puzzled captain, sorry that he had spoken. 'Didn't you know?'

'Captain,' there was hysteria in the woman's voice. 'You *must* not land. If you do, I shall make trouble – plenty of trouble. I will *not* be exposed to hordes of those terrible Lhasinu – those awful reptiles from Vega.'

'You need not fear, Madam Surat,' observed Filip Sanat, coldly. 'The vast majority of Earth's population is very much human. It is only the one per cent that rules that is Lhasinuic.'

'Oh –' A pause, and then, in a wounded manner, 'Well, I don't think Earth can be so important, if it is not even ruled by Humans. Loarism indeed! Silly waste of time, I call it!'

Sanat's face flushed suddenly, and for a moment he seemed to struggle vainly for speech. When he did speak, it was in an agitated tone, 'You have a very superficial view. The fact that the Lhasinu control Earth has nothing to do with the fundamental problem of Loarism which –'

He turned on his heel and left.

Sammel Maronni drew a long breath as he watched the retreating figure. 'You hit him in a sore spot, Madam Surat, I never saw him squirm away from an argument or an attempt at an explanation in that way before.'

'He's not a bad looking chap,' said Captain Drake.

Maronni chuckled, 'Not by a long shot. We're from the same planet, that young fellow and I. He's a typical Lactonian, like me.'

The widow cleared her throat grumpily, 'Oh, let us change the subject by all means. That person seems to have cast a shadow over the entire room. Why do they wear those awful purple robes? So unstylish!'

Loara Broos Porin glanced up as his young acolyte entered.

'Well?'

'In less than forty-five minutes, Loara Broos.'

And throwing himself into a chair, Sanat leaned a flushed and frowning face upon one balled fist.

Porin regarded the other with an affectionate smile, 'Have you been arguing with Samuel Maronni again, Filip?'

'No, not exactly.' He jerked himself upright. 'But what's the use, Loara Broos? There, on the upper level, are hundreds of Humans, thoughtless, gaily dressed, laughing, frolicking; and there outside is Earth, disregarded. Only we two of the entire ship's company are stopping there to view the world of our ancient days.'

His eyes avoided those of the older man and his voice took on a bitter tinge, 'And once thousands of Humans from every corner of the Galaxy landed on Earth every day. The great days of Loarism are over.'

Loara Broos laughed. One would not have thought such a hearty laugh to be in his spindly figure. 'That is at least the hundredth time I have heard that said by you. Foolish! The day will come when Earth will once more be remembered. People will yet again flock. By the thousands and millions they'll come.'

'No! It is over!'

'Bah! The croaking prophets of doom have said that over and over again through history. They have yet to prove themselves right.'

'This time they will.' Sanat's eyes blazed suddenly, 'Do you know why? It is because Earth is profaned by the reptile conquerors. A woman has just said to me – a vain, stupid, shallow woman – that "I don't think Earth can be so important if it is not even ruled by Humans." She said what billions must say unconsciously, and I hadn't the words to refute her. It was one argument I couldn't answer.'

'And what would your solution be, Filip? Come, have you thought it out?'

'Drive them from Earth! Make it a Human planet once more! We fought them once during the First Galactic Drive two thousand years ago, and stopped them when it seemed as if they might absorb the Galaxy. Let us make a Second Drive of our own and hurl them back to Vega.'

Porin sighed and shook his head, 'You young hothead! There never was a young Loarist who didn't eat fire on the subject. You'll outgrow it. You'll outgrow it.'

'Look, my boy!' Loara Broos arose and grasped the other by the shoulders, 'Man and Lhasinu have intelligence, and are the *only* two intelligent races of the Galaxy. They are brothers in mind and spirit. Be at peace with them. Don't hate; it is the most unreasoning emotion. Instead, strive to understand.'

Filip Sanat stared stonily at the ground and made no indication that he heard. His mentor clicked his tongue in gentle rebuke.

'Well, when you are older, you will understand. Now, forget all this, Filip. Remember that the ambition of every real Loarist is about to be fulfilled for you. In two days, we shall reach Earth and its soil shall be under your feet. Isn't that enough to make you happy? Just think! When you return, you shall be awarded the title "Loara." You shall be one who has visited Earth. The golden sun will be pinned to your shoulder.'

Porin's hand crept to the staring yellow orb upon his own tunic, mute witness of his three previous visits to Earth.

'Loara Filip Sanat,' said Sanat slowly, eyes glistening. 'Loara Filip Sanat. It has a wonderful sound, hasn't it? And only a little ways off.'

'Now, then, you feel better. But come, in a few moments we shall leave hyper-space and we will see Sol.'

Already even as he spoke, the thick, choking cloak of hyper-stuff that clung so closely to the sides of the *Flaming Nova* was going through those curious changes that marked the beginning of the shift to normal space. The blackness lightened a bit and concentric rings of various shades of gray chased each other across the port-view with gradually hastening speed. It was a weird and beautiful optical illusion that science has never succeeded in explaining.

Porin clicked off the lights in the room, and the two sat quietly in the dark, watching the feeble phosphorescence of the racing ripples as they sped into a blur. Then, with a terrifying silent suddenness, the whole structure of hyper-stuff seemed to burst apart in a whirling madhouse of brilliant color. And then all was peaceful again. The stars sparkled quietly, against the curved backdrop of normal space.

And up in the corner of the port blazed the brightest spark of the sky with a luminous yellow flame that lit up the faces of the two men into pale, waxen masks. It was Sol!

The birth-star of Man was so distant that it lacked a perceptible disc, yet it was incomparably the brightest object to be seen. In its feeble yellow light, the two remained in quiet thought, and Filip Sanat grew calmer.

In two days, the *Flaming Nova* landed on Earth.

Filip Sanat forgot the delicious thrill that had seized him at the moment when his sandals first came into contact with the firm green sod of Earth, when he caught his first glimpse of a Lhasinuic official.

They seemed actually *human* – or humanoid, at least.

At first glance, the predominantly Manlike characteristics drowned out all else. The body plan differed in no essential from Man's. The four-limbed, bipedal body; the middling-well proportioned arms and legs; the well-defined neck, were all astonishingly in evidence. It was only after a few minutes that the smaller details marking the difference between the two races were noticed at all.

Chief of these were the scales covering the head and a thick line down the backbone, halfway to the hips. The face itself, with its flat, broad, thinly-scaled nose and lidless eyes was rather repulsive, but in no way bestial. Their clothes were few and simple, and their speech quite pleasant to the ear. And, what was more important, there was no masking the intelligence that showed forth in their dark, luminous eyes.

Porin noted Sanat's surprise at this first glimpse of the Vegan reptiles with every sign of satisfaction.

'You see,' he remarked, 'their appearance is not at all monstrous. Why should hate exist between Human and Lhasinu, then?'

Sanat didn't answer. Of course, his old friend was right. The word 'Lhasinu' had so long been coupled with the words 'alien' and 'monster' in his mind, that against all knowledge and reason, he had subconsciously expected to see some weird lifeform.

Yet, overlying the foolish feeling this realization induced was the same haunting hate that clung closely to him, growing to fury as they passed inspection by an over-bearing English-speaking Lhasinu.

The next morning, the two left for New York, the largest city of the planet. In the historic lore of the unbelievably ancient metropolis, Sanat forgot for a day the troubles of the Galaxy outside. It was a great moment for him when he finally stood before a towering structure and said to himself, '*This* is the Memorial.'

The Memorial was Earth's greatest monument, dedicated to the birthplace of the Human race, and this was Wednesday, the day of the week when two men 'guarded the Flame.' Two men, alone in the Memorial, watched over the flickering yellow fire that symbolized Human courage and Human initiative – and Porin had already arranged that the choice should fall that day upon himself and Sanat, as being two newly-arrived Loarists.

And so, in the fading twilight, the two sat alone in the spacious Flame Room of the Memorial. In the murky semi-darkness, lit only by the fitful glare of a dancing yellow flame, a quiet peace descended upon them.

There was something about the brooding aura of the place that wiped all mental disturbance clean away. There was something about the wavering shadows as they weaved through the pillars of the long colonnade on either side, that cast a hypnotic spell.

Gradually, he fell into a half doze, and out of sleepy eyes regarded the Flame intently, until it became a living being of light weaving a dim, silent figure beside him.

But tiny sounds are sufficient to disturb a reverie, especially when contrasted with a hitherto deep silence. Sanat stiffened suddenly, and grasped Porin's elbow in a fierce grip.

'Listen,' he hissed the warning quietly.

Porin started violently out of a peaceful day-dream, regarded his young companion with uneasy intentness, then without a word, trumpeted one ear. The silence was thicker than ever – also a tangible cloak. Then the faintest possible scraping of feet upon marble, far off. A low whisper, down at the limits of audibility, and then silence again.

'What is it?' he asked bewilderedly of Sanat, who had already risen to his feet.

'Lhasinu!' ground out Sanat, face a mask of hate-filled indignation.

'Impossible!' Porin strove to keep his voice coldly steady, but it trembled in spite of itself. 'It would be an unheard-of event. We are just imagining things, now. Our nerves are rubbed raw by this silence, that is all. Perhaps it is some official of the Memorial.'

'After sunset, on Wednesday?' came Sanat's strident voice. 'That is as illegal as the entrance of Lhasiniuc lizards, and far more unlikely. It is my duty as a Guardian of the Flame to investigate this.'

He made as if to walk toward the shadowed door, and Porin caught his wrist fearfully, 'Don't Filip. Let us forget this until sunrise. One can never tell what will happen. What can you do, even supposing that Lhasinu have entered the Memorial? If you –'

But Sanat was no longer listening. Roughly, he shook off the other's desperate grasp, 'Stay here! The Flame must be guarded. I shall be back soon.'

He was already halfway across the wide, marble-floored hall. Cautiously, he approached the glass-paned door to the dark, twisting staircase that circled its way upwards through the twilit gloom into the desert recesses of the tower.

Slipping off his sandals, he crept up the stairs, casting one last look back toward the softly luminous Flame, and toward the nervous, frightened figure standing beside it.

The two Lhasinu stared about them in the pearly light of the Atomo lamp.

'Dreary old place,' said Threg Ban Sola. His wrist camera clicked three times. 'Take down a few of those books on the walls. They'll serve as additional proof.'

'Do you think we ought to,' asked Cor Wen Hasta. 'These Human apes may miss them.'

'Let them!' came the cool response. 'What can they do? Here, sit down!' He flicked a hasty glance upon his chronometer. 'We'll get fifty credits for every minute we stay, so we might as well pile up enough to last us for a while.'

'Pirat For is a fool. What made him think we wouldn't take the bet?'

'I think,' said Ban Sola, 'he's heard about the soldier torn to pieces last year for looting a European museum. The Humans didn't like it, though Loarism is filthy rich, Vega knows. The Humans were disciplined, of course, but the soldier was dead. Anyway, what Pirat For doesn't know is that the Memorial is deserted Wednesday. This is going to cost him money.'

'Fifty credits a minute. And it's been seven minutes now.'

'Three hundred and fifty credits. Sit down. We'll play a game of cards and watch our money mount.'

Threg Ban Sola drew forth a worn pack of cards from his pouch which, though they were typically and essentially Lhasinuic, bore unmistakable traces of their Human derivation.

'Put the Atomo-light on the table and I'll sit between it and the window,' he continued peremptorily, shuffling the cards as he spoke. 'Hah! I'll warrant no Lhasinu ever gamed in such an atmosphere. Why, it will triple the zest of the play.'

Cor Wen Hasta seated himself, and then rose again, 'Did you hear anything?' He stared into the shadows beyond the half-open door.

'No,' Ban Sola frowned and continued shuffling. 'You're not getting nervous, are you?'

'Of course not. Still, if they *were* to catch us here in this blasted tower, it might not be pleasant.'

122

'Not a chance. The shadows are making you jumpy.' He dealt the hands.

'Do you know,' said Wen Hasta, studying his cards carefully, 'it wouldn't be so nice if the Viceroy were to get wind of this, either. I imagine he wouldn't deal lightly with offenders of the Loarists, as a matter of policy. Back on Sirius, where I served before I was shifted, the scum –'

'Scum, all right,' grunted Ban Sola. 'They breed like flies and fight each other like mad bulls. Look at the creatures!' He turned his cards downward and grew argumentative. 'I mean, look at them scientifically and impartially. What are they? Only mammals! Mammals that can think, in a way; but mammals just the same. That's all.'

'I know. Did you ever visit one of the Human worlds?'

Ban Sola smiled, 'I may, pretty soon.'

'Furlough?' Wen Hasta registered polite astonishment.

'Furlough, my scales. With my ship! And with guns shooting!'

'What do you mean?' There was a sudden glint in Wen Hasta's eyes.

Ban Sola's grin grew mysterious. 'This isn't supposed to be known, even among us officers, but you know how things leak out.'

Wen Hasta nodded, 'I know.' Both had lowered their voices instinctively.

'Well. The Second Drive will be on, now, any time.'

'No!'

'Fact! And we're starting right here. By Vega, the Viceregal Palace is buzzing with nothing else. Some of the officers have even started a lottery on the exact date of the first move. I've got a hundred credits at twenty to one myself. But then, I drew only to the nearest week. You can get a hundred and fifty to one, if you're nervy enough to pick a particular day.'

'But why here on this Galaxy-forsaken planet?'

'Strategy on the part of the Home Office.' Ban Sola leaned forward. 'The position we're in now has us facing a numerically superior enemy hopelessly divided amongst itself. If we can keep them so, we can take them over one by one. The Human Worlds would just naturally rather cut their own throats than co-operate with each other.'

Wen Hasta grinned agreement, 'That's typical mammalian behavior for you. Evolution must have laughed when she gave a brain to an ape.'

'But Earth has particular significance. It's the center of Loarism, because the Humans originated here. It corresponds to our own Vegan system.'

'Do you mean that? But you couldn't! This little two-by-four fly-speck?'

'That's what they say. I wasn't here at the time, so I wouldn't know. But anyway, if we can destroy Earth, we can destroy Loarism, which is centered here. It was Loarism, the historians say, that united the Worlds against us at the end of the First Drive. No Loarism; the last fear of enemy unification is gone; and victory is easy.'

'Damned clever! How are we going to go about it?'

'Well, the word is that they're going to pack up every last Human on Earth and scatter them through the subject worlds. Then we can remove everything else on Earth that smells of the Mammals and make it an entirely Lhasinuic world.'

'But when?'

'We don't know; hence the lottery. But no one has placed his bet at a period more than two years in the future.'

'Hurrah for Vega! I'll give you two to one I riddle a Human cruiser before you do, when the time comes.'

'Done,' cried Ban Sola. 'I'll put up fifty credits.'

They rose to touch fists in token and Wen Hasta grinned at his chronometer, 'Another minute and we'll have an even thousand credits coming to us. Poor Pirat For. He'll groan. Let's go now; more would be extortionate.'

There was low laughter as the two Lhasinu left, long cloaks swishing softly behind them. They did not notice the slightly darker shadow hugging the wall at the head of the stairs, though they almost brushed it as they passed. Nor did they sense the burning eyes focused upon them as they descended noiselessly.

Loara Broos Porin jerked to his feet with a sob of relief as he saw the figure of Filip Sanat stumble across the hall toward him. He ran to him eagerly, grasping both hands tightly.

'What kept you, Filip? You don't know what wild thoughts have passed through my head this past hour. If you had been gone another five minutes, I would have gone mad for sheer suspense and uncertainty. But what's wrong?'

It took several moments for Loara Broos' wild relief to subside sufficiently to note the other's trembling hands, his disheveled hair, his feverishly-glinting eyes; but when it did, all his fears returned.

He watched Sanat in dismay, scarcely daring to press his question for fear of the answer. But Sanat needed no urging. In short, jerky sentences he related the conversation he had overheard and his last words trailed into a despairing silence.

Loara Broos' pallor was almost frightening, and twice he tried to talk with no success other than a few hoarse gasps. Then, finally, 'But it is the death of Loarism! What is to be done?'

Filip Sanat laughed as men laugh when they are at last convinced that nothing remains to laugh at. 'What *can* be done? Can we inform the Central Council? You know only too well how helpless they are. The various Human governments? You can imagine how effective *those* divided fools would be.'

'But it can't be true! It simply can't be!'

Sanat remained silent for seconds, and then his face twisted agonizedly and in a voice thick with passion, he shouted, 'I won't have it! Do you hear? It shan't be! I'll stop it!'

It was easy to see that he had lost control of himself; that wild emotion was driving him. Porin, large drops of perspiration on his brow, grasped him about the waist, 'Sit down, Filip, sit down! Are you going crazy?'

'No!' With a sudden push, he sent Porin stumbling backwards into a sitting position, while the Flame wavered and flickered madly in the rush of air, 'I'm going sane. The time for idealism and compromise and subservience is gone! The time for force has come! We will fight and, by Space, we will win!'

He was leaving the room at a dead run.

Porin limped after, 'Filip! Filip!' He stopped at the doorway in frightened despair. He could go no further. Though the Heavens fell, someone must guard the Flame.

But – but what was Filip Sanat going to do? And through Porin's tortured mind flickered visions of a certain night, five hundred years before, when a careless word, a blow, a shot, had lit a fire over Earth that was finally drowned in Human blood.

Loara Paul Kane was alone that night. The inner office was empty; the dim, blue light upon the severely simple desk the only illumination in the room. His thin face was bathed in the ghastly light, and his chin buried musingly between his hands.

And then there was a crushing interruption as the door was flung open and a disheveled Russell Tymball knocked off the restraining hands of half a dozen men and catapulted in. Kane whirled in dismay at the intrusion and one hand flew up to his throat as his eyes widened in apprehension. His face was one startled question.

Tymball waved his arm in a quieting gesture. 'It's all right.

Just let me catch my breath.' He wheezed a bit and seated himself gently before continuing, 'Your catalyst has turned up, Loara Paul – and guess where. Here on Earth! Here in New York! Not half a mile from where we're sitting now!'

Loara Paul Kane eyed Tymball narrowly, 'Are you mad?'

'Not so you can notice it. I'll tell you about it, if you don't mind turning on a light or two. You look like a ghost in the blue.' The room whitened under the glare of Atomos, and Tymball continued, 'Ferni and I were returning from the meeting. We were passing the Memorial when it happened, and you can thank Fate for the lucky coincidence that led us to the right spot at the right moment.

'As we passed, a figure shot out the side entrance, jumped on the marble steps in front, and shouted, 'Men of Earth!' Everyone turned to look – you know how filled Memorial Sector is at eleven – and inside of two seconds, he had a crowd.'

'Who was the speaker, and what was he doing inside the Memorial? This is Wednesday night, you know.'

'Why,' Tymball paused to consider, 'now that you mention it, he must have been one of the two Guardians. He was a Loarist – you couldn't mistake the tunic. He wasn't Terrestrial, either!'

'Did he wear the yellow orb?'

'No.'

'Then I know who he was. He's Porin's young friend. Go ahead.'

'There he stood!' Tymball was warming to his task. 'He was some twenty feet above street level. You have no idea what an impressive figure he made with the glare of the Luxites lighting his face. He was handsome, but not in an athletic, brawny way. He was the ascetic type, if you know what I mean. Pale, thin face, burning eyes, long, brown hair.

'And when he spoke! It's no use describing it; in order to appreciate it really, you would have to hear him. He began telling the crowd of the Lhasinuic designs; shouting what *I* had been whispering. Evidently, he had gotten them from a good source, for he went into details – and how he put them! He made them sound real and frightening. He frightened *me* with them; had me standing there scared blue at what he was saying; and as for the crowd, after the second sentence, they were hypnotized. Every one of them had had "Lhasinuic Menace" drilled into them over and over again, but this was the first time they listened – actually *listened*.

'Then he began damning the Lhasinu. He rang the changes

on their bestiality, their perfidy, their criminality – only he had a vocabulary that raked them into the lowest mud of a Venusian ocean. And every time he let loose with an epithet, the crowd stood upon its hind legs and let out a roar. It began to sound like a catechism. "Shall we allow this to go on?" cried he. "Never!" yelled the crowd. "Must we yield?" "Never!" "Shall we resist?" "To the end!" "Down with the Lhasinu!" he shouted. "Kill them!" they howled.

'I howled as loud as any of them – forgot myself entirely.

'I don't know how long it lasted before Lhasinuic guards began closing in. The crowd turned on them, with the Loarist urging them on. Did you ever hear a mob yell for blood? No? It's the most awful sound you can imagine. The guards thought so, too, for one look at what was before them made them turn and run for their lives, in spite of the fact that they were armed. The mob had grown into a matter of thousands and thousands by then.

'But in two minutes, the alarm siren sounded – for the first time in a hundred years. I came to my senses at last and made for the Loarist, who had not stopped his tirade a moment. It was plain that we couldn't let him fall into the hands of the Lhasinu.

'The rest is pretty much of a mixup. Squadrons of motorized police were charging down on us, but somehow, Ferni and I managed between the two of us to grab the Loarist, slip out, and bring him here. I have him in the outer room, gagged and tied, to keep him quiet.'

During all the last half of the narrative, Kane had paced the floor nervously, pausing every once in a while in deep consideration. Little flecks of blood appeared on his lower lip.

'You don't think,' he asked, 'that the riot will get out of hand? A premature explosion–'

Tymball shook his head vigorously, 'They're mopping up already. Once the young fellow disappeared, the crowd lost its spirit, anyway.'

'There will be many killed or hurt, but – Well, bring in the young firebrand.' Kane seated himself behind his desk and composed his face into a semblance of tranquility.

Filip Sanat was in sad shape as he knelt before his superior. His tunic was in tatters, and his face scratched and bloody, but the fire of determination shone as brilliantly as ever in his fierce eyes. Russell Tymball regarded him breathlessly as though the previous hour's magic still lingered.

Kane extended his arm gently, 'I have heard of your wild escapade, my boy. What was it that impelled you to do so foolish an act? It might very well have cost you your life, to say nothing of the lives of thousands of others.'

For the second time that night, Sanat repeated the conversation he had overheard – dramatically and in the minutest detail.

'Just so, just so,' said Kane, with a grim smile, upon the conclusion of the tale, 'and did you think we knew nothing of this? For a long time we have been preparing against this danger, and you have come near to upsetting all our carefully laid plans. By your premature appeal, you might have worked irreparable harm to our cause.'

Filip Sanat reddened, 'Pardon my inexperienced enthusiasm –'

'Exactly,' exclaimed Kane. 'Yet, properly directed, you might be of great aid to us. Your oratory and youthful fire might work wonders if well managed. Would you be willing to dedicate yourself to the task?'

Sanat's eyes flashed, 'Need you ask?'

Loara Paul Kane laughed and cast a jubilant side-glance at Russell Tymball. 'You'll do. In two days, you will leave for the outer stars. With you, will go several of my own men. And now, you are tired. You will be taken to where you may wash and treat your cuts. Then, you had better sleep, for you shall need your strength in the days to come.'

'But – but Loara Broos Porin – my companion at the Flame?'

'I shall send a messenger to the Memorial immediately. He will tell Loara Broos of your safety and serve as the second Guardian for the remainder of the night. Go, now!'

But even as Sanat, relieved and deliriously happy, rose to go, Russell Tymball leaped from his chair and grasped the older Loarist's wrist in a convulsive grip.

'Great Space! Listen!'

The shrill, keening whine that pierced to the inner sanctum of Kane's offices told its own story. Kane's face turned haggard.

'It's martial law!'

Tymball's very lips had turned bloodless, 'We lost out, after all. They're using tonight's disturbance to strike the first blow. They're after Sanat, and they'll have him. A mouse couldn't get through the cordon they're going to throw about the city now.'

'But they mustn't have him.' Kane's eyes glittered. 'We'll take him to the Memorial by the Passageway. They won't dare violate the Memorial.'

'They have done it once already,' came Sanat's impassioned cry. 'I won't hide from the lizards. Let us fight.'

'Quiet,' said Kane, 'and follow silently.'

A panel in the wall had slid aside, and toward it Kane motioned.

And as the panel closed noiselessly behind them, leaving them in the cold glow of a pocket Atomo lamp. Tymball muttered softly, 'If they are ready, even the Memorial will yield no protection.'

New York was in ferment. The Lhasinuic garrison had mustered its full strength and placed it in a state of siege. No one might enter. No one might leave. Through the key avenues, rolled the ground cars of the army, while overhead poised the Strato-cars that guarded the airways.

The Human population stirred restlessly. They percolated through the streets, gathering in little knots that broke up at the approach of the Lhasinu. The spell of Sanat lingered, and here and there frowning men exchanged angry whispers.

The atmosphere crackled with tension.

The Viceroy of New York realized that as he sat behind his desk in the Palace, which raised its spires upon Washington Heights. He stared out the window at the Hudson River, flowing darkly beneath, and addressed the uniformed Lhasinu before him.

'There must be positive action, Captain. You are right in that. And yet, if possible, an outright break must be avoided. We are woefully undermanned and we haven't more than five third-rate war-vessels on the entire planet.'

'It is not our strength but their own fear that keeps them helpless, Excellency. Their spirit has been thoroughly broken in these last centuries. The rabble would break before a single unit of Guardsmen. That is precisely the reason why we must strike hard now. The population has reared and they must feel the whip immediately. The Second Drive may as well begin tonight.'

'Yes,' the Viceroy grimaced wryly. 'We are caught off-stride, but the – er – rabble-rouser must be made an example of. You have him, of course.'

The captain smiled grimly, 'No. The Human dog had powerful friends. He is a Loarist you know. Kane –'

'Is Kane standing against us?' Two red spots burnt over the Viceroy's eyes. 'The fool presumes! The troops are to arrest the rebel in spite of him – and him, too, if he objects.'

'Excellency!' the captain's voice rang metallically. 'We have reason to believe the rebel may be skulking in the Memorial.'

The Viceroy half-rose to his feet. He scowled in indecision and seated himself once more, 'The Memorial! That presents difficulties!'

'Not necessarily!'

'There are some things those Humans won't stand.' His voice trailed off uncertainly.

The Captain spoke decisively, 'The nettle seized firmly does not sting. Quickly done – a criminal could be dragged from the Hall of the Flame itself – and we kill Loarism at a stroke. There could be no struggle after that supreme defiance.'

'By Vega! Blast me, if you're not right. Good! Storm the Memorial!'

The Captain bowed stiffly, turned on his heel, and left the Palace.

Filip Sanat re-entered the Hall of Flame, thin face set angrily, 'The entire Sector is patrolled by the lizards. All avenues of approach to the Memorial have been shut off.'

Russell Tymball rubbed his jaw, 'Oh, they're not fools. They've treed us, and the Memorial won't stop them. As a matter of fact, they may have decided to make this The Day.'

Filip frowned and his voice was thickly furious, 'And we're to wait here, are we? Better to die fighting, than to die hiding.'

'Better not to die at all, Filip,' responded Tymball quietly.

There was a moment of silence. Loara Paul Kane sat staring at his fingers.

Finally, he said, 'If you were to give the signal to strike now, Tymball, how long could you hold out?'

'Until Lhasinuic reinforcements could arrive in sufficient numbers to crush us. The Terrestrial garrison, including the entire Solar Patrol, is not enough to stop us. Without outside help, we can fight effectively for six months at the very least. Unfortunately it's out of the question.' His composure was unruffled.

'Why is it out of the question?'

And his face reddened suddenly, as he sprang angrily to his feet, 'Because you can't just push buttons. The Lhasinu are weak. My men know that, but Earth doesn't. The lizards have one weapon, fear! We can't defeat them, unless the populace is with us, at least passively.' His mouth twisted, 'You don't know the practical difficulties involved. Ten years, now, I've been planning, working, trying. I have an army; and a respectable fleet in the Appalachians. I could set the wheels in motion in all five continents simultaneously. But what good would it do? It would be useless. If I had New York, now – if I were able to prove to the rest of Earth that the Lhasinu were not invincible.'

'If I could banish fear from the hearts of Humans?' said Kane softly.

'I would have New York by dawn. But it would take a miracle.'

'Perhaps! Do you think you can get through the cordon and reach your men?'

'I could if I had to. What are you going to do?'

'You will know when it happens.' Kane was smiling fiercely. 'And when it does happen, strike!'

There was a Tonite gun in Tymball's hand suddenly, as he backed away. His plump face was not at all gentle, 'I'll take a chance, Kane. Good-bye!'

The captain strode up the deserted marble steps of the Memorial arrogantly. He was flanked on each side by an armed adjutant.

He paused an instant before the huge double-door that loomed up before him and stared at the slender pillars that soared gracefully upwards at its sides.

There was faint sarcasm in his smile, 'Impressive, all this, isn't it?'

'Yes, Captain!' was the double reply.

'And mysteriously dark, too, except for the dim yellow of their Flame. You see its light?' He pointed toward the stained glass of the bottom windows, which glinted flickeringly.

'Yes, Captain!'

'It's dark, and mysterious, and impressive – and it is about to fall in ruins.' He laughed, and suddenly brought the butt end of his saber down upon the metal carvings on the door in a clanging salvo.

It echoed through the emptiness within and sounded hollowly in the night, but there was no answer.

The adjutant at his left raised his televisor to his ear and caught the faint words issuing therefrom. He saluted, 'Captain, the Humans are crowding into the sector.'

The captain sneered, 'Let them! Order the guns placed in readiness and aimed along the avenues. Any Human attempting to pass the cordon is to be rayed mercilessly.'

His barked command was murmured into the televisor, and a hundred yards beyond, Lhasinuic Guardsmen put guns in order and aimed them carefully. A low, inchoate murmur went up – a murmur of fear. Men pressed back.

'If the door does not open,' said the captain, grimly, 'it is to be broken down.' He raised his saber again, and again there was the thunder of metal on metal.

Slowly, noiselessly, the door yawned wide, and the captain recognized the stern, purple-clad figure that stood before him.

'Who disturbs the Memorial on the night of the Guarding of the Flame?' demanded Loara Paul Kane solemnly.

'Very dramatic, Kane. Stand aside!'

'Back!' The words rang out loudly and clearly. 'The Memorial may not be approached by the Lhasinu.'

'Yield us our prisoner, and we leave. Refuse, and we will take him by force.'

'The Memorial yields no prisoner. It is inviolate. You may not enter.'

'Make way!'

'Stand back!'

The Lhasinu growled throatily and became aware of a dim roaring. The streets about him were empty, but a block away in every direction was the thin line of Lhasinuic troops, stationed at their guns, and beyond were the Humans. They were massed in noisy thickness and the whites of their faces shone palely in the Chromolights.

'What,' gritted the captain to himself, 'do the scum yet snarl?' His tough skin ridged at the jaws and the scales upon his head up-tilted sharply. He turned to the adjutant with the televisor. 'Order a round over their heads.'

The night was split in two by the purple blasts of energy and the Lhasinu laughed aloud at the silence that followed.

He turned to Kane, who remained standing upon the threshold. 'So you see that if you expect help from your people, you will be disappointed. The next round will be aimed at head level. If you think that bluff, try me!'

Teeth clicked together sharply, 'Make way!' A Tonite was leveled in his hand, and thumb was firm upon the trigger.

Loara Paul Kane retreated slowly, eyes upon the gun. The captain followed. And as he did so, the inner door of the anteroom swung open and the Hall of the Flame stood revealed. In the sudden draft, the Flame staggered, and at the sight of it, there came a huge shout from the distant spectators.

Kane turned toward it, face raised upwards. The motion of one of his hands was all but imperceptible.

And the Flame suddenly changed. It steadied and roared up to the vaulted ceiling, a blazing shaft fifty feet high. Loara Paul Kane's hand moved again, and as it did so, the Flame turned carmine. The color deepened and the crimson light of that flaming pillar streamed out into the city and turned the Memorial's windows into staring, bloody eyes.

Long seconds passed, while the captain froze in bewilderment; while the distant mass of Humanity fell into awed silence.

And then there was a confused murmur, which strengthened and grew and split itself into one vast shout.

'Down with the Lhasinu!'

There was the purple flash of a Tonite from somewhere high above, and the captain came to life an instant too late. Caught squarely, he bent slowly to his death; cold, reptilian face a mask of contempt to the last.

Russell Tymball brought down his gun and smiled sardonically, 'A perfect target against the Flame. Good for Kane! The changing of the Flame was just the emotion-stirring thing we needed. Let's go!'

From the roof of Kane's dwelling he aimed down upon the Lhasinu below. And as he did, all Hell erupted. Men mushroomed from the very ground, it seemed, weapons in hand. Tonites blazed from every side, before the startled Lhasinu could spring to their triggers.

And when they did so, it was too late, for the mob, white-hot with flaring rage, broke its bounds. Someone shrieked, 'Kill the lizards!' and the cry was taken up in one roaring ululation that swelled to the sky.

Like a many-headed monster, the stream of Humanity surged forward, weaponless. Hundreds withered under the belated fury of the defending guns, and tens of thousands scrambled over the corpses, charging to the very muzzles.

The Lhasinu never wavered. Their ranks thinned steadily under the deadly sharp-shooting of the Tymballists, and those that remained were caught by the Human flood that surged over them and tore them to horrible death.

The Memorial sector gleamed in the crimson of the bloody Flame and echoed to the agony of the dying, and the shrieking fury of the triumphant.

It was the first battle of the Great Rebellion, but it was not really a battle, or even madness. It was concentrated anarchy.

Throughout the city, from the tip of Long Island to the mid-Jersey flatlands, rebels sprang from nowhere and Lhasinu went to their death. And as quickly as Tymball's orders spread to raise the snipers, so did the news of the changing of the Flame speed from mouth to mouth and grow in the telling. All New

York heaved, and poured its separate lives into the single giant crucible of the 'mob.'

It was uncontrollable, unanswerable, iresistible. The Tymballists followed helplessly where it led, all efforts at direction hopeless from the start.

Like a mighty river, it lashed its way through the metropolis, and where it passed no living Lhasinu remained.

The sun of that fateful morning arose to find the masters of Earth occupying a shrinking circle in upper Manhattan. With the cool courage of born soldiers, they linked arms and withstood the charging, shrieking millions. Slowly, they backed away; each building a skirmish; each block a desperate battle. They split into isolated groups; defending first a building, and then its upper stories, and finally its roof.

With the noonday sun boiling down, only the Palace itself remained. Its last desperate stand held the Humans at bay. The withering circle of fire about it paved the grounds with blackened bodies. The Viceroy himself from his throneroom directed the defense; his own hand upon the butt of a semi-portable.

And then, when the mob had finally come to a pause, Tymball seized his opportunity and took the lead. Heavy guns clanked to the front. Atomos and delta-rays, from the rebel stock and from the stores captured the previous night, pointed their death-laden muzzles at the Palace.

Gun answered gun, and the first organized battle of machines flared into desperate fury. Tymball was an omnipresent figure, shouting, directing, leaping from gun-emplacement to gun-emplacement, firing his own hand Tonite defiantly at the Palace.

Under a barrage of the heaviest fire, the Humans charged once more and pierced to the walls as the defenders fell back. An Atomo projectile smashed its way into the central tower and there was a sudden inferno of fire.

That blaze was the funeral pyre of the last of the Lhasinu in New York. The blackening walls of the palace crumbled in, in one vast crash; but to the very last, room blazing about him, face horribly cut, the Viceroy stood his ground, aiming into the thick of the besieging force. And when his semi-portable expended the last dregs of its power and expired, he heaved it out the window in a last futile gesture of defiance, and plunged into the burning Hell at his back.

Above the Palace grounds at sunset, with a yet-roaring furnace as the background, there floated the green flag of independent Earth.

New York was once more Human.

Russell Tymball was a sorry figure when he entered the Memorial once more that night. Clothes in tatters, and bloody from head to foot from the undressed cut on his cheek, he surveyed the carnage about him with sated eyes.

Volunteer squads, occupied in removing the dead and tending to the wounded had not yet succeeded in making more than a dent in the deadly work of the rebellion.

The Memorial was an improvised hospital. There were few wounded, for energy weapons deal death; and of these few, almost none slightly. It was a scene of indescribable confusion, and the moans of the hurt and dying mingled horribly with the distant yells of celebrating war-drunk survivors.

Loara Paul Kane pushed through the crowding attendants to Tymball.

'Tell me; is it over?' His face was haggard.

'The beginning is. The Terrestrial Flag flies over the ruins of the Palace.'

'It was horrible! The day has – has –' He shuddered and closed his eyes, 'If I had known in advance, I would rather have seen Earth dehumanized and Loarism destroyed.'

'Yes, it was bad. But the results might have been much more dearly bought, and yet have remained cheap at the price. Where's Sanat?'

'In the courtyard – helping with the wounded. We all are. It – it –' Again his voice failed him.

There was impatience in Tymball's eyes, and he shrugged weary shoulders, 'I'm not a callous monster, but it had to be done, and as yet it is only the beginning. Today's events mean little. The uprising has taken place over most of Earth, but without the fanatic enthusiasm of the rebellion in New York. The Lhasinu aren't defeated, or anywhere near defeated; make no mistake about that. Even now the Solar Guard is flashing to Earth, and the forces on the outer planets are being called back. In no time at all, the entire Lhasinuic Empire will converge upon Earth and the reckoning will be a terrible and bloody one. We must have help!'

He grasped Kane by the shoulders and shook him roughly. 'Do you understand? We must have help! Even here in New York the first flush of victory will fade by tomorrow. *We must have help!*'

'I know,' said Kane tonelessly. 'I'll get Sanat and he can leave today.' He sighed, 'If today's action was any criterion of his power as a catalyst, we may expect great events.'

Sanat climbed into the little two-man cruiser half an hour later and took his seat beside Petri at the controls.

He extended his hand to Kane a last time, 'When I come back it will be with a navy behind me.'

Kane grasped the young man's hand tightly, 'We depend upon you, Filip.' He paused and said slowly, 'Good luck, Loara Filip Sanat!'

Sanat flushed with pleasure at the title as he resumed his seat once more. Petri waved and Tymball called out, 'Watch out for the Solar Guard!'

The airlock clanged shut, and then with a coughing roar, the pygmy cruiser was off into the heavens.

Tymball followed it to where it dwindled into a speck and less and then turned to Kane, 'All is now in the hands of Fate. And, Kane, just how was that Changing of the Flame worked? Don't tell me the Flame turned red of itself.'

Kane shook his head slowly, 'No! That carmine blaze was the result of opening a hidden pocket of strontium salts, originally placed there to impress the Lhasinu in case of need. The rest was chemistry.'

Tymball laughed grimly, 'You mean the rest was mob psychology! And the Lhasinu, I think, were impressed – and *how*!'

Space itself gave no warning, but the mass-detector buzzed. It buzzed peremptorily and insistently. Petri stiffened in his seat and said, 'We're in none of the meteor zones.'

Filip Sanat held his breath as the other turned the knob that rotated the peri-rotor. The star-field in the 'visor shifted with slow dignity, and then they saw it.

It glinted in the sun like half a tiny, orange football, and Petri growled, 'If they've spotted us, we're sunk.'

'Lhasinuic ship?'

'Ship? That's no *ship*! That's a fifty-thousand ton battle cruiser! What in the Galaxy it's doing here, I don't know. Tymball said the Patrol had made for Earth.'

Sanat's voice was calm, 'That one hasn't. Can we outrace it?'

'Fat chance!' Petri's fist clenched white on the G-stick. 'They're coming closer.'

The words might have been a signal. The audiomitter jiggled and the harsh Lhasinuic voice started from a whisper and rose to stridence as the radio beam sharpened, 'Fire reverse motors and prepare for boarding!'

Petri released the controls and shot a look at Sanat, 'I'm

only the chauffeur. What do you want to do? We haven't the chance of a meteor against the sun – but if you like the gamble –'

'Well,' said Sanat, simply, 'we're not going to surrender, are we?'

The other grinned, as the decelerating rockets blasted, 'Not bad for a Loarist! Can you shoot a mounted Tonite?'

'I've never tried!'

'Well, then, learn how. Grab that little wheel over there and keep your eye on the small 'visor above. See anything?' Speed was steadily dropping and the enemy ship was approaching.

'Just stars!'

'All right, rotate the wheel – go ahead, further. Try the other direction. Do you see the ship now?'

'Yes! There it is.'

'Good! Now center it. Get it where the hairlines cross, and for the sake of Sol, keep it there. Now I'm going to turn toward the lizard scum,' siderockets blasted as he spoke, 'and you keep it centered.'

The Lhasinuic ship was bloating steadily, and Petri's voice descended to a tense whisper, 'I'm dropping our screen and lunging directly at her. It's a gamble. If they're sufficiently startled, they may drop *their* screen and shoot; and if they shoot in a hurry, they may miss.'

Sanat nodded silently.

'Now the second you see the purple flash of the Tonite, pull back on the wheel. Pull back *hard*; and pull back *fast*. If you're the tiniest trifle late, we're through.' He shrugged, 'It's a gamble!'

With that, he slammed the G-stick forward hard and shouted, 'Keep it centered!'

Acceleration pushed Sanat back gaspingly, and the wheel in his sweating hands responded reluctantly to pressure. The orange football wobbled at the center of the 'visor. He could feel his hands trembling, and that didn't help any. Eyes winced with tension.

The Lhasinuic ship was swelling terribly now, and then, from its prow, a purple sword leaped toward them. Sanat closed his eyes and jerked backwards.

He kept his eye closed and waited. There was no sound.

He opened them and started to his feet; for Petri, arms akimbo, was laughing down upon him.

'A beginner's own luck,' he laughed. 'Never held a gun before in his life and knocks out a heavy cruiser in as pretty a pink as I ever saw.'

'I hit it?' gasped Sanat.

'Not on the button, but you did disable it. That's good enough. And now, just as soon as we get far enough away from the sun, we're going into hyperspace.'

The tall, purple-clad figure standing by the central portview gazed longingly at the silent globe without. It was Earth, huge, gibbous, glorious.

Perhaps his thoughts were just a trifle bitter as he considered the six-month period that had just passed. It had begun with a nova-blaze. Enthusiasm kindled to white heat and spread, leaping the stellar gulfs from planet to planet as fast as the hyperatomic beam. Squabbling governments, sudden putty before the outraged clamoring of their peoples, outfitted fleets. Enemies of centuries made sudden peace and flew under the same green flag of Earth.

Perhaps it would have been too much to expect this love-feast to continue. While it did the Humans were irresistible. One fleet was not two parsecs from Vega itself; another had captured Luna and hovered one light-second above the Earth, where Tymball's ragged revolutionaries still held on doggedly.

Filip Sanat sighed and turned at the sound of a step. White-haired Ion Smitt of the Lactonian contingent entered.

'Your face tells the story,' said Sanat.

Smitt shook his head, 'It seems hopeless.'

Sanat turned away again, 'Did you know that we've gotten word from Tymball today? They're fighting on what they can filch from the Lhasinu. The lizards have captured Bucnos Aires, and all South America seems likely to go under their heel. They're disheartened – the Tymballists – and disgusted, and I am, too.' He whirled suddenly, 'You say that our new needle-ships insure victory. Then, why don't we attack?'

'Well, for one thing,' the grizzled soldier planted one booted leg on the chair next to him, 'the reinforcements from Santanni are not coming.'

Sanat started, 'I thought they were on their way. What happened?'

'The Santannian government has decided its fleet is required for home defense.' A wry smile accompanied his words.

'What home defense? Why, the Lhasinu are five hundred parsecs away from them.'

Smitt shrugged, 'An excuse is an excuse and need not make sense. I didn't say that was the real reason.'

Sanat brushed his hair back and his fingers strayed to the yellow sun upon his shoulder, 'Even so! We could still fight, with over a hundred ships. The enemy outnumbers us two to one, but with the needle ships and with Lunar Base at our backs and the rebels harassing them in the rear –' He fell into a brooding reverie.

'You won't get them to fight, Filip. The Trantorian squadron favors retreat.' His voice was suddenly savage, 'Of the entire fleet, I can trust only the twenty ships of my own squadron – the Lactonian. Oh, Filip, you don't know the dirt of it – you never have known. You've won the people to the Cause, but you've never won the governments. Popular opinion forced them in, but now that they are in, they're in only for what they can get.'

'I can't believe that, Smitt. With victory in their grasp –'

'Victory? Victory for whom? It is exactly over that bone that the planets are squabbling. At a secret convention of the nations, Santanni demanded control of all the Lhasinuic worlds of the Sirius sector – none of which have been recognized as yet – and was refused. Ah, you didn't know that. Consequently, she decides that she must take care of her home defense, and withdraws her various squadrons.'

Filip Sanat turned away in pain, but Ion Smitt's voice hammered on, hard, unmerciful.

'And then Trantor realizes that she hates and fears Santanni more than ever she did the Lhasinu and any day now she will withdraw *her* fleet to refrain from crippling them while her enemy's ships remain quietly and safely in port. The Human nations are falling apart,' the soldier's fist came down upon the table, 'like rotten cloth. It was a fool's dream to think that the selfish idiots could ever unite for any worthy purpose long.'

Sanat's eyes were suddenly calculating slits, 'Wait a while! Things will yet work out all right, if we can only manage to seize control of Earth. Earth is the key to the whole situation.' His fingers drummed upon the table edge. 'Its capture would provide the vital spark. It would drum up Human enthusiasm, now lagging, to the boiling point, and the Governments, – well, they would either have to ride the wave, or be dashed to pieces.'

'I know that. If we fought today, you have a soldier's word we'd be on Earth tomorrow. They realize it, too, but they won't fight.'

'Then – then they must be *made* to fight. The only way they can be made to fight is to leave no alternative. They won't fight now, because they can retreat whenever they wish, but if –'

He suddenly looked up, face aglow, 'You know, I haven't been out of the Loarist tunic in years. Do you suppose your clothes will fit me?'

Ion Smitt looked down upon his ample girth and grinned, 'Well, they might not fit you, but they'll cover you all right. What are you thinking of doing?'

'I'll tell you. It's a terrible chance, but – Relay the following orders immediately to the Lunar Base Garrison –'

The admiral of the Lhasinuic Solar squadron was a war-scarred veteran who hated two things above all else: Humans and civilians. The combination, in the person of the tall, slender Human in ill-fitted clothing, put a scowl of dislike upon his face.

Sanat wriggled in the grasp of the two Lhasinuic soldiers. 'Tell them to let go,' he cried in the Vegan tongue. 'I am unarmed.'

'Speak,' ordered the admiral in English. 'They do not understand your language.' Then, in Lhasinuic to the soldiers, 'Shoot when I give the word.'

Sanat subsided, 'I came to discuss terms.'

'I judged as much when you hoisted the white flag. Yet you come in a one-man cruiser from the night side of your own fleet, like a fugitive. Surely, you cannot speak for your fleet.'

'I speak for myself.'

'Then I give you one minute. If I am not interested by the end of that time, you will be shot.' His expression was stony.

Sanat tried once more to free himself, with little success. His captors tightened their grips.

'Your situation,' said the Earthman, 'is this. You can't attack the Human squadron as long as they control Lunar Base, without serious damage to your own fleet, and you can't risk that with a hostile Earth behind you. At the same time, I happen to know that the order from Vega is to drive the Humans from the Solar System at all costs, and that the Emperor dislikes failures.'

'You have ten seconds left,' said the admiral, but tell-tale red spots appeared above his eyes.

'All right, then,' came the hurried response, 'how's this? What if I offer you the entire Human Fleet caught in a trap?'

There was silence. Sanat went on, 'What if I show you how you can take over Lunar Base, and surround the Humans?'

'Go on!' It was the first sign of interest the admiral had permitted himself.

'I am in command of one of the squadrons and I have certain powers. If you'll agree to our terms, we can have the Base deserted within twelve hours. Two ships,' the Human raised two fingers impressively, 'will take it.'

'Interesting,' said the Lhasinu, slowly, 'but your motive? What is your reason for doing this?'

Sanat thrust out a surly under-lip, 'That would not interest you. I have been ill-treated and deprived of my rights. Besides,' his eyes glittered, 'Humanity's is a lost cause, anyway. For this I shall expect payment – ample payment. Swear to that, and the fleet is yours.'

The admiral glared his contempt. 'There is a Lhasinuic proverb: The Human is steadfast in nothing but his treachery. Arrange your treason, and I shall repay. I swear by the word of a Lhasinuic soldier. You may return to your ships.'

With a motion, he dismissed the soldiers and then stopped them at the doorway, 'But remember, I risk two ships. They mean little as far as my fleet's strength is concerned, but, nevertheless, if harm comes to a Lhasinuic head through Human treachery –' The sales on his head were stiffly erect and Sanat's eyes dropped beneath the other's cold stare.

For a long while, the admiral sat alone and motionless. Then he spat. 'This Human filth! It is a disgrace even to fight them!'

The Flagship of the Human fleet lazed one hundred miles above Luna, and within it the captains of the Squadrons sat about the table and listened to Ion Smitt's shouted indictment.

'– I tell you your actions amount to treason. The battle off Vega is progressing, and if the Lhasinu win, their Solar squadron will be strengthened to the point where we must retreat. And if the Humans win, our treachery here exposes their flank and renders the victory worthless. We can win, I tell you. With these new needle-ships –'

The sleepy-eyed Trantorian leader spoke up. 'The needle-ships have never been tried before. We cannot risk a major battle on an experiment, when the odds are against us.'

'That wasn't your original view, Porcut. You – yes, and the rest of you as well – are a cowardly traitor. Cowards! Cravens!'

A chair crashed backwards as one arose in anger and others followed. Loara Filip Sanat, from his vantage-point at the central port, from where he watched the bleak landscape of Luna below with devouring concentration, turned in alarm. But Jem Porcut raised a gnarled hand for order.

'Let's stop fencing,' he said. 'I represent Trantor, and I take orders only from her. We have eleven ships here, and Space knows how many at Vega. How many has Santanni got? None! Why is she keeping them at home? Perhaps to take advantage of Trantor's preoccupation. Is there anyone who hasn't heard of her designs against us? We're not going to destroy our ships here for her benefit. Trantor will not fight! My division leaves tomorrow! Under the circumstances, the Lhasinu will be glad to let us go in peace.'

Another spoke up, 'And Poritta, too. The treaty of Draconis has hung like neutronium around our neck these twenty years. The imperialist planets refuse revision, and we will not fight a war which is to their interests only.'

One after another, surly exclamations dinned the perpetual refrain, 'Our interests are against it! We will not fight!'

And suddenly, Loara Filip Sanat smiled. He had turned away from Luna and laughed at the snarling arguers.

'Sirs,' he said, 'no one is leaving.'

Ion Smitt sighed with relief and sank back in his chair.

'Who will stop us?' asked Porcut with disdain.

'The Lhasinu! They have just taken Lunar Base and we are surrounded.'

The room was a babble of dismay. Shouting confusion held sway and then one roared above the rest, 'What of the garrison?'

'The garrison had destroyed the fortifications and evacuated hours before the Lhasinu took over. The enemy met with no resistance.'

The silence that followed was much more terrifying than the cries that had preceded. 'Treason,' whispered someone.

'Who is at the bottom of this?' One by one they approached Sanat. Fists clenched. Faces flushed. 'Who did this?'

'I did,' said Sanat, calmly.

A moment of stunned disbelief. 'Dog!' 'Pig of a Loarist!' 'Tear his guts out!'

And then they shrank back at the pair of Tonite guns that appeared in Ion Smitt's fists. The burly Lactonian stepped before the younger man.

'I was in on this, too,' he snarled. 'You'll *have* to fight now. It is necessary to fight fire with fire sometimes, and Sanat fought treason with treason.'

Jem Porcut regarded his knuckles carefully and suddenly chuckled, 'Well, we can't wriggle out now, so we might as well fight. Except for orders, I wouldn't mind taking a crack at the damn lizards.'

The reluctant pause was followed by shamefaced shouts – proof-positive of the willingness of the rest.

In two hours, the Lhasinuic demand for surrender had been scornfully rejected and the hundred ships of the Human squadron spread outwards on the expanding surface of an imaginary sphere – the standard defense formation of a surrounded fleet – and the Battle for Earth was on.

A space-battle between approximately equal forces resembles in almost every detail a gigantic fencing match in which controlled shafts of deadly radiation are the rapiers and impermeable walls of etheric inertia are the shields.

The two forces advance to battle and maneuver for position. Then the pale purple of a Tonite beam lashes out in a blaze of fury against the screen of an enemy ship, and in so doing, its own screen is forced to blink out. For that one instant it is vulnerable and is a perfect target for an enemy ray, which, when loosed, renders *its* ship open to attack for the moment. In widening circles, it spreads. Each unit of the fleet, combining speed of mechanism with speed of human reaction, attempts to slip through at the crucial moment and yet maintain its own safety.

Loara Filip Sanat knew all this and more. Since his encounter with the battle cruiser on the way out from Earth, he had studied space war, and now, as the battle fleets fell into line, he felt his very fingers twitch for action.

He turned and said to Smitt, 'I'm going down to the big guns.'

Smitt's eye was on the grand 'visor, his hand on the etherwave sender, 'Go ahead, if you wish, but don't get in the way.'

Sanat smiled. The captain's private elevator carried him to the gun levels, and from there it was five hundred feet through an orderly mob of gunners and engineers to Tonite One. Space is at a premium in a battleship. Sanat could feel the crampedness of the room in which individual Humans dove-tailed their work smoothly to create the gigantic machine that was a giant dreadnaught.

He mounted the six steep steps to Tonite One and motioned the gunner away. The gunner hesitated; his eye fell upon the purple tunic, and then he saluted and backed reluctantly down the steps.

Sanat turned to the co-ordinator at the gun's visiplate. 'Do you mind working with me? My speed of reaction has been tested and grouped 1–A. I have my rating card, if you'd care to see it.'

The co-ordinator flushed and stammered, 'No, *sir*! It's an honor to work with you, sir.'

The amplifying system thundered, 'To your stations!' and a deep silence fell, in which the cold purr of machinery sounded its ominous note.

Sanat spoke to the co-ordinator in a whisper, 'This gun covers a full quadrant of space, doesn't it?"

'Yes, sir.'

'Good, see if you can locate a dreadnaught with the sign of a double sun in partial eclipse.'

There was a long silence. The co-ordinator's sensitive hands were on the Wheel, delicate pressure turning it this way and that, so that the field in view on the visiplate shifted. Keen eyes scanned the ordered array of enemy ships.

'There it is,' he said. 'Why, it's the flagship.'

'Exactly! Center that ship!'

As the Wheel turned, the space-field reeled, and the enemy flagship wobbled toward the point where the hairlines crossed. The pressure of the co-ordinator's fingers became lighter and more expert.

'Centered!' he said. Where the hairlines crossed the tiny oval globe remained impaled.

'Keep it that way!' ordered Sanat, grimly. 'Don't lose it for a second as long as it stays in our quadrant. The enemy admiral is on that ship and we're going to get him, you and I.'

The ships were getting within range of each other and Sanat felt tense. He knew it was going to be close – very close. The Humans had the edge in speed, but the Lhasinu were two to one in numbers.

A flickering beam shot out, another, ten more.

There was a sudden blinding flash of purple intensity!

'First hit,' breathed Sanat. He relaxed. One of the enemy ships drifted off helplessly, its stern a mass of fused and glowing metal.

The opposing ships were not at close grips. Shots were being exchanged at blinding speed. Twice, a purple beam showed at the extreme limits of the visiplate and Sanat realized with a queer sort of shiver down his spine that it was one of the adjacent Tonites of their own ship that was firing.

The fencing match was approaching a climax. Two flashes blazed into being, almost simultaneously, and Sanat groaned. One of the two had been a Human ship. And three times there came that disquieting hum as Atomo-engines in the lower level shot into high gear – and that meant that an enemy beam directed at their own ship had been stopped by the screen.

And, always, the co-ordinator kept the enemy flagship centered. An hour passed; an hour in which six Lhasinu and four

Human ships had been whiffed to destruction; an hour in which the Wheel turned fractions of a degree this way, that way; in which it swivelled on its universal socket mere hairlines in half a dozen directions.

Sweat matted the co-ordinator's hair and got into his eyes; his fingers half-lost all sensation, but that flagship never left the ominous spot where the hairlines crossed.

And Sanat watched; finger on trigger – watched – and waited.

Twice the flagship had glowed into purple luminosity, its guns blazing and its defensive screen down; and twice Sanat's finger had quivered on the trigger and refrained. He hadn't been quick enough.

And then Sanat rammed it home and rose to his feet tensely. The co-ordinator yelled and dropped the Wheel.

In a gigantic funeral pyre of purple-hued energy, the flagship with the Lhasinuic Admiral inside had ceased to exist.

Sanat laughed. His hand went out, and the co-ordinator's came to meet it in a firm grasp of triumph.

But the triumph did not last long enough for the co-ordinator to speak the first jubilant words that were welling up in his throat, for the visiplate burst into a purple bombshell as five Human ships detonated simultaneously at the touch of deadly energy shafts.

The amplifiers thundered, 'Up screens! Cease firing! Ease into Needle formation!'

Sanat felt the deadly pall of uncertainty squeeze his throat. He knew what had happened. The Lhasinu had finally managed to set up their big guns on Lunar Base; big guns with three times the range of even the largest ship guns – big guns that could pick off Human ships with no fear of reprisal.

And so the fencing match was over, and the real battle was to start. But it was to be a real battle of a type never before fought, and Sanat knew that that was the thought in every man's mind. He could see it in their grim expressions and feel it in their silence.

It might work! And it might not!

The Earth squadron had resumed its spherical formation and drifted slowly outwards, its offensive batteries silent. The Lhasinu swept in for the kill. Cut off from power supply as the Earthmen were, and unable to retaliate with the gigantic guns of the Lunar batteries commanding near-by space, it seemed only a matter of time before either surrender or annihilation.

The enemy Tonite beams lashed out in continuous blasts of

energy, and tortured screens on Human ships sparked and fluoresced under the harsh whips of radiation.

Sanat could hear the buzz of the Atomo-engines rise to a protesting squeal. Against his will, his eye flicked to the energy gauge, and the quivering needle sank as he watched, moving down the dial at perceptible speed.

The co-ordinator licked dry lips, 'Do you think we'll make it, sir?'

'Certainly!' Sanat was far from feeling his expressed confidence. 'We need hold out for an hour – provided they don't fall back.'

And the Lhasinu didn't. To have fallen back would have meant a thinning of the lines, with a possible break-through and escape on the part of the Humans.

The Human ships were down to crawling speed – scarcely above a hundred miles an hour. Idling along, they crept up the purple beams of energy, the imaginary sphere increasing in size, the distance between the opposing forces ever narrowing.

But inside the ship, the gauge-needle was dropping rapidly, and Sanat's heart dropped with it. He crossed the gunlevel to where hard-bitten soldiers waited at a gigantic and gleaming lever, in anticipation of an order that had to come soon – or never.

The distance between opponents was now only a matter of one or two miles – almost contact from the viewpoint of space warfare – and then that order shot over the shielded etheric beams from ship to ship.

It reverberated through the gun level:

'Out needles!'

A score of hands reached for the lever, Sanat's among them, and jerked downwards. Majestically, the lever bent in a curving arc to the floor and as it did so, there was a vast scraping noise and a sharp thud that shook the ship.

The dreadnaught had become a 'needle ship!'

At the prow, a section of armor plate had slid aside and a glittering shaft of metal had lunged outward viciously. One hundred feet long, it narrowed gracefully from a base ten feet in diameter to a needle-sharp diamond point. In the sunlight, the chrome-steel of the shaft gleamed in flaming splendor.

And every other ship of the Human squadron was likewise equipped. Each had become ten, fifteen, twenty, fifty thousand tons of driving rapier.

Swordfish of space!

Somewhere in the Lhasinuic fleet, frantic orders must have been issued. Against this oldest of all naval tactics – old even in the dim dawn of history when rival triremes had maneuvered and rammed each other to destruction with pointed prows – the super-modern equipment of a space-fleet has no defense.

Sanat forced his way to the visiplate and strapped himself into an anti-acceleration seat, and he felt the springs absorb the backward jerk as the ship sprang into sudden acceleration.

He didn't bother with that, though. He wanted to watch the battle! There wasn't one here, nor anywhere in the Galaxy, that risked what he did. They risked only their lives; and he risked a dream that he had, almost single-handed, created out of nothing.

He had taken an apathetic Galaxy and driven it into revolt against the reptile. He had taken an Earth on the point of destruction and dragged it from the brink, almost unaided. A Human victory would be a victory for Loara Filip Sanat and no one else.

He, and Earth, and the Galaxy were now lumped into one and thrown into the scale. And against it was weighed the outcome of this last battle, a battle hopelessly lost by his own purposeful treachery, unless the needles won.

And if they lost, the gigantic defeat – the ruin of Humanity – was also his.

The Lhasinuic ships were jumping aside, but not fast enough. While they were slowly gathering momentum and drifting away, the Human ships had cut the distance by three-quarters. On the screen, a Lhasinuic ship had grown to colossal proportions. Its purple whip of energy had gone out as every ounce of power had gone into a man-killing attempt at rapid acceleration.

And nevertheless its image grew and the shining point that could be seen at the lower end of the screen aimed like a glittering javelin at its heart.

Sanat felt he could not bear the tension. Five minutes and he would take his place as the Galaxy's greatest hero – or its greatest traitor! There was a horrible, unbearable pounding of blood in his temples.

Then it came.

Contact!!

The screen went wild in a chaotic fury of twisted metal. The anti-acceleration seats shrieked as springs absorbed the shock. Things clearly slowly. The screenview veered wildly as the ship slowly steadied. The ship's needle had broken, the jagged stump twisted awry, but the enemy vessel it had pierced was a gutted wreck.

Sanat held his breath as he scanned space. It was a vast sea of wrecked ships, and on the outskirts tattered remnants of the enemy were in flight, with Human ships in pursuit.

There was the sound of colossal cheering behind him and a pair of strong hands on his shoulders.

He turned. It was Smitt – Smitt, the veteran of five wars, with tears in his eyes.

'Filip,' he said, 'we've won. We've just received word from Vega. The Lhasinuic Home Fleet has been smashed – and also with the needles. The war is over, and we've won. *You've* won, Filip! *You!*'

His grip was painful, but Loara Filip Sanat did not mind that. For a single, ecstatic moment, he stood motionless, face transfigured.

Earth was free! Humanity was saved!

THE END

For some reason, possibly because of the awful title, for which I emphatically disclaim responsibility, 'Black Friar of the Flame' is taken as the quintessence of my early incompetence. At least, fans who come across a copy think they can embarrass me by referring to it.

Well, it isn't good, I admit, but it has its interesting points.

For one thing, it is an obvious precursor to my successful 'Foundation' series. In 'Black Friar of the Flame,' as in the 'Foundation' series, human beings occupy many planets; and two worlds mentioned in the former, Trantor and Santanni, also play important roles in the latter. (Indeed, the first of the 'Foundation series was to appear only a couple of months after 'Black Friar of hte Flame,' thanks to the delay in selling the latter.)

Furthermore, there is also a strong suggestion in 'Black Friar of the Flame' of my first book-length novel, *Pebble in the Sky*, which was to appear eight years later. In both, the situation I pictured on Earth was inspired by that of Judea under the Romans. The climactic battle in 'Black Friar of the Flame,' however, was inspired by that of the Battle of Salamis, the great victory of the Greeks over the Persians. (In telling future-history I always felt it wisest to be guided by past-history. This was true in the 'Foundation' series, too.)

'Black Friar of the Flame' cured me forever, by the way, of attempting repeated revisions. There may well be a connection between the consensus that the story is a poor one and the fact that it was revised six times. I know that there are writers who revise and revise and revise, polishing everything to a high gloss, but I can't do that.

It is my habit now to begin by typing a first draft without an outline. I compose freely on the typewriter though I am frequently questioned about this by readers who seem to think an initial draft can be only in pencil. Actually, writing by hand begins to hurt my wrist after fifteen minutes or so, is very slow, and is hard to read. I can type, on the other hand, ninety words a minute and keep that up for hours without difficulty. As for outlines, I tried one once and it was disastrous, like trying to play the piano from inside a straitjacket.

Having completed the first draft, I go over it and correct it in pen and ink. I then retype the whole thing as the final copy. I revise no more, of my own volition. If an editor asks for a clearly defined revision of a minor nature, with the philosophy of which I agree, I oblige. A request for a major, top-to-bottom revision, or a second revision after the first, is another matter altogether. Then I *do* refuse.

This is not out of arrogance or temperament. It is just that too large a revision, or too many revisions, indicate that the piece of writing is a failure. In the time it would take to salvage such a failure, I could write a new piece altogether and have infinitely more fun in the process. (Doing a revision is something like chewing used gum.) Failures are therefore put to one side and held for possible sale elsewhere – for what is a failure to one editor is not necessarily a failure to another.

About the time I was working on 'Black Friar of the Flame' I was becoming enmeshed in fan activities. I had joined an organization called 'The Futurians,' which contained a group of ardent science fiction readers, almost all of whom were to become important in the field as writers or editors or both. Included among them were Frederik Pohl, Donald A. Wollheim, Cyril Kornbluth, Richard Wilson, Damon Knight, and so on.

As I had occasion to say before, I became particularly friendly with Pohl. During the spring and summer of 1939, he visited me periodically, looking over my manuscripts and announcing that I had the 'best bunch of rejected stories' he had ever seen.

The possibility began to arise that he might be my agent. He was no older than myself, but he had a great deal more practical experience with editors and knew a great deal more about the field. I was tempted, but was afraid this might mean I would not be allowed to see Campbell any more, and I valued my monthly visits with him too much to risk it.

In May 1939 I wrote a story I called 'Robbie,' and on the twenty-third of that month I submitted it to Campbell. It was the first robot story I had ever written and it contained the germ of what later came to be known as the 'Three Laws of Robotics.' Fred read my carbon and at once said it was a good story but that Campbell would reject it because it had a weak ending plus other shortcomings. Campbell *did* reject it on June 6, for precisely the reasons Pohl had given me.

I was very impressed by that, and any hesitation I had with respect to letting him represent me vanished – but I specified that his agentship must be confined to editors other than Campbell.

I gave him 'Robbie' after the rejection, but he didn't succeed in selling it either, though he even submitted it to a British science fiction magazine (something I would myself never have thought of doing). In October 1939, however, he himself became editor of *Astonishing Stories* and *Super Science Stories,* and he therefore ceased being my agent.*

On March 25, 1940, however, he did as editor what he couldn't do as agent. He placed the story – by taking it himself.

It appeared in *Super Science Stories* under a changed title. (Pohl was always changing titles.) He called the story 'Strange Playfellow,' a miserable choice, in my opinion. Eventually the story was included as the first of the nine connected 'positronic robot' series that made up my book *I, Robot.* In the book, I restored the title to the original 'Robbie,' and it has appeared as 'Robbie' in every form in which the story has been published since.

Fifteen years later, a daughter was born to me. She was named Robyn and I call her Robbie. I have been asked more than once whether there is a connection. Did I deliberately give her a name close to 'robot' because I made such a success of my robot stories? The answer is a flat negative. The whole thing is pure coincidence.

One more thing – In the course of my meeting with Campbell on June 6, 1939 (the one in which he rejected 'Robbie'), I met a by then quite well established science fiction writer, L. Sprague de Camp. That started a close friendship – perhaps

* A decade later he became my agent again for a few years. I never enjoyed being represented, however, and except for Pohl on these two occasions, I have never had an agent, despite the vast and complicated nature of my writing commitments. Nor do I intend ever having one.

my closest within the science fiction fraternity – that has continued to this day.

In June 1939 I wrote 'Half-Breed' and decided to give Fred Pohl a fair chance. I did not submit it to Campbell, but gave it to Pohl directly to see what he could do with it. He tried *Amazing*, which rejected it. So I took it back and tried Campbell in the usual direct fashion. Campbell rejected it, too.

When Pohl became an editor, however, he announced the fact to me (on October 27, 1939) by saying that he was taking 'Half-Breed.' In later months he also took first 'Robbie,' then 'The Callistan Menace.' He bought seven stories from me altogether during his editorial tenure.

Jefferson Scanlon wiped a perspiring brow and took a deep breath. With trembling finger, he reached for the switch – and changed his mind. His latest model, representing over three months of solid work, was very nearly his last hope. A good part of the fifteen thousand dollars he had been able to borrow was in it. And now the closing of a switch would show whether he won or lost.

Scanlon cursed himself for a coward and grasped the switch firmly. He snapped it down and flicked it open again with one swift movement. And nothing happened – his eyes, strain though they might, caught no flash of surging power. The pit of his stomach froze, and he closed the switch again savagely, and left it closed. Nothing happened: the machine, again, was a failure.

He buried his aching head in his hands, and groaned. 'Oh, God! It should work – it should. My math is right and I've produced the fields I want. By every law of science, those fields should crack the atom.' He arose, opening the useless switch, and paced the floor in deep thought.

His theory was right. His equipment was cut neatly to the pattern of his equations. If the theory was right, the equipment must be wrong. But the equipment was right, so the theory must. . . . 'I'm getting out of here before I go crazy,' he said to the four walls.

He snatched his hat and coat from the peg behind the door and was out of the house in a whirlwind of motion, slamming the door behind him in a gust of fury.

Atomic power. Atomic power! *Atomic power!*

The two words repeated themselves over and over again, singing a monotonous, maddening song in his brain. A siren song! It was luring him to destruction; for this dream he had given up a safe and comfortable professorship at M.I.T. For it, he had become a middle-aged man at thirty – the first flush of youth long gone, – an apparent failure.

And now his money was vanishing rapidly. If the love of money is the root of all evil, the need of money is most certainly the root of all despair. Scanlon smiled a little at the

Astonishing Stories, February 1940
Copyright © 1939 by Fictioneers, Inc.
Copyright renewed © 1966 by Isaac Asimov

thought – rather neat.

Of course, there were the beautiful prospects in store if he could ever bridge the gap he had found between theory and practice. The whole world would be his – Mars too, and even the unvisited planets. All his. All he had to do was to find out what was wrong with his mathematics – no, he'd checked that, it was in the equipment. Although – He groaned aloud once more.

The gloomy train of his thoughts was broken as he suddenly became aware of a tumult of boyish shouts not far off. Scanlon frowned. He hated noise especially when he was in the dumps.

The shouts became louder and dissolved into scraps of words, 'Get him, Johnny!' 'Whee – look at him run!'

A dozen boys careened out from behind a large frame building, not two hundred yards away, and ran pell-mell in Scanlon's general direction.

In spite of himself, Scanlon regarded the yelling group curiously. They were chasing something or other, with the heartless glee of children. In the dimness he couldn't make out just what it was. He screened his eyes and squinted. A sudden motion and a lone figure disengaged itself from the crowd and ran frantically.

Scanlon almost dropped his solacing pipe in astonishment, for the fugitive was a Tweenie – an Earth–Mars half-breed. There was no mistaking that brush of wiry, dead-white hair that rose stiffly in all directions like porcupine-quills. Scanlon marvelled – what was one of *those* things doing outside an asylum?

The boys had caught up with the Tweenie again, and the fugitive was lost to sight. The yells increased in volume, Scanlon, shocked, saw a heavy board rise and fall with a thud. A profound sense of the enormity of his own actions in standing idly by while a helpless creature was being hounded by a crew of gamins came to him, and before he quite realized it he was charging down upon them, fists waving threateningly in the air.

'Scat, you heathens! Get out of here before I –' the point of his foot came into violent contact with the seat of the nearest hoodlum, and his arms sent two more tumbling.

The entrance of the new force changed the situation considerably. Boys, whatever their superiority in numbers, have an instinctive fear of adults, – especially such a shouting, ferocious adult as Scanlon appeared to be. In less time than it took Scanlon to realize it they were gone, and he was left alone with the Tweenie, who lay half-prone, and who between panting sobs cast fearful and uncertain glances at his deliverer.

'Are you hurt?' asked Scanlon gruffly.

'No, sir.' The Tweenie rose unsteadily, his high silver crest of hair swaying incongruously. 'I twisted my ankle a bit, but I can walk. I'll go now. Thank you very much for helping me.'

'Hold on! Wait!' Scanlon's voice was much softer, for it dawned on him that the Tweenie, though almost full-grown, was incredibly gaunt; that his clothes were a mere mass of dirty rags; and that there was a heart-rending look of utter weariness on his thin face.

'Here,' he said, as the Tweenie turned towards him again, 'Are you hungry?'

The Tweenie's face twisted as though he were fighting a battle within himself. When he spoke it was in a low, embarrassed voice. 'Yes – I am, a little.'

'You look it. Come with me to my house,' he jerked a thumb over his shoulder. 'You ought to eat. Looks like you can do with a wash and change of clothes, too.' He turned and led the way.

He didn't speak again until he had opened his front door and entered the hall. 'I think you'd better take a bath first, boy. There's the bathroom. Hurry into it and lock the door before Beulah sees you.'

His admonition came too late. A sudden, startled gasp caused Scanlon to whirl about, the picture of guilt, and the Tweenie to shrink backwards into the shadow of a hat-rack.

Beulah, Scanlon's housekeeper, scurried towards them, her mild face aflame with indignation and her short, plump body exuding exasperation at every pore.

'Jefferson Scanlon! Jefferson!' She glared at the Tweenie with shocked disgust. 'How can you bring such a thing into this house! Have you lost your sense of morals?'

The poor Tweenie was washed away with the flow of her anger, but Scanlon, after his first momentary panic, collected himself. 'Come come, Beulah. This isn't like you. Here's a poor fellow-creature, starved, tired, beaten by a crowd of boys, and you have no pity for him. I'm really disappointed in you, Beulah.'

'Disappointed!' sniffed the housekeeper, though touched. 'Because of *that* disgraceful thing. He should be in an institution where they keep such monsters!'

'All right, we'll talk about it later. Go ahead, boy, take your bath. And, Beulah, see if you can't rustle up some old clothes of mine.'

With a last look of disapproval, Beulah flounced out of the

room.

'Don't mind her, boy,' Scanlon said when she left. 'She was my nurse once and she still has a sort of proprietary interest in me. She won't harm you. Go take your bath.'

The Tweenie was a different person altogether when he finally seated himself at the dining-room table. Now that the layer of grime was removed, there was something quite handsome about his thin face, and his high, clear forehead gave him a markedly intellectual look. His hair still stood erect, a foot tall, in spite of the moistening it had received. In the light its brilliant whiteness took an imposing dignity, and to Scanlon it seemed to lose all ugliness.

'Do you like cold chicken?' asked Scanlon.

'Oh, *yes!*' enthusiastically.

'Then pitch in. And when you finish that, you can have more. Take anything on the table.'

The Tweenie's eyes glistened as he set his jaws to work; and, between the two of them, the table was bare in a few minutes.

'Well, now,' exclaimed Scanlon when the repast had reached its end, 'I think you might answer some questions now. What's your name?'

'They called me Max.'

'Ah! And your last name?'

The Tweenie shrugged his shoulders. 'They never called me anything but Max – when they spoke to me at all. I don't suppose a half-breed needs a name.' There was no mistaking the bitterness in his voice.

'But what were you doing running wild through the country? Why aren't you where you live?'

'I was in a home. Anything is better than being in a home – even the world outside, which I had never seen. Especially after Tom died.'

'Who was Tom, Max?' Scanlon spoke softly.

'He was the only other one like me. He was younger – fifteen – but he died.' He looked up from the table, fury in his eyes. '*They* killed him, Mr. Scanlon. He was such a young fellow, and so friendly. He couldn't stand being alone the way I could. He needed friends and fun, and – all he had was me. No one else would speak to him, because he was a half-breed. And when he died I couldn't stand it anymore either. I left.'

'They meant to be kind, Max. You shouldn't have done that. You're not like other people; they don't understand you. And they must have done something for you. You talk as though you've had some education.'

'I could attend classes, all right,' he assented gloomily. 'But I had to sit in a corner away from all the others. They let me read all I wanted, though, and I'm thankful for *that*.'

'Well, there you are, Max. You weren't so badly off, were you?'

Max lifted his head and stared at the other suspiciously. 'You're not going to send me back, are you?' He half rose, as though ready for instant flight.

Scanlon coughed uneasily. 'Of course, if you don't want to go back I won't make you. But it would be the best thing for you.'

'It wouldn't!' Max cried vehemently.

'Well, have it your own way. Anyway, I think you'd better go to sleep now. You need it. We'll talk in the morning.'

He led the still suspicious Tweenie up to the second floor, and pointed out a small bedroom. 'That's yours for the night. I'll be in the next room later on, and if you need anything just shout.' He turned to leave, then thought of something. 'But remember, you mustn't try to run away during the night.'

'Word of honor. I won't.'

Scanlon retired thoughtfully to the room he called his study. He lit a dim lamp and seated himself in a worn armchair. For ten minutes he sat without moving, and for the first time in six years thought about something besides his dream of atomic power.

A quiet knock sounded, and at his grunted acknowledgement Beulah entered. She was frowning, her lips pursed. She planted herself firmly before him.

'Oh, Jefferson! To think that you should do this! If your dear mother knew ...'

'Sit down, Beulah,' Scanlon waved at another chair, 'and don't worry about my mother. She wouldn't have minded.'

'No. Your father was a good-hearted simpleton, too. You're just like him, Jefferson. First you spend all your money on silly machines that might blow the house up any day – and now you pick up that awful creature from the streets. ... Tell me, Jefferson,' there was a solemn and fearful pause, 'are you thinking of *keeping* it?'

Scanlon smiled moodily. 'I think I am, Beulah. I can't very well do anything else.'

A week later Scanlon was in his workshop. During the night before, his brain, rested by the change in the monotony brought about by the presence of Max, had thought of a possible solution to the puzzle of why his machine wouldn't work. Perhaps some of the parts were defective, he thought. Even a very slight flaw in some of the parts could render the machine inoperative.

He plunged into work ardently. At the end of half an hour the machine lay scattered on his workbench, and Scanlon was sitting on a high stool, eying it disconsolately.

He scarcely heard the door softly open and close. It wasn't until the intruder had coughed twice that the absorbed inventor realized another was present.

'Oh – it's Max.' His abstracted gaze gave way to recognition. 'Did you want to see me?'

'If you're busy I can wait, Mr. Scanlon.' The week had not removed his shyness. 'But there were a lot of books in my room...'

'Books? Oh, I'll have them cleaned out, if you don't want them. I don't suppose you do, – they're mostly textbooks, as I remember. A bit too advanced for you just now.'

'Oh, it's not too difficult,' Max assured him. He pointed to a book he was carrying. 'I just wanted you to explain a bit here in Quantum Mechanics. There's some math with Integral Calculus that I don't quite understand. It bothers me. Here – wait till I find it.'

He ruffled the pages, but stopped suddenly as he became aware of his surroundings. 'Oh say – are you breaking up your model?'

The question brought the hard facts back to Scanlon at a bound. He smiled bitterly. 'No, not yet. I just thought there might be something wrong with the insulation or the connections that kept it from functioning. There isn't – I've made a mistake somewhere.'

'That's too bad, Mr. Scanlon.' The Tweenie's smooth brow wrinkled mournfully.

'The worst of it is that I can't imagine what's wrong. I'm positive the theory's perfect – I've checked every way I can. I've gone over the mathematics time and time again, and each time it says the same thing. Space-distortion fields of such and such an intensity will smash the atom to smithereens. Only they don't.'

'May I see the equations?'

Scanlon gazed at his ward quizzically, but could see nothing in his face other than the most serious interest. He shrugged his shoulders. 'There they are – under that ream of yellow paper on the desk. I don't know if you can read them, though. I've been too lazy to type them out, and my handwriting is pretty bad.'

Max scrutinized them carefully and flipped the sheets one by one. 'It's a bit over my head, I guess.'

The inventor smiled a little. 'I rather thought they would be, Max.'

He looked around the littered room, and a sudden sense of anger came over him. Why wouldn't the thing work? Abruptly he got up and snatched his coat. 'I'm going out of here, Max,' he said. 'Tell Beulah not to make me anything hot for lunch. It would be cold before I got back.'

It was afternoon when he opened the front door, and hunger was sharp enough to prevent him from realizing with a puzzled start that someone was at work in his laboratory. There came to his ears a sharp buzzing sound followed by a momentary silence and then again the buzz which this time merged into a sharp crackling that lasted an instant and was gone.

He bounded down the hall and threw open the laboratory door. The sight that met his eyes froze him into an attitude of sheer astonishment – stunned incomprehension.

Slowly, he understood the message of his senses. His precious atomic motor had been put together again, but this time in a manner so strange as to be senseless, for even his trained eye could see no reasonable relationship among the various parts.

He wondered stupidly if it were a nightmare or a practical joke, and then everything became clear to him at one bound, for there at the other end of the room was the unmistakable sight of a brush of silver hair protruding from above a bench, swaying gently from side to side as the hidden owner of the brush moved.

'Max!' shouted the distraught inventor, in tones of fury. Evidently the foolish boy had allowed his interest to inveigle him into idle and dangerous experiments.

At the sound, Max lifted a pale face which upon the sight of his guardian turned a dull red. He approached Scanlon with reluctant steps.

'What have you done?' cried Scanlon, staring about him angrily. 'Do you know what you've been playing with? There's enough juice running through this thing to electrocute you twice over.'

'I'm sorry, Mr. Scanlon. I had a rather silly idea about all this when I looked over the equations, but I was afraid to say anything because you know so much more than I do. After you went away, I couldn't resist the temptation to try it out, though I didn't intend to go this far. I thought I'd have it apart again before you came back.'

There was a silence that lasted a long time. When Scanlon spoke again, his voice was curiously mild, 'Well, what have you done?'

'You won't be angry?'

'It's a little too late for that. You couldn't have made it much worse, anyway.'

'Well, I noticed here in your equations,' he extracted one sheet and then another and pointed, 'that whenever the expression representing the space-distortion fields occurs, it is always referred to as a function of x^2 plus y^2 plus z^2. Since the fields, as far as I could see, were always referred to as constants, that would give you the equation of a sphere.'

Scanlon nodded, 'I noticed that, but it has nothing to do with the problem.'

'Well, *I* thought it might indicate the necessary *arrangement* of the individual fields, so I disconnected the distorters and hooked them up again in a sphere.'

The inventor's mouth fell open. The mysterious rearrangement of his device seemed clear now – and what was more, eminently sensible.

'Does it work?' he asked.

'I'm not quite sure. The parts haven't been made to fit this arrangement so that it's only a rough set-up at best. Then there's the constant error –'

'But does it *work*? Close the switch, damn it!' Scanlon was all fire and impatience once more.

'All right, stand back. I cut the power to one-tenth normal so we won't get more output than we can handle.'

He closed the switch slowly, and at the moment of contact, a glowing ball of blue-white flame leaped into being from the recesses of the central quartz chamber. Scanlon screened his eyes automatically, and sought the output gauge. The needle was climbing steadily and did not stop until it was pressing the upper limit. The flame burned continuously, releasing no heat seemingly, though beside its light, more intensely brilliant than a magnesium flare, the electric lights faded into dingy yellowness.

Max opened the switch once more and the ball of flame reddened and died, leaving the room comparatively dark and red. The output gauge sank to zero once more and Scanlon felt his knees give beneath him as he sprawled onto a chair.

He fastened his gaze on the flustered Tweenie and in that look there was respect and awe, and something more, too, for there was *fear*. Never before had he really realized that the Tweenie was not of Earth or Mars but a member of a race apart. He noticed the difference now, not in the comparatively minor physical changes, but in the profound and searching mental gulf that he only now comprehended.

'Atomic power!' he croaked hoarsely. 'And solved by a boy, not yet twenty years old.'

Max's confusion was painful, 'You did all the real work, Mr. Scanlon, years and years of it. I just happened to notice a little detail that you might have caught yourself the next day.' His voice died before the fixed and steady stare of the inventor.

'Atomic power – the greatest achievement of man so far, and we actually have it, we two.'

Both – guardian and ward – seemed awed at the grandeur and power of the thing they had created.

And in that moment – the age of Electricity died.

Jefferson Scanlon sucked at his pipe contentedly. Outside, the snow was falling and the chill of winter was in the air, but inside, in the comfortable warmth, Scanlon sat and smoked and smiled to himself. Across the way, Beulah, likewise quietly happy, hummed softly in time to clicking knitting needles, stopping only occasionally as her fingers flew through an unusually intricate portion of the pattern. In the corner next the window sat Max, occupied in his usual pastime of reading, and Scanlon reflected with faint surprise that of late Max had confined his reading to light novels.

Much had happened since that well-remembered day over a year ago. For one thing, Scanlon was now a world-famous and world-adored scientist, and it would have been strange had he not been sufficiently human to be proud of it. Secondly, and scarcely less important, atomic power was remaking the world.

Scanlon thanked all the powers that were, over and over again, for the fact that war was a thing of two centuries past, for otherwise atomic power would have been the final ruination of civilization. As it was, the coalition of World Powers that now controlled the great force of Atomic Power proved it a real blessing and were introducing it into Man's life in the slow, gradual stages necessary to prevent economic upheaval.

Already, interplanetary travel had been revolutionized. From hazardous gambles, trips to Mars and Venus had become holiday jaunts to be negotiated in a third of the previous time, and trips to the outer planets were at last feasible.

Scanlon settled back further in his chair, and pondered once more upon the only fly in his wonderful pot of ointment. Max had refused all credit; stormily and violently refused to have his name as much as mentioned. The injustice of it galled Scanlon, but aside from a vague mention of 'capable assistants' he had said nothing; and the thought of it still made him feel an ace of a cad.

A sharp explosive noise brought him out of his reverie and he turned startled eyes towards Max, who had suddenly closed his book with a peevish slap.

'Hello,' exclaimed Scanlon, 'and what's wrong now?'

Max tossed the book aside and stood up, his underlip thrust out in a pout, 'I'm lonely, that's all.'

Scanlon's face fell, and he felt at an uncomfortable loss for words. 'I guess I know that, Max,' he said softly, at length. 'I'm sorry for you, but the conditions – are so –'

Max relented, and brightening up, placed an affectionate arm about his foster-father's shoulder, 'I didn't mean it that way, you know. It's just – well, I can't say it but it's that – you get to wishing you had someone your own age to talk to – someone of your own kind.'

Beulah looked up and bestowed a penetrating glance upon the young Tweenie but said nothing.

Scanlon considered, 'You're right, son, in a way. A friend and companion is the best thing a fellow can have, and I'm afraid Beulah and I don't qualify in that respect. One of your own kind, as you say, would be the ideal solution, but that's a tough proposition.' He rubbed his nose with one finger and gazed at the ceiling thoughtfully.

Max opened his mouth as if he were going to say something more, but changed his mind and turned pink for no evident reason. Then he muttered, barely loud enough for Scanlon to hear, 'I'm being silly!' With an abrupt turn he marched out of the room, banging the door loudly as he left.

The older man gazed after him with undisguised surprise, 'Well! What a funny way to act. What's got into him lately, anyway?'

Beulah halted the nimbly-leaping needles long enough to remark acidly, 'Men are born fools and blind into the bargain.'

'Is that so?' was the somewhat nettled response, 'And do *you* know what's biting him?'

'I certainly do. It's as plain as that terrible tie you're wearing. I've seen it for months now. Poor fellow!'

Scanlon shook his head, 'You're speaking in riddles, Beulah.'

The housekeeper laid her knitting aside and glanced at the inventor wearily, 'It's very simple. The boy is twenty. He needs company.'

'But that's just what he said. Is *that* your marvelous penetration?'

'Good land, Jefferson. Has it been so long since you were twenty yourself? Do you mean to say that you honestly think he's referring to *male* company?'

'Oh,' said Scanlon, and then brightening suddenly, 'Oh!' He giggled in an inane manner.

'Well, what are you going to do about it?'

'Why – why, nothing. What *can* be done?'

'That's a fine way to speak of your ward, when you're rich enough to buy five hundred orphan asylums from basement to roof and never miss the money. It should be the easiest thing in the world to find a likely-looking young lady Tweenie to keep him company.'

Scanlon gazed at her, a look of intense horror on his face, 'Are you serious, Beulah? Are you trying to suggest that I go shopping for a female Tweenie for Max? Why – why, what do I know about women – especially Tweenie women. I don't know his standards. I'm liable to pick one he'll consider an ugly hag.'

'Don't raise silly objections, Jefferson. Outside of the hair, they're the same in looks as anyone else, and I'll leave it to you to pick a pretty one. There never was a bachelor old and crabbed enough not to be able to do *that*.'

'No! I won't do it. Of all the horrible ideas –'

'Jefferson! You're his guardian. You owe it to him.'

The words struck the inventor forcibly, 'I owe it to him,' he repeated. 'You're right there, more right than you know.' He sighed, 'I guesss it's got to be done.'

Scanlon shifted uneasily from one trembling foot to the other under the piercing stare of the vinegar-faced official, whose name-board proclaimed in large letters – Miss Martin, Superintendent.

'Sit down, sir,' she said sourly. 'What do you wish?'

Scanlon cleared his throat. He had lost count of the asylums visited up to now and the task was rapidly becoming too much for him. He made a mental vow that this would be the last – either they would have a Tweenie of the proper sex, age, and appearance or he would throw up the whole thing as a bad job.

'I have come to see,' he began, in a carefully-prepared, but stammered speech, 'if there are any Twee – Martian half-breeds in your asylum. It is –'

'We have three,' interrupted the superintendent sharply.

'Any females?' asked Scanlon, eagerly.

'*All* females,' she replied, and her eye glittered with disapproving suspicion.

'Oh, good. Do you mind if I see them. It is —'

Miss Martin's cold glance did not waver, 'Pardon me, but before we go any further, I would like to know whether you're thinking of adopting a half-breed.'

'I *would* like to take out guardianship papers if I am suited. Is that so very unusual?'

'It certainly is,' was the prompt retort. 'You understand that in any such case, we must first make a thorough investigation of the family's status, both financial and social. It is the opinion of the government that these creatures are better off under state supervision, and adoption would be a difficult matter.'

'I know, madam, I know. I've had practical experience in this matter about fifteen months ago. I believe I can give you satisfaction as to my financial and social status without much trouble. My name is Jefferson Scanlon —'

'Jefferson Scanlon!' her exclamation was half a scream. In a trice, her face expanded into a servile smile, 'Why of course. I should have recognized you from the many pictures I've seen of you. How stupid of me. Pray do not trouble yourself with any further references. I'm sure that in your case,' this with a particularly genial expression, 'no red tape need be necessary.'

She sounded a desk-bell furiously. 'Bring down Madeline and the two little ones as soon as you can,' she snapped at the frightened maid who answered. 'Have them cleaned up and warn them to be on their best behavior.'

With this, she turned to Scanlon once more, 'It will not take long, Mr. Scanlon. It is really such a great honor to have you here with us, and I am so ashamed at my abrupt treatment of you earlier. At first I didn't recognize you, though I saw immediately that you were someone of importance.'

If Scanlon had been upset by the superintendent's former harsh haughtiness, he was entirely unnerved by her effusive geniality. He wiped his profusely-perspiring brow time and time again, answering in incoherent monosyllables the vivacious questions put to him. It was just as he had come to the wild decision of taking to his heels and escaping from the she-dragon by flight that the maid announced the three Tweenies and saved the situation.

Scanlon surveyed the three half-breeds with interest and sudden satisfaction. Two were mere children, perhaps ten years of age, but the third, some eighteen years old, was eligible from every point of view.

Her slight form was lithe and graceful even in the quiet attitude of waiting that she had assumed, and Scanlon, 'dried-up, dyed-in-the-wool bachelor' though he was, could not restrain a light nod of approval.

Her face was certainly what Beulah would call 'likely-looking' and her eyes, now bent towards the floor in shy confusion, were of a deep blue, which seemed a great point to Scanlon.

Even her strange hair was beautiful. It was only moderately high, not nearly the size of Max's lordly male crest, and its silky-white sheen caught the sunbeams and sent them back in glistening highlights.

The two little ones grasped the skirt of their elder companion with tight grips and regarded the two adults in wide-eyed fright which increased as time passed.

'I believe, Miss Martin, that the young lady will do,' remarked Scanlon. 'She is exactly what I had in mind. Could you tell me how soon guardianship papers could be drawn up?'

'I could have them ready for you tomorrow, Mr. Scanlon. In an unusual case such as yours, I could easily make special arrangements.'

'Thank you. I shall be back then –' he was interrupted by a loud sniffle. One of the little Tweenies could stand it no longer and had burst into tears, followed soon by the other.

'Madeline,' cried Miss Martin to the eighteen-year-old. 'Please keep Rose and Blanche quiet. This is an abominable exhibition.'

Scanlon intervened. It seemed to him that Madeline was rather pale and though she smiled and soothed the youngsters he was certain that there were tears in her eyes.

'Perhaps,' he suggested, 'the young lady has no wish to leave the institution. Of course, I wouldn't think of taking her on any but a purely voluntary basis.'

Miss Martin smiled superciliously, 'She won't make any trouble.' She turned to the young girl, 'You've heard of the great Jefferson Scanlon, haven't you?'

'Ye-es, Miss Martin,' replied the girl, in a low voice.

'Let me handle this, Miss Martin,' urged Scanlon. 'Tell me, girl, would you really prefer to stay here?'

'Oh, no,' she replied earnestly, 'I would be very glad to leave though,' with an apprehensive glance at Miss Martin, 'I have been very well treated here. But you see – what's to be done with the two little ones? I'm all they have, and if I left, they – they –'

She broke down and snatched them to her with a sudden, fierce grip, 'I don't want to leave them, sir!' She kissed each softly, 'Don't cry, children. I won't leave you. They won't take me away.'

Scanlon swallowed with difficulty and groped for a handkerchief with which to blow his nose. Miss Martin gazed on with disapproving hauteur.

'Don't mind the silly thing, Mr. Scanlon,' said she. 'I believe I can have everything ready by tomorrow noon.'

'Have ready guardianship papers for all three,' was the gruff reply.

'What? All three? Are you serious?'

'Certainly. I can do it if I wish, can't I?' he shouted.

'Why, of course, but –'

Scanlon left precipitately, leaving both Madeline and Miss Martin petrified, the latter with utter stupefaction, the former in a sudden upsurge of happiness. Even the ten-year-olds sensed the change in affairs and subsided into occasional sobs.

Beulah's surprise, when she met them at the airport and saw three Tweenies where she had expected one, is not to be described. But, on the whole, the surprise was a pleasant one, for little Rose and Blanche took to the elderly housekeeper immediately. Their first greeting was to bestow great, moist kisses upon Beulah's lined cheeks at which she glowed with joy and kissed them in turn.

With Madeline she was enchanted, whispering to Scanlon that he knew a little more about such matters than he pretended.

'If she had decent hair,' whispered Scanlon in reply, 'I'd marry her myself. That I would,' and he smiled in great self-satisfaction.

The arrival at home in mid-afternoon was the occasion of great excitement on the part of the two oldsters. Scanlon inveigled Max into accompanying him on a long walk together in the woods, and when the unsuspecting Max left, puzzled but willing, Beulah busied herself with setting the three newcomers at their ease.

They were shown over the house from top to bottom, the rooms assigned to them being indicated. Beulah prattled away continuously, joking and chaffing, until the Tweenies had lost all their shyness and felt as if they had known her forever.

Then, as the winter evening approached, she turned to

Madeline rather abruptly and said, 'It's getting late. Do you want to come downstairs with me and help prepare supper for the men?'

Madeline was taken aback, 'The *men*. Is there, then, someone besides Mr. Scanlon?'

'Oh, yes. There's Max. You haven't seen him yet.'

'Is Max a relation of yours?'

'No, child. He's another of Mr. Scanlon's wards.'

'Oh, I see.' She blushed and her hand rose involuntarily to her hair.

Beulah saw in a moment the thoughts passing through her head and added in a softer voice, 'Don't worry, dear. He won't mind your being a Tweenie. He'll be *glad* to see you.'

It turned out, though, that 'glad' was an entirely inadequate adjective when applied to Max's emotions at the first sight of Madeline.

He tramped into the house in advance of Scanlon, taking off his overcoat and stamping the snow off his shoes as he did so.

'Oh, boy,' he cried at the half-frozen inventor who followed him in, 'why you were so anxious to saunter about on a freezer like today I don't know.' He sniffed the air appreciatively, 'Ah, do I smell lamb chops?' and he made for the dining-room in double-quick time.

It was at the threshold that he stopped suddenly, and gasped for air as if in the last throes of suffocation. Scanlon slipped by and sat down.

'Come on,' he said, enjoying the other's brick-red visage. 'Sit down. We have company today. This is Madeline and this is Rose and this is Blanche. And this,' he turned to the seated girls and noted with satisfaction that Madeline's pink face was turning a fixed glance of confusion upon the plate before her, is my ward, Max.'

'How do you do,' murmured Max, eyes like saucers, 'I'm pleased to meet you.'

Rose and Blanche shouted cheery greetings in reply but Madeline only raised her eyes fleetingly and then dropped them again.

The meal was a singularly quiet one. Max, though he had complained of a ravenous hunger all afternoon, allowed his chop and mashed potatoes to die of cold before him, while Madeline played with her food as if she did not know what it was there for. Scanlon and Beulah ate quietly and well, exchanging sly glances between bites.

Scanlon sneaked off after dinner, for he rightly felt that the more tactful touch of a woman was needed in these matters, and when Beulah joined him in his study some hours later, he saw at a glance that he had been correct.

'I've broken the ice,' she said happily, 'they're telling each other their life histories now and are getting along wonderfully. They're still afraid of each other, though, and insist on sitting at opposite ends of the room, but that'll wear off – and pretty quickly, too.'

'It's a fine match, Beulah, eh?'

'A finer one I've never seen. And little Rose and Blanche are angels. I've just put them to bed.'

There was a short silence, and then Beulah continued softly, 'That was the only time you were right and I was wrong – that time you first brought Max into the house and I objected – but that one time makes up for everything else. You are a credit to your dear mother, Jefferson.'

Scanlon nodded soberly, 'I wish I could make all Tweenies on earth so happy. It would be such a simple thing. If we treated them like humans instead of criminals and gave them homes built especially for them and calculated especially for their happiness –'

'Well, why don't *you* do it?' interrupted Beulah.

Scanlon turned a serious eye upon the old housekeeper, 'That's exactly what I was leading up to.' His voice lapsed into a dreamy murmur, 'Just think. A town of Tweenies – run by them and for them – with its own governing officials and its own schools and its own public utilities. A little world within a world where the Tweenie can consider himself a human being – instead of a freak surrounded and looked down upon by endless multitudes of pure-bloods.'

He reached for his pipe and filled it slowly, 'The world owes a debt to *one* Tweenie which it can never repay – and I owe it to him as well. I'm going to do it. I'm going to create Tweenie-town.'

That night he did not go to sleep. The stars turned in their grand circles and paled at last. The grey dawn came and grew, but still Scanlon sat unmoving – dreaming and planning.

At eighty, age sat lightly upon Jefferson Scanlon's head. The spring was gone from his step, the sturdy straightness from his shoulders, but his robust health had not failed him, and his mind, beneath the shock of hair, now as white as any Tweenie's, still worked with undiminished vigor.

A happy life is not an aging one, and for forty years now,

Scanlon had watched Tweenietown grow, and in the watching, had found happiness.

He could see it now stretched before him like a large, beautiful painting as he gazed out the window. A little gem of a town with a population of slightly more than a thousand, nestling amid three hundred square miles of fertile Ohio land.

Neat and sturdy houses, wide, clean streets, parks, theatres, schools, stores, – a model town, bespeaking decades of intelligent effort and co-operation.

The door opened behind him and he recognized the soft step without needing to turn, 'Is that you, Madeline?'

'Yes, father,' for by no other title was he known to any inhabitant of Tweenietown. 'Max is returning with Mr. Johanson.'

'That's good,' he gazed at Madeline tenderly. 'We've seen Tweenietown grow since those days long ago, haven't we?'

Madeline nodded and sighed.

'Don't sigh, dear. It's been well worth the years we've given to it. If only Beulah had lived to see it now.'

He shook his head as he thought of the old housekeeper, dead now a quarter of a century.

'Don't think such sad thoughts,' admonished Madeline in her turn. 'Here comes Mr. Johanson. Remember it's the fortieth anniversary and a happy day; not a sad one.'

Charles B. Johanson was what is known as a 'shrewd' man. That is, he was an intelligent, far-seeing person, comparatively well-versed in the sciences, but one who was wont to put these good qualities into practice only in order to advance his own interest. Consequently, he went far in politics and was the first appointee to the newly created Cabinet post of Science and Technology.

It was the first official act of his to visit the world's greatest scientist and inventor, Jefferson Scanlon, who, in his old age, still had no peer in the number of useful inventions turned over to the government every year. Tweenietown was a considerable surprise to him. It was known rather vaguely in the outside world that the town existed, and it was considered a hobby of the old scientist – a harmless eccentricity. Johanson found it a well-worked-out project of sinister connotations.

His attitude, however, when he entered Scanlon's room in company with his erstwhile guide, Max, was one of frank geniality, concealing well certain thoughts that swept through his mind.

'Ah, Johanson,' greeted Scanlon, 'you're back. What do you

think of all this?' his arm made a wide sweep.

'It is surprising – something marvelous to behold,' Johanson assured him.

Scanlon chuckled, 'Glad to hear it. We have a population of 1154 now and growing every day. You've seen what we've done already but it's nothing to what we are going to do in the future – even after my death. However, there is something I wish to see done *before* I die and for that I'll need your help.'

'And that is?' questioned the Secretary of Science and Technology guardedly.

'Just this. That you sponsor measures giving these Tweenies, these so long despised half-breeds, full equality, – political, – legal, – economic, – social, – with Terrestrials and Martians.'

Johanson hesitated, 'It would be difficult. There is a certain amount of perhaps understandable prejudice against them, and until we can convince Earth that the Tweenies deserve equality –' he shook his head doubtfully.

'Deserve equality!' exclaimed Scanlon, vehemently, 'Why, they deserve more. I am *moderate* in my demands.' At these words, Max, sitting quietly in a corner, looked up and bit his lip, but said nothing as Scanlon continued, 'You don't know the true worth of these Tweenies. They combine the best of Earth and Mars. They possess the cold, analytical reasoning powers of the Martians together with the emotional drive and boundless energy of the Earthman. As far as intellect is concerned, they are your superior and mine, every one of them. I ask only equality.'

The Secretary smiled soothingly, 'Your zeal misleads you perhaps, my dear Scanlon.'

'It does not. Why do you suppose I turned out so many successful gadgets – like this gravitational shield I created a few years back. Do you think I could have done it without my Tweenie assistants? It was Max here,' Max dropped his eyes before the sudden piercing gaze of the Cabinet member, 'that put the final touch upon my discovery of atomic power itself.'

Scanlon threw caution to the winds, as he grew excited, 'Ask Professor Whitsun of Stanford and he'll tell you. He's a world authority on psychology and knows what he's talking about. He *studied* the Tweenie and he'll tell you that the Tweenie is the *coming* race of the Solar System, destined to take the supremacy away from us pure-bloods as inevitably as night follows day. Don't you think they deserve equality in that case?'

'Yes, I do think so, – definitely,' replied Johanson. There was a strange glitter in his eyes, and a crooked smile upon his lips, 'This is of extreme importance, Scanlon. I shall attend to it immediately. So immediately, in fact, that I believe I had better leave in half an hour, to catch the 2:10 strato-car.'

Johanson had scarcely left, when Max approached Scanlon and blurted out with no preamble at all, 'There is something I have to show you, father – something you have not known about before.'

Scanlon stared his surprise, 'What do you mean?'

'Come with me, please, father. I shall explain.' His grave expression was almost frightening. Madeline joined the two at the door, and at a sign from Max, seemed to comprehend the situation. She said nothing but her eyes grew sad and the lines in her forehead seemed to deepen.

In utter silence, the three entered the waiting Rocko-car and were sped across the town in the direction of the Hill o' the Woods. High over Lake Clare they shot to come down once more in the wooded patch at the foot of the hill.

A tall, burly Tweenie sprang to attention as the car landed, and started at the sight of Scanlon.

'Good afternoon, father,' he whispered respectfully, and cast a questioning glance at Max as he did so.

'Same to you, Emmanuel,' replied Scanlon absently. He suddenly became aware that before him was a cleverly-camouflaged opening that led into the very hill itself.

Max beckoned him to follow and led the way into the opening which after a hundred feet opened into an enormous man-made cavern. Scanlon halted in utter amazement, for before him were three giant space-ships, gleaming silvery-white and equipped, as he could plainly see, with the latest atomic power.

'I'm sorry, father,' said Max, 'that all this was done without your knowledge. It is the only case of the sort in the history of Tweenietown.' Scanlon scarcely seemed to hear, standing as if in a daze, and Max continued, 'The center one is the flagship – the *Jefferson Scanlon*. The one to the right is the *Beulah Goodkin* and the one to the left the *Madeline*.'

Scanlon snapped out of his bemusement, 'But what does this all mean and why the secrecy?'

'These ships have been lying ready for five years now, fully fuelled and provisioned, ready for instant take-off. Tonight, we blast away the side of the hill and shoot for Venus – tonight. We have not told you till now, for we did not wish to disturb your peace of mind with a misfortune we knew long ago to be inevitable. We had thought that perhaps,' his voice sank lower, 'its fulfillment might have been postponed until after you were

170

no longer with us.'

'Speak out,' cried Scanlon suddenly. 'I want the full details. Why do you leave just as I feel sure I can obtain full equality for you?'

'Exactly,' answered Max, mournfully. 'Your words to Johanson swung the scale. As long as Earthmen and Martians merely thought us different and inferior, they despised us and tolerated us. You have told Johanson we were superior and would ultimately supplant Mankind. They have no alternative now but to hate us. There shall be no further toleration; of that I can assure you. We leave before the storm breaks.'

The old man's eyes widened as the truth of the other's statements became apparent to him, 'I see. I must get in touch with Johanson. Perhaps, we can together correct that terrible mistake.' He clapped a hand to his forehead.

'Oh, Max', interposed Madeline, tearfully, 'why don't you come to the point? We want you to come with us, father. In Venus, which is so sparsely settled, we can find a spot where we can develop unharmed for an unlimited time. We can establish our nation, free and untrammeled, powerful in our own right, no longer dependent on –'

Her voice died away and she gazed anxiously at Scanlon's face, now grown drawn and haggard. 'No,' he whispered, 'no! My place is here with my own kind. Go, my children, and establish your nation. In the end, your descendants shall rule the System. But I – I shall stay here.'

'Then I shall stay, too,' insisted Max. 'You are old and someone must care for you. I owe you my life a dozen times over.'

Scanlon shook his head firmly, 'I shall need no one. Dayton is not far. I shall be well taken care of there or anywhere else I go. You, Max, are needed by your race. You are their leader. Go!'

Scanlon wandered through the deserted streets of Tweenietown and tried to take a grip upon himself. It was hard. Yesterday, he had celebrated the fortieth anniversary of its founding – it had been at the peak of its prosperity. Today, it was a ghost town.

Yet, oddly enough, there was a spirit of exultation about him. His dream had shattered – but only to give way to a brighter dream. He had nourished foundlings and brought up a race in its youth and for that he was someday to be recognized as the founder of the *super-race*.

It was *his* creation that would someday rule the system.

Atomic power – gravity nullifiers – all faded into insignificance. *This* was his real gift to the Universe.

This, he decided, was how a God must feel.

THE END

As in 'The Weapon Too Dreadful to Use,' the story dealt with racial prejudice on an interplanetary scale. I kept coming back to this theme very frequently – something not surprising in a Jew growing up during the Hitler era.

Once again my naïveté shows, since I assume not only an intelligent race on Mars, where such a thing is most unlikely even by 1939 evidence, but assume the Martians to be sufficiently like Earthmen to make interbreeding possible. (I can only shake my head wearily. I knew better in 1939; I really did. I just accepted science fictional clichés, that's all. Eventually, I stopped doing that.)

My treatment of atomic power was also primitive in the extreme, and I knew better than that, too, even though at the time I wrote the story, uranium fission had not been discovered. The Tweenie's mysterious reference to 'a function of x^2 plus y^2 plus z^2' merely means that I had taken analytic geometry at Columbia not too long before and was flaunting my knowledge of the equation for the sphere.

This was the first story in which I tried to introduce the romantic motif, however light. It *had* to be a failure. At the time of the writing of this story, I had still never had a date with a girl.

And yet the greatest embarrassment in a story simply littered with embarrassments was the following line in the seventh paragraph: '... For it, he had become a middle-aged man at thirty – the first flush of youth long gone –'

Well, I wrote it at nineteen. To me, the first flush of youth was long gone by the time one reached thirty. I know better now, of course, since more than thirty years later, I find that I am *still* in the first flush of youth.

There was some reason for self-congratulation in connection with 'Half-Breed,' however. My fourth published story, it was the longest to appear up to then. With a length of nine thousand words, it was listed on the table of contents as a 'novelette,' my first published story in that class.

My name also appeared on the cover of the magazine. It was the first time that had ever happened.

Almost immediately after finishing 'Half-Breed,' I began 'The Secret Sense,' submitting it to John Campbell on June 21, 1939, and receiving it back on the twenty-eighth. Pohl could not place it either.

Toward the end of 1940, however, a pair of sister magazines, *Cosmic Stories* and *Stirring Science Stories*, were being planned, with Don Wollheim, a fellow Futurian, selected as editor. The magazines were starting on a micro-budget, however, and the only way they could come into being was to get stories for nothing – at least for the initial issues. For the purpose, Wollheim appealed to the Futurians and they came through. The first issues consisted entirely (I think) of stories by Futurians, under their own names or pseudonyms.

I, too, was asked, and since by that time I was convinced I could sell 'The Secret Sense' nowhere, I donated it to Wollheim, who promptly accepted it.

That was that, except that, at the time, yet another magazine, *Comet Stories*, was coming into existence, under the editorship of F. Orlin Tremaine, who had been Campbell's predecessor at *Astounding*.

I went to see Tremaine several times, since I thought I might sell him a story or two. On the second visit, on December 5, 1940, Tremaine spoke with some heat concerning the forthcoming birth of Wollheim's magazines. While he himself was paying top rates, he said, Wollheim was getting stories for nothing and with these could put out magazines that would siphon readership from those magazines that paid. Any author who donated stories to Wollheim, and thus contributed to the destruction of competing magazines who paid, should be blacklisted in the field.

I listened with horror, knowing that I had donated a story for nothing. It was a story, to be sure, that I had felt to be worth nothing, but it had not occurred to me that I was undercutting other authors by setting up unfair competition.

I did not quite have the nerve to tell Tremaine I was one of the guilty ones, but as soon as I got home I wrote to Wollheim asking him to accept one of two alternatives: either he could run the story under a pseudonym so that my guilt would be hidden, or if he insisted on using my name, he could pay me five dollars so that if the question ever arose I could honestly deny having given him the story for nothing.

Wollheim chose to use my name and sent me a check for five dollars, but did so with remarkably poor grace (and, to be sure, he was not, in those days, noted for any suavity of character). He accompanied the check with an angry letter that said, in part, that I was being paid an enormous word rate because it was only my name that had value and for that I was receiving $2.50 a word. Perhaps he was correct. If so, the word rate was indeed a record, one that I have not surpassed to this very day. On the other hand, the total payment also set a record. No other story I have ever written commanded so low a payment.

Years later, the well-known science fiction historian Sam Moskowitz wrote a short biography of me, which appeared in the April 1962 *Amazing*. In the course of the biography, he describes a version of the above events and mistakenly states that it was John Campbell who was angry at the donation of stories without pay and that it was he who threatened me with blacklisting.

Not so!

Campbell had nothing to do with it, and, what's more, would have been incapable of making threats. If he had known in advance that I intended to donate a story for nothing to a competing magazine, he would have pointed out my stupidity to me in a perfectly friendly way and I would have let it go at that.

As a matter of fact, while I tried to keep my guilt a secret from Tremaine, I had no intention of hiding it from Campbell. On my very next visit to him, on December 16, 1940, I confessed in full, and he shrugged it off.

Campbell, I imagine, was quite certain that no magazine that had to depend on free stories could last for long, since the only stories so available would have been rejected by everyone else. And he would be right. *Cosmic Stories* lasted only three issues, and *Stirring Science Stories* only four. 'The Secret Sense' remained the only story of mine they published.

As for *Comet Stories*, that lasted five issues, and though Tremaine hesitated over a couple of my stories, he never bought one.

The lilting strains of a Strauss waltz filled the room. The music waxed and waned beneath the sensitive fingers of Lincoln Fields, and through half-closed eyes he could almost see whirling figures pirouetting about the waxed floor of some luxurious salon.

Music always affected him that way. It filled his mind with dreams of sheer beauty and transformed his room into a paradise of sound. His hands flickered over the piano in the last delicious combinations of tones and then slowed reluctantly to a halt.

He sighed and for a moment remained absolutely silent as if trying to extract the last essence of beauty from the dying echoes. Then he turned and smiled faintly at the other occupant of the room.

Garth Jan smiled in turn but said nothing. Garth had a great liking for Lincoln Fields, though little understanding. They were worlds apart – literally – for Garth hailed from the giant underground cities of Mars while Fields was the product of sprawling Terrestrial New York.

'How was that, Garth, old fellow?' questioned Fields doubtfully.

Garth shook his head. He spoke in his precise, painstaking manner, 'I listened attentively and can truly say that it was not unpleasant. There is a certain rhythm, a cadence of sorts, which, indeed, is rather soothing. But beautiful? No!'

There was pity in Fields' eyes – pity almost painful in its intensity. The Martian met the gaze and understood all that it meant, yet there was no answering spark of envy. His bony giant figure remained doubled up in a chair that was too small for him and one thin leg swung leisurely back and forth.

Fields lunged out of his seat impetuously and grasped his companion by the arm. 'Here! Seat yourself on the bench.'

Garth obeyed genially. 'I see you want to carry out some little experiment.'

'You've guessed it. I've read scientific works which tried to explain all about the difference in sense-equipment between Earthman and Martian, but I never could quite grasp it all.'

He tapped the notes C and F in a single octave and glanced

Cosmic Stories, March 1941
Copyright © 1941 by Albing Publications
Copyright renewed © 1968 by Isaac Asimov

at the Martian inquiringly.

'If there's a difference,' said Garth doubtfully, 'it's a very slight one. If I were listening casually, I would certainly say you had hit the same note twice.'

The Earthman marvelled. 'How's this?' He tapped C and G. 'I can hear the difference this time.'

'Well, I suppose all they say about your people is true. You poor fellows – to have such a crude sense of hearing. You don't know what you're missing.'

The Martian shrugged his shoulders fatalistically. 'One misses nothing that one has never possessed.'

Garth Jan broke the short silence that followed. 'Do you realize that this period of history is the first in which two intelligent races have been able to communicate with each other? The comparison of sense equipment is highly interesting – and rather broadens one's views on life.'

'That's right,' agreed the Earthman, 'though we seem to have all the advantage of the comparison. You know a Terrestrial biologist stated last month that he was amazed that a race so poorly equipped in the matter of sense-perception could develop so high a civilization as yours.'

'All is relative, Lincoln. What we have is sufficient for us.'

Fields felt a growing frustration within him. 'But if you only *knew*, Garth, if you only *knew* what you were missing.

'You've never seen the beauties of a sunset or of dancing fields of flowers. You can't admire the blue of the sky, the green of the grass, the yellow of ripe corn. To you the world consists of shades of dark and light.' He shuddered at the thought. 'You can't smell a flower or appreciate its delicate perfume. You can't even enjoy such a simple thing as a good, hearty meal. You can't taste nor smell nor see color. I pity you for your drab world.'

'What you say is meaningless, Lincoln. Waste no pity on me, for I am as happy as you.' He rose and reached for his cane – necessary in the greater gravitational field of Earth.

'You must not judge us with such easy superiority, you know.' That seemed to be the galling aspect of the matter. 'We do not boast of certain accomplishments of our race of which you know nothing.'

And then, as if heartily regretting his words, a wry grimace overspread his face, and he started for the door.

Fields sat puzzled and thoughtful for a moment, then jumped up and ran after the Martian, who was stumping his way towards the exit. He gripped Garth by the shoulder and insisted that he return.

'What did you mean by that last remark?'

The Martian turned his face away as if unable to face his questioner. 'Forget it, Lincoln. That was just a moment of indiscretion when your unsolicited pity got on my nerves.'

Fields gave him a sharp glance. 'It's true, isn't it? It's logical that Martians possess senses Earthmen do not, but it passes the bounds of reason that your people should want to keep it secret.'

'That is as it may be. But now that you've found me out through my own utter stupidity, you will perhaps agree to let it go no further?'

'Of course! I'll be as secret as the grave, though I'm darned if I can make anything of it. Tell me, of what nature is this secret sense of yours?'

Garth Jan shrugged listlessly. 'How can I explain? Can you define color to me, who cannot even conceive it?'

'I'm not asking for a definition. Tell me its uses. Please,' he gripped the other's shoulder, 'you might as well. I have given my promise of secrecy.'

The Martian sighed heavily. 'It won't do you much good. Would it satisfy you to know that if you were to show me two containers, each filled with a clear liquid, I could tell you at once whether either of the two were poisonous? Or, if you were to show me a copper wire, I could tell instantly whether an electric current were passing through it, even if it were as little as a thousandth of an ampere? Or I could tell you the temperature of any substance within three degrees of the true value even if you held it as much as five yards away? Or I could – well, I've said enough.'

'Is that all?' demanded Fields, with a disappointed cry.

'What more do you wish?'

'All you've described is very useful – but where is the beauty in it? Has this strange sense of yours no value to the spirit as well as to the body?'

Garth Jan made an impatient movement. 'Really, Lincoln, you talk foolishly. I have given you only that for which you asked – the uses I put this sense to. I certainly didn't attempt to explain its nature. Take your color sense. As far as I can see its only use is in making certain fine distinctions which I cannot. You can identify certain chemical solutions, for instance, by something you call color when I would be forced to run a chemical analysis. Where's the beauty in that?'

Fields opened his mouth to speak but the Martian motioned him testily into silence. 'I know. You're going to babble foolishness about sunsets or something. But what do you know of beauty? Have you ever known what it was to witness the beauty of the naked copper wires when an AC current is turned on? Have you sensed the delicate loveliness of induced currents set up in a solenoid when a magnet is passed through it? Have you ever attended a Martian *portwem*?'

Garth Jan's eyes had grown misty with the thoughts he was conjuring up, and Fields stared in utter amazement. The shoe was on the other foot now and his sense of superiority left him of a sudden.

'Every race has its own attributes,' he mumbled with a fatalism that had just a trace of hypocrisy in it, 'but I see no reason why you should keep it such a blasted secret. We Earthmen have kept no secrets from your race.'

'Don't accuse us of ingratitude,' cried Garth Jan vehemently. According to the Martian code of ethics, ingratitude was the supreme vice, and at the insinuation of that Garth's caution left him. 'We never act without reason, we Martians. And certainly it is not for our own sake that we hide this magnificent ability.'

The Earthman smiled mockingly. He was on the trail of something – he felt it in his bones – and the only way to get it out was to *tease* it out.

'No doubt there is some nobility behind it all. It is a strange attribute of your race that you can always find some altruistic motive for your actions.'

Garth Jan bit his lip angrily. 'You have no right to say that.' For a moment he thought of pleading worry over Fields' future peace of mind as a reason for silence, but the latter's mocking reference to 'altruism' had rendered that impossible. A feeling of anger crept over him gradually and that forced him to his decision.

There was no mistaking the note of frigid unfriendliness that entered his voice. 'I'll explain by analogy.' The Martian stared straight ahead of him as he spoke, eyes half-closed.

'You have told me that I live in a world that is composed merely of shades of light and dark. You try to describe a world of your own composed of infinite variety and beauty. I listen but care little concerning it. I have never known it and never can know it. One does not weep over the loss of what one has never owned.

'*But* – what if you were able to give me the ability to see color for five minutes? What if, for five minutes, I reveled in wonders undreamed of? What if, after those five minutes,

I have to return it *forever*? Would those five minutes of paradise be worth a lifetime of regret afterwards – a lifetime of dissatisfaction because of my own shortcomings? Would it not have been the kinder act never to have told me of color in the first place and so have removed its ever-present temptation?'

Fields had risen to his feet during the last part of the Martian's speech and his eyes opened wide in a wild surmise. 'Do you mean an Earthman could possess the Martian sense if so desired?'

'For five minutes in a lifetime,' Garth Jan's eyes grew dreamy, 'and in those five minutes sense –'

He came to a confused halt and glared angrily at his companion, 'You know more than is good for you. See that you don't forget your promise.'

He rose hastily and hobbled away as quickly as he could, leaning heavily upon the cane. Lincoln Fields made no move to stop him. He merely sat there and thought.

The great height of the cavern shrouded the roof in misty obscurity in which, at fixed intervals, there floated luminescent globes of radite. The air, heated by this subterranean volcanic stratum, wafted past gently. Before Lincoln Fields stretched the wide, paved avenue of the principal city of Mars, fading away into the distance.

He clumped awkwardly up to the entrance of the home of Garth Jan, the six-inch-thick layer of lead attached to each shoe a nuisance unending. Though it was still better than the uncontrollable bounding Earth muscles brought about in this lighter gravity.

The Martian was surprised to see his friend of six months ago but not altogether joyful. Fields was not slow to notice this but he merely smiled to himself. The opening formalities passed, the conventional remarks were made, and the two seated themselves.

Fields crushed the cigarette in the ash-tray and sat upright, suddenly serious. 'I've come to ask for those five minutes you claim you can give me! May I have them?'

'Is that a rhetorical question? It certainly doesn't seem to require an answer.' Garth's tone was openly contemptuous.

The Earthman considered the other thoughtfully. 'Do you mind if I outline my position in a few words?'

The Martian smiled indifferently. 'It won't make any difference,' he said.

'I'll take my chance on that. The situation is this: I've been born and reared in the lap of luxury and have been most disgustingly spoiled. I've never yet had a reasonable desire that I have not been able to fulfill, and I don't know what it means *not* to get what I want. Do you see?'

There was no answer and he continued, 'I have found my happiness in beautiful sights, beautiful words, and beautiful sounds. I have made a cult of beauty. In a word, I am an aesthete.'

'Most interesting,' the Martian's stony expression did not change a whit, 'but what bearing has all this on the problem at hand?'

'Just this: You speak of a new form of beauty – a form unknown to me at present and entirely inconceivable even, but one which could be known if you so wished. The notion attracts me. It more than attracts me – it makes its demands of me. Again I remind you that when a notion begins to make demands of me, I yield – I always have.'

'You are not the master of this case,' reminded Garth Jan. 'It is crude of me to remind you of this, but you cannot force *me*, you know. Your words, in fact, are almost offensive in their implications.'

'I am glad you said that, for it allows me to be crude in my turn without offending my conscience.'

Garth Jan's only reply to this was a self-confident grimace.

'I make my demand of you,' said Fields, slowly, 'in the name of gratitude.'

'Gratitude?' The Martian started violently.

Fields grinned broadly, 'It's an appeal no honourable Martian can refuse – by your own ethics. You owe me gratitude, now, because it was through me you gained entrance into the houses of the greatest and most honorable men of Earth.'

'I know that,' Garth Jan flushed angrily. 'You are impolite to remind me of it.'

'I have no choice. You acknowledged the gratitude you owe me in actual words, back on Earth. I demand the chance to possess this mysterious sense you keep so secret – in the name of this acknowledged gratitude. Can you refuse now?'

'You know I can't,' was the gloomy response. 'I hesitated only for your own sake.'

The Martian rose and held out his hand gravely, 'You have me by the neck, Lincoln. It is done. Afterwards, though, I owe you nothing more. This will pay my debt of gratitude. Agreed?'

'Agreed!' The two shook hands and Lincoln Fields continued in an entirely different tone. 'We're still friends, though, aren't we? This little altercation won't spoil things?'

'I hope not. Come! Join me at the evening meal and we can discuss the time and place of your – er – five minutes.'

Lincoln Fields tried hard to down the faint nervousness that filled him as he waited in Garth Jan's private 'concert'-room. He felt a sudden desire to laugh as the thought came to him that he felt exactly as he usually did in a dentist's waiting room.

He lit his tenth cigarette, puffed twice and threw it away, 'You're doing this very elaborately, Garth.'

The Martian shrugged, 'You have only five minutes so I might as well see to it that they are put to the best possible use. You're going to "hear" part of a *portwem*, which is to our sense what a great symphony (is that the word?) is to sound.'

'Have we much longer to wait? The suspense, to be trite, is terrible.'

'We're waiting for Novi Lon, who is to play the *portwem*, and for Done Vol, my private physician. They'll be along soon.'

Fields wandered onto the low dais that occupied the center of the room and regarded the intricate mechanism thereupon with curious interest. The fore-part was encased in gleaming aluminum leaving exposed only seven tiers of shining black knobs above and five large white pedals below. Behind, however, it lay open, and within there ran crossings and recrossings of finer wires in incredibly complicated paths.

'A curious thing, this,' remarked the Earthman.

The Martian joined him on the dais, 'It's an expensive instrument. It cost me ten thousand Martian credits.'

'How does it work?'

'Not so differently from a Terrestrial piano. Each of the upper knobs controls a different electric circuit. Singly and together an expert *portwem* player could, by manipulating the knobs, form any conceivable pattern of electric current. The pedals below control the strength of the current.'

Fields nodded absently and ran his fingers over the knobs at random. Idly, he noticed the small galvanometer located just above the keys kick violently each time he depressed a knob. Aside from that, he sensed nothing.

'Is the instrument really playing?'

The Martian smiled, 'Yes, it is. And a set of unbelievably atrocious discords too.'

He took a seat before the instrument and with a murmured 'Here's how!' his fingers skimmed rapidly and accurately over the gleaming buttons.

The sound of a reedy Martian voice crying out in strident accents broke in upon him, and Garth Jan ceased in sudden embarrassment. 'This is Novi Lon,' he said hastily to Fields, 'As usual, he does not like my playing.'

Fields rose to meet the newcomer. He was bent of shoulder and evidently of great age. A fine tracing of wrinkles, especially about eyes and mouth, covered his face.

'So this is the young Earthman,' he cried, in a strongly-accented English. 'I disapprove of your rashness but sympathize with your desire to attend a *portwem*. It is a great pity you can own our sense for no more than five minutes. Without it no one can truly be said to live.'

Garth Jan laughed, 'He exaggerates, Lincoln. He's one of the greatest musicians of Mars, and thinks anyone doomed to damnation who would not rather attend a *portwem* than breathe.' He hugged the older man warmly, 'He was my teacher in my youth and many were the long hours in which he struggled to teach me the proper combinations of circuits.'

'And I have failed after all, you dunce,' snapped the old Martian. 'I heard your attempt at playing as I entered. You still have not learned the proper *fortgass* combination. You were desecrating the soul of the great Bar Danin. My pupil! Bah! It is a disgrace!'

The entrance of the third Martian, Done Vol, prevented Novi Lon from continuing his tirade. Garth, glad of the reprieve, approached the physician hastily.

'Is all ready?'

'Yes,' growled Vol surlily, 'and a particularly uninteresting experiment this will be. We know all the results beforehand.' His eyes fell upon the Earthman, whom he eyed contemptuously. 'Is this the one who wishes to be inoculated?'

Lincoln Fields nodded eagerly and felt his throat and mouth go dry suddenly. He eyed the newcomer uncertainly and felt uneasy at the sight of a tiny bottle of clear liquid and hypodermic which the physician had extracted from a case he was carrying.

'What are you going to do?' he demanded.

'He'll merely inoculate you. It'll take a second,' Garth Jan assured him. 'You see, the sense-organs in this case are several groups of cells in the cortex of the brain. They are activated by a hormone, a synthetic preparation of which is used to stimulate the dormant cells of the occasional Martian who is born – er – "blind." You'll receive the same treatment.'

'Oh! – then Earthmen possess those cortex cells?'

'In a very rudimentary state. The concentrated hormone will

activate them, but only for five minutes. After that time, they are literally blown out as a result of their unwonted activity. After that, they can't be re-activated under *any* circumstances.'

Done Vol completed his last-minute preparations and approached Fields. Without a word, Fields extended his right arm and the hypodermic plunged in.

With the operation completed, the Terrestrial waited a moment or two and then essayed a shaky laugh, 'I don't feel any change.'

'You won't for about ten minutes,' explained Garth. 'It takes time. Just sit back and relax. Novi Lon has begun Bar Danin's "Canals in the Desert" – it is my favorite – and when the hormone begins its work you will find yourself in the very middle of things.'

Now that the die was cast irrevocably, Fields found himself stonily calm. Novi Lon played furiously, and Garth Jan, at the Earthman's right, was already lost in the composition. Even Done Vol, the fussy doctor, had forgotten his peevishness for the nonce.

Fields snickered under his breath. The Martians listened attentively but to him the room was devoid of sound and – almost – of all other sensation as well. What – no, it was impossible, of course – but what if it were just an elaborate practical joke? He stirred uneasily and put the thought from his mind angrily.

The minutes passed; Novi Lon's fingers flew; Garth Jan's expression was one of unfeigned delight.

Then Lincoln Fields blinked his eyes rapidly. For a moment a nimbus of color seemed to surround the musician and his instrument. He couldn't identify it – but it was there. It grew and spread until the room was full of it. Other hues came to join it and still others. They wove and wavered; expanding and contracting; changing with lightning speed and yet staying the same. Intricate patterns of brilliant tints formed and faded, beating in silent bursts of color upon the young man's eyeballs.

Simultaneously, there came the impression of sound. From a whisper it rose into a glorious, ringing shout that wavered up and down the scale in quivering tremolos. He seemed to hear every instrument from fife to bass viol simultaneously, and yet, paradoxically, each rang in his ear in solitary clearness.

And together with this, there came the more subtle sensation of odor. From a suspicion, a mere trace, it waxed into a phantasmal field of flowers. Delicate spicy scents followed each other in ever stronger succession; in gentle wafts of pleasure.

Yet all this was nothing. Fields knew that. Somehow, he *knew* that what he saw, heard, and smelt were mere delusions – mirages of a brain that frantically attempted to interpret an entirely new conception in the old, familiar ways.

Gradually, the colors and the sounds and the scents died. His brain was beginning to realize that that which beat upon it was something hitherto unexperienced. The effect of the hormone became stronger, and suddenly – in one burst – Fields realized what it was he sensed.

He didn't see it – nor hear it – nor smell it – nor taste it – nor feel it. He knew what it was but he couldn't think of the word for it. Slowly, he realized that there wasn't any word for it. Even more slowly, he realized that there wasn't even any *concept* for it.

Yet he knew what it was.

There beat upon his brain something that consisted of pure waves of enjoyment – something that lifted him out of himself and pitched him headlong into a universe unknown to him earlier. He was falling through an endless eternity of – something. It wasn't sound or sight but it was – something. Something that enfolded him and hid his surroundings from him – that's what it was. It was endless and infinite in its variety, and with each crashing wave, he glimpsed a farther horizon, and the wonderful cloak of sensation became thicker – and softer – and more beautiful.

Then came the discord. Like a little crack at first – marring a perfect beauty. Then spreading and branching and growing wider, until, finally, it split apart thunderously – though without a sound.

Lincoln Fields, dazed and bewildered, found himself back in the concert room again.

He lurched to his feet and grasped Garth Jan by the arm violently, 'Garth! Why did he stop? Tell him to continue! Tell him!'

Garth Jan's startled expression faded into pity, 'He is still playing, Lincoln.'

The Earthman's befuddled stare showed no signs of understanding. He gazed about him with unseeing eyes. Novi Lon's fingers sped across the keyboard as nimbly as ever; the expression on his face was as rapt as ever. Slowly, the truth seeped in, and the Earthman's empty eyes filled with horror.

He sat down, uttering one hoarse cry, and buried his head in his hands.

The five minutes had passed! There could be no return!

Garth Jan was smiling – a smile of dreadful malice, 'I had

pitied you just a moment ago, Lincoln, but now I'm glad – glad! You forced this out of me – you made me do this. I hope you're satisfied, because I certainly am. For the rest of your life,' his voice sank to a sibilant whisper, 'you'll remember these five minutes and know what it is you're missing – what it is you can never have again. You are blind, Lincoln – blind!'

The Earthman raised a haggard face and grinned, but it was no more than a horrible baring of the teeth. It took every ounce of willpower he possessed to maintain an air of composure.

He did not trust himself to speak. With wavering step, he marched out of the room, head held high to the end.

And within, that tiny, bitter voice, repeating over and over again, 'You entered a normal man! You leave blind – *blind* – BLIND.'

THE END

APPENDIX—The Sixty Stories of the Campbell Years

STORY (WORDS)	MAGAZINE ISSUE	COLLECTION
1. Cosmic Corkscrew (9,000)	—	—
2. THE CALLISTAN MENACE (6,500)	*Astonishing Stories* April 1940	*The Early Asimov* (Vol. I)
3. Marooned off Vesta (6,400)	*Amazing Stories* March 1939	*Asimov's Mysteries*
4. This Irrational Planet (3,000)	—	—
5. RING AROUND THE SUN (5,000)	*Future Fiction* March 1940	*The Early Asimov* (Vol. I)
6. The Weapon (4,000)	—	—
7. Paths of Destiny (6,000)	—	—
8. Knossos in Its Glory (6,000)	—	—
9. THE MAGNIFICENT POSSESSION (5,000)	*Future Fiction* July 1940	*The Early Asimov* (Vol. I)
10. TRENDS (6,900)	*Astounding Science Fiction* July 1939	*The Early Asimov* (Vol. I)
11. THE WEAPON TOO DREADFUL TO USE (6,500)	*Amazing Stories* May 1939	*The Early Asimov* (Vol. I)
12. The Decline and Fall (6,000)	—	—
13. BLACK FRIAR OF THE FLAME (16,000)	*Planet Stories* Spring 1942	*The Early Asimov* (Vol. I)
14. Robbie (Strange Playfellow) (6,500)	*Super Science Stories* September 1940	*I, Robot*
15. HALF-BREED (9,000)	*Astonishing Stories* February 1940	*The Early Asimov* (Vol. I)
16. THE SECRET SENSE (5,000)	*Cosmic Stories* March 1941	*The Early Asimov* (Vol. I)
17. Life Before Birth (6,000)	—	—
18. The Brothers (6,000)	—	—
19. HOMO SOL (7,200)	*Astounding Science Fiction* September 1940	*The Early Asimov* (Vol. II)
20. HALF-BREEDS ON VENUS (10,000)	*Astonishing Stories* December 1940	*The Early Asimov* (Vol. II)
21. THE IMAGINARY (7,200)	*Super Science Stories* November 1942	*The Early Asimov* (Vol. II)
22. The Oak (6,000)	—	—
23. HEREDITY (10,500)	*Astonishing Stories* April 1941	*The Early Asimov* Vol. II)
24. HISTORY (5,000)	*Super Science Stories* March 1941	*The Early Asimov* (Vol. II)
25. Reason (7,000)	*Astounding Science Fiction* April 1941	*I, Robot*
26. CHRISTMAS ON GANYMEDE (6,000)	*Startling Stories* January 1942	*The Early Asimov* (Vol. II)
27. THE LITTLE MAN ON THE SUBWAY (4,000)	*Fantasy Book* Vol. 1, No. 6	*The Early Asimov* (Vol. II)
28. Liar! (7,000)	*Astounding Science Fiction* May 1941	*I, Robot*
29. Masks (1,500)	—	—
30. THE HAZING (5,000)	*Thrilling Wonder Stories* October 1942	*The Early Asimov* (Vol. II)
31. SUPER-NEUTRON (5,000)	*Astonishing Stories* September 1941	*The Early Asimov* (Vol. II)
32. Nightfall (13,200)	*Astounding Science Fiction* September 1941	*Nightfall and Other Stories*

Other Panthers For Your Enjoyment

Asimov in Panther

☐ **THE STARS LIKE DUST**   30p
A great Utopian story of a chase through the length and breadth
of the galaxy in search of a secret document which may be the key
to the overthrow of tyranny.

☐ **THE END OF ETERNITY**   30p
Mankind is spreading through the galaxy – and meets an alien
intelligence which is moving in from the shadowy 'outside'. How to
stop them? Simple – you modify the past: except that nothing ever
is as simple as that in Isaac Asimov's stupendous cosmology.

☐ **THE CAVES OF STEEL**   30p
Many writers have tried to merge science fiction with the
detective story, but only Asimov has supremely succeeded.
THE CAVES OF STEEL has a detective – an unusual one –
operating in the deep-down warrens of an over-populated metropolis
– and if you think you know what over-population means . . . read
Asimov.

☐ **THE NAKED SUN**   30p
Another science fiction/detective story masterpiece. A tec from
over-crowded Earth has to take off to a sparsely populated
way-out planet. After the teeming dens of Earth – a sort of womb
existence – the wide open spaces make him literally sick.
Nevertheless, there's a killer on the loose – to be run down.

☐ **ASIMOV'S MYSTERIES**   30p
Short, sharp stories about murders, mayhems, crooks and
detectives fouling up Asimov's cleanly organised science fiction
worlds. This deep, dark space collection rounds off the author's
excursion into the s.f./thriller field.

☐ **THE MARTIAN WAY**   30p
Four novellas by Asimov. The author races along – taking Mars
in his stride (the title is a misnomer) as he slams his penetrating
imagination into the deeps of space and time.

Asimov in Panther

☐ **FOUNDATION**   30p
The first volume of an astounding sweep through 30,000 years
of galactic history. A shadowy figure – called Hari Seldon –
establishes a mysterious foundation. Its objective – to save
galactic civilisation from coming disaster.

☐ **FOUNDATION AND EMPIRE**   30p
The galaxy is rent by space adventurers staking out their claims to
ephemeral kingdoms. Then a mutant known as The Mule makes
his appearance and imposes his brutal overlordship across the
whole galaxy.

☐ **SECOND FOUNDATION**   30p
To the entire galaxy comes the grim final reckoning. The Seldon
Foundation reveals itself and its cosmic aims, and order is at last
imposed on chaos. As the magazine *Vector* wrote, 'The *Foundation*
trilogy is the prime example of straight SF published to date. No
other work can compare with the magnificent scope that this
series offers'.

☐ **I, ROBOT**   30p
Almost single-handed Isaac Asimov invented 'robotics', and
practically every famous author in the SF field has acknowledged
his indebtedness to this splendidly imaginative novel and its
famous sequel –

☐ **THE REST OF THE ROBOTS**   30p
Although these stories can be read in their own right they also
complete Asimov's fantastic imaginings of a robot universe.

☐ **EARTH IS ROOM ENOUGH**   30p
Fifteen stories, each one built on an impeccable set of facts (which
is the only way to write really convincing SF). And Dr Asimov, a
practising scientist himself, is a master of bizarre facts.

Science Fiction and Fantasy

☐ **H. P. Lovecraft** **AT THE MOUNTAINS OF MADNESS** **25p**
A great collection of sinister and uncanny tales for connoisseurs of terror.

☐ **H. P. Lovecraft** **THE CASE OF CHARLES DEXTER WARD** **25p**
A short macabre novel by the 20th century's undisputed master of horror.

☐ **Keith Roberts** **PAVANE** **30p**
An alternative universe in which 20th century England is still under the grimly reactionary rule of the Roman Church. 'His blend of telling detail, gripping story line and pure exalted fantasy is little short of miraculous' – *Tribune*. 'Brilliant' – *SF Review*

☐ **Roger Zelazny** **LORD OF LIGHT** **40p**
'A triumph' said the *Magazine of Fantasy and Science Fiction*. 'A rare work of SF imagination' added the *Sunday Telegraph*. And the final accolade – the Hugo Award. In an era yet to come and a planet far distant from this one a group of way-out men and women, backed by a powerful technology that makes ours look primitive, take over the role of the ancient Hindu pantheon.

☐ **Roger Zelazny** **THE DREAM MASTER 25p**
A mind-stretching story of a lonely voyager's nightmare journey into the infinity of inner space. By a master of contemporary SF.

☐ **John Blackburn** **CHILDREN OF THE NIGHT** **30p**
A pothole on the Yorkshire moors and an ancient race emerging from it to once more – after eons of time – take its 'rightful' place on Earth's surface – 'rightfully' meaning that humans go to the wall. One of the eeriest thrillers published in years. John Blackburn is streets ahead of all his competitors in this field.

Obtainable from all booksellers and newsagents. If you have any difficulty please send purchase price plus 7p postage per book to Panther Cash Sales, P.O. Box 11, Falmouth, Cornwall.

I enclose a cheque/postal order for titles ticked above plus 7p. a book to cover postage and packing.

Name——————————————————————

Address——————————————————————

——————————————————————